DRAKE UNBOUND

BOOK THREE IN THE DRAKE SERIES

S. E. LUND

ACADIAN PUBLISHING LIMITED

FOREWARD

"Have enough courage to trust love one more time and always one more time."

Maya Angelou

CHAPTER 1

AS I LED her through the gate and to the baggage carousel, Kate's expression showed a mixture of excitement and anxiety. Her cheeks were slightly flushed from the heat. Her hand was closed tightly around mine, and when I put our carry-on bags down, I glanced at Kate again, trying to see her from the perspective of someone who didn't know her. She appeared a bit lost, and at that moment, I felt an incredible sense of responsibility for her. She was here with me, dependent on me. It was both incredibly rewarding to someone like me who liked to be in control, but at the same time, it made me consider that responsibility seriously.

As an independent woman of some personal wealth, although she tried not to be dependent on her father, Kate could buy a ticket back to Manhattan any time she desired. It wasn't the fact of being financially dependent on me for she never would be, but she was emotionally dependent on me. She was here *with* me. As my lover and partner. Her happiness depended, at least in part, on our relationship.

I wanted to make her happy. I promised Ethan before we

1

left that I would do everything in my power to make her happy and I meant it.

We stood in the crush of people meeting their friends and relatives, our arms around each other.

"We're here," I whispered, squeezing her closer. I tilted her chin up and kissed her tenderly. When I pulled back, I ran a finger over her bottom lip, touching the tiny scar. "I thought I'd be here by myself when I accepted Michael's offer back in December. I'm so glad you're with me, future Mrs. Morgan."

"I'm so glad you asked me."

It was true. When I accepted Michael's offer, Kate and I were briefly broken up as a couple. I expected to arrive here alone and to spend my days immersed in my caseload, keeping my head down, using the distance between Nairobi and Manhattan to mend my wounds. They were wounds. I wanted Kate so badly when we first met at Ethan's party. Despite the difference in our age and the fact she was Ethan's beloved daughter, I wanted her as my own. When I realized she was the young woman Lara was trying to hook me up with, I wanted her even more for I knew then that we were compatible sexually.

She wanted a Dom. I wanted a submissive. I wanted *her*.

Now, here she was. All mine. My submissive in heart and mind, even if she wasn't the best-behaved sub and I was a terrible Dom, letting her get away with murder. I couldn't help it. I loved her for her resistance. She was a challenge. Truth be told, if she had been too compliant right away, if she had been fully submissive, I think I wouldn't have fallen as hard or as fast.

"I guess we should get our bags," I said and ended the embrace. "Why don't you have a seat and wait for me. I'll get a cart. Michael and Claire should be here soon."

Kate nodded and sat in a chair by the floor-to-ceiling

2

window while I went to the baggage area, pushing a cart in front of me.

While I waited for our bags, I thought about Kate. I hoped that while she was here, she could take some time to explore herself, find out what she wanted to do with her life—besides be with me. She was the daughter of a very powerful man and had always felt she was in her brother's shadow. It was all of her own making, for Ethan adored Kate and only wanted her happiness, but Kate never felt secure in her father's approval. She always tried to second guess him and please him, but resented it at the same time.

I hoped she would have the freedom to do whatever she wanted. Write. Paint. Explore the city and go on safari. I wanted her to see Africa in a different light. The way my father and I saw it—as a place of great possibility and hope.

I picked up my suitcase when it emerged and turned to glance at Kate, still seated by the windows. She smiled back, her tiny wave so sweet. While I was loading one of my own bags onto the baggage cart, Michael Owiti walked up, his hand extended, a huge smile on his friendly face.

His wife Claire followed, looking impeccable as usual. Michael and I shook and embraced. He was a mentor of mine and felt like a favorite uncle or big brother. Michael was Chief of Surgery at the Aga Khan Hospital where I would work. He was also Dean of the Faculty of Medicine at the Aga Khan University Medical College where I would teach.

I was finally making good on a promise I made Michael several years earlier, that I would take time off from my practice in Manhattan, come teach at the university and take on a surgical caseload at the hospital. I had come briefly for a couple of months a year earlier, but Michael wanted me to stay longer. Then my father died and I was a year in mourning before I met Kate.

Things seemed to have worked out for the best for now I'd be able to devote six months to Michael instead of four. Maybe longer, depending on Kate.

I gave Claire a hug and pointed to Kate, who sat up, eager to meet our hosts.

Kate stood and smiled, waving hesitantly. Being a natural extrovert, Michael strode over to her with his arms out.

"There you are, lovely Miss *Katherine*," he said. "Welcome to Kenya!"

He shook Kate's hand, smiling broadly at her.

"Nice to meet you," Kate said, her cheeks flushed. "You must be Dr. Owiti. Drake spoke so highly of you."

"Please, call me Michael," he said. "And Drake has spoken so highly of *you* as well. My wife Claire and I have been so excited to meet the woman who finally stole *Drake the Rake's* heart. We thought he might be a playboy forever after the divorce, but you proved us wrong."

Michael turned and wagged his eyebrows at me. I cringed inwardly when he used the old title *Drake the Rake*. It was what the nurses called me when I had been at Michael's hospital for a term.

"Drake the *Rake*?" Kate said and laughed, turning to me with a gleam in her eye. I draped an arm around her shoulders and pulled her close, giving her my best guilty smile.

"That was his nickname for me when we worked together a couple of years ago," I said.

Claire arrived and smiled at Kate, extending her hand. The two women shook hands while Michael introduced Claire.

"We met in a philosophy class on Heidegger," Claire said, her British accent impeccable. "Back when Michael was still a rebellious son trying to be anything but a doctor, the way his father wanted and expected."

"Sounds familiar," Kate said and raised her eyebrows at

me. "Drake studied psychology before he became a surgeon." She turned to Michael. "Philosophy is a long way from neurosurgery. How did you end up studying the brain?"

"The philosopher is obsessed with the theory of the mind; the neurosurgeon with the brain," Michael said. "It's actually a very easy jump."

Michael and Claire led us to the car and while Michael loaded our suitcases into the trunk of the black Mercedes, I opened Kate's door, leaning in close to kiss her cheek before she entered.

"Drake the Rake, *hmm?*" she said quietly when I pulled away. I caught the gleam in her eyes.

"Michael's exaggerating of course," I said, feigning innocence, although I had a few partners while I was in Nairobi before. Not as many as Michael might suggest, but enough for an old married man like him to take note.

"You must have been seen as a rake, for it to be your nickname, though."

I grinned. "I was notorious," I admitted, "but Michael had better stop telling tales or he'll scare you off."

"Not likely," she said. "Drake the Rake is pretty mild, considering the other nicknames you have."

"It *is* mild," I said and nodded. "And I'm the farthest thing from a rake now. I'm a committed monogamist soon-to-be newly-wed husband."

She smiled at that and entered the car. I closed the door and went around to the other side and took my seat beside her. I checked her seat belt to make sure it was fastened properly and then fastened my own, my arm slipping across the back of the seat so I could touch her.

Michael drove through the streets of Nairobi, an expert at managing its busy roadways.

"You know, Katherine," Michael said from the driver's seat. "When I first heard that you'd broken poor Drake's

5

heart back in December and he wanted to come to Kenya to escape, I was so happy for myself and for our hospital, although of course I felt bad for Drake. I'm very glad you two worked things out because I was feeling very guilty that my happiness came at Drake's expense."

"I'm glad as well," Kate said and smiled at me. I squeezed her hand, wanting to show her affection and that I felt the same way.

"How is that young son of yours?" Claire said from the front seat. "We were so surprised to get the news, and so worried for you about his diagnosis. Your last email said that he was doing well, that the graft was taking and he was improving."

"He's doing very well," I said, thinking of the last report I had from Liam's doctors. "I wouldn't have left if there was any doubt, but they'll keep a close eye on him for the next weeks and months."

"We didn't expect that you were bringing Kate with you, you bad boy," Claire said chidingly. I glanced at her, surprised that she was bringing it up. I hadn't said anything about Kate to Claire, although I did finally email Michael and tell him. "You never told us that in your emails!" Claire turned to Kate and looked at her pointedly. "He kept the fact you two reconciled a secret. We only found out a few days ago. Imagine our surprise that you were back together."

I held Kate's hand up, wanting to silence Claire once and for all. "And engaged."

Claire smiled icily. "And engaged?" She turned to Michael and hit him playfully on the shoulder. "Did you know this? Why didn't you tell me?" She turned back to me. "How quick was that?!"

I shrugged. "Sorry I didn't tell you sooner about Kate, but I was pretty preoccupied with Liam for the past month so I wasn't thinking about coming here." I turned to Michael.

6

"You didn't have to pick us up," I said, appreciating it all the same. "We could have taken a taxi to the hotel."

"Nonsense," Michael said, shaking his head. "The driver would take you all over the place to extend his fare and then given you the wrong change. Claire and I are only too pleased to give you a ride to the hotel. I hope you're not too tired, because we have the new student-faculty mixer tonight at the faculty club. I thought we'd go so Drake could meet the new students and a few of the residents, have a glass of wine and some appetizers. Then we'll take you out for some good street food, and give you a proper introduction to Nairobi."

I turned to Kate and squeezed her hand once more. "What do you think? Are you up to it?

Kate smiled, but I could see fatigue in her eyes.

"Of course we can go," she said. "Don't want to keep you from your students."

Claire turned to face us from the front seat. "Oh, by the way, Drake, you'll *never* guess who decided to come back to Nairobi for specialization in pediatric neurosurgery."

"Who?" I said, curious about my new crop of residents.

"Sam Cuttington."

Christ... I said nothing for a moment as I thought about Sam. Samantha Cuttington. A medical student, specializing in surgery when I was in Nairobi before. We had an affair that lasted for most of the time I was in Nairobi. We kept it quiet because technically, I was faculty and she was a student. We could have gotten in trouble—I could have gotten in trouble if anyone besides Michael and Claire had found out.

I cleared my throat. "When did this happen?"

"Only recently," Michael said from the front seat. He caught my eye in the rear view mirror. "We contacted Sam at Christmas that you were coming to teach the robotic surgery class, but didn't hear back until now. Sam's a great student

7

and wants to specialize in robotic surgery. We'll all work closely together."

I nodded, and then looked out the window. Sam was a great student, very bright and competent. Driven. We were too much alike to click. I was very committed to my lifestyle as a Dominant, but she was very adamant about seducing me.

I let her seduce me for I was lonely, without a submissive, and the sex was good.

Kate squeezed my hand and I turned and smiled at her, but I wasn't happy that Sam had returned and would be a student once more. She had probably returned when she knew I was going to be teaching for the semester. She and Michael were close and he had mentored her while she was in Nairobi before, but we had parted on less than agreeable terms.

She wanted more and I couldn't give it. I was already cutting my ties to Nairobi for my return to Manhattan. I had already pushed her out of my mind and it took her a while to realize it.

I felt guilty, but she had to know a long distance relationship just wouldn't work between us, aside from the fact that I wanted to be in control sexually and she wanted to share it.

It didn't end as well as I would have liked, but it had to end.

Now she'd be back and I hoped she knew that I had Kate with me and we were engaged. I'd have to make that clear to her if she came to Nairobi with any hopes of rekindling our previous relationship. If we were going to be anything, it would be colleagues and professionals.

Nothing more.

WE ARRIVED AT THE HOTEL, and I was excited to see Kate's response. I picked the Hemmingway because it was perhaps

8

the nicest hotel I had been in. Picturesque, it resembled an old estate from a bygone era.

A porter helped me with the luggage and while Kate sat with Michael and Claire, I checked in.

One of the perks of the hotel was a butler, who was assigned to us during our stay. He led the way to the hotel room and got us settled. Kate glanced around the suite, her face flushed. When she stopped and glanced in a circle, her face bore a look of pleasure that made me very happy.

While Michael and Claire waited in the living room, I spoke with the butler and Kate freshened up in the bathroom. I joined her, and then took a quick shower. When I was done, I pulled a towel around my waist and went to where she stood by the sink.

"So, what do you think, Ms. Bennet?" I pulled her into my arms. "Does the hotel meet your expectations?"

She slipped her arms around my neck. "It's fantastic. Looks like a place where Hemingway himself would stay, except brand new."

I kissed her. "Good. I want you in the lap of luxury while we find a place to live. You've been working hard at college for five years and now it's time to relax and do whatever you feel like. Paint. Sightsee. Go on safari."

"What about you?" Kate said, stroking her fingers through my hair. "You've been working hard at your surgical practice, your foundation, the business, and your band..."

"I only work as hard as I want," I said, for it was true. I worked the cases I wanted. "I want you to rest, sleep in as late as you want. Stay up as late as you want, painting or writing. Whatever your heart desires."

She smiled. "I might like to do some wildlife art while I'm here. When I was in high school, I did a lot of bird paintings so it makes sense to paint wildlife since we're in Africa."

"I'd love to go on Safari," I said, squeezing her. "Maybe

some weekend when I'm not on call. Claire and Michael will know some good places to go and good tour guides."

She pushed a hank of hair from my forehead. "I'm pretty tired. I hope we won't be out late."

I shook my head, and pulled her more tightly into my arms. "Don't worry. We'll go to the mixer, go for some local food and then come back early. I think I might like a late-night swim in the pool, though."

"Sounds good to me," she said and smiled.

I pulled her up for a kiss and when it ended, she frowned.

"You didn't seem all that pleased that this Sam fellow was coming back to the college to work with you and Michael."

I shook my head and wondered how to handle the next part of our discussion. How much should I tell Kate? I wanted to be truthful, but I didn't want her to be worried that there would be any reason for jealousy.

"Not a *he*." I stroked her cheek. "Samantha Cuttington, one of Michael's former students."

Kate frowned, her expression one of shock.

"*Tell* me," she said, her face blanching a bit.

"I met her when she was a resident two years ago," I said, deciding to be as truthful as I could. "I volunteered at the hospital for a couple of months. At Michael's request, I was here to help deal with a backlog of cases the foundation brought in from Somalia. It was before my father died. We," I said and shrugged. "Sam and I had a fling."

"A 'fling'?" she said, her voice soft. "I didn't think you had flings."

"I don't. Sam and I," I said and hesitated as I tried to use the right words. "We went out a few times, had sex a few times. But she wasn't interested in anything to do with BDSM so nothing more developed."

Kate nodded, and I could tell she was trying hard to stay calm. I pulled on some clothes and waited for her questions.

She played with the collar on my shirt, straightening the tie knot. "So you broke up."

"There was nothing really to break," I said, although I knew Sam thought there was. "It was only a few times."

"How many is a few? Twice? Three times?"

I shook my head. "I can't remember exactly. I was here for a couple of months. Maybe a dozen times." I finished fastening my cuffs and then focused on Kate. "There was nothing other than sexual release for me, Kate. She's not my type and was very upset at the thought I was into D/s."

She had been upset, claiming D/s was anti-feminist. I had told her that feminism meant freedom for women in all aspects of their lives, including desire. She didn't seem to understand.

"You must have liked something about her. I thought you only had submissives."

"I do, I *did* only have submissives. She was here when I was here, and well, it was just opportunity…"

"Did *she* feel that way?" Kate asked, her voice very soft now. "That it was just opportunity?"

I shrugged, and remembered back when we ended things. Or rather, when *I* ended things. "She wasn't happy when I left without continuing the relationship," I said, a sense of relief that Kate seemed okay with it. "She thought she'd be enough to tempt me to give up my kinky ways. She wasn't. End of story."

"You're not very kinky, Master D. She must be pretty vanilla."

"She's pretty dominant herself. We clashed."

"Not enough to keep you out of each others arms."

"Too much to keep me with her."

Kate exhaled. "Did Michael know about you two? Does he know about you being part of the lifestyle?"

"We tried to keep it private," I said, "because I was in a

supervisory role even though I was only here for a few months. I want it to stay that way, Kate. It's not that I think it would matter. It's not something I want getting around."

"Of course," Kate said. "I know that better than anyone. But *she* knows…"

"Look," I said and took hold of her shoulders. "This was several years ago before my father died. I've moved on. She's moved on and so there's nothing to be concerned about."

"It sounds like she came back to study with you."

"She came back to study with *Michael*. He's the one who specializes in pediatrics," I said but I suspected that she also came back because she heard I'd be in Nairobi for the term. "Let's forget about her and what happened and enjoy ourselves."

"I'm sorry." Kate held up a hand and forced a smile. "You don't have to say anything more. I was surprised, that's all."

I shook my head. "You have nothing to worry about. Like I said it was just sex. Plain old vanilla sex out of convenience."

I bent down and kissed her again, hoping that I had dispelled any worries she felt about an old flame being in town. I had no interest in seeing Sam again and would have preferred that she went somewhere else for the last years of her residency. I knew that she really liked Michael and wanted to specialize in pediatric neurosurgery. Michael was the obvious choice. If anything, the fact that I was here was just icing on the cake.

After pushing Sam out of my mind, I took Kate's hand and together, we went out to join Claire and Michael.

CHAPTER 2

MICHAEL DROVE us to the college.

"Hang on," Michael said from the front seat, a grin on his face in the rear view mirror. "This could be extra fun."

I took Kate's hand and smiled. "You haven't lived until you've survived driving in Nairobi."

"Oh, *God*," she said, biting her bottom lip. "I'm used to Manhattan traffic."

"Don't worry." Claire turned around to watch us. "Michael's an expert. He's been driving in Nairobi most of his life and took his driver's license here so he knows the roads, the traffic and how to deal with the idiots."

For the next fifteen minutes, we wove through traffic, moving from side streets to the main roadway and then to the Aga Khan University Medical College faculty club where the mixer was being held.

Michael led us inside the building to an elegant room with overstuffed sofas and chairs, tables with white linen, located at the back of the faculty club. There were perhaps two-dozen students there along with faculty. While Michael

13

took me to a group of students, Claire took Kate's arm and led her over to a table filled with treats and drinks.

"Kate can come with us," I said to Michael but he waved a hand. "Let Claire take care of Kate. I'm sure it will be a huge bore to have to meet everyone. She and Claire can get to know one another."

I didn't argue although I was upset that Kate wouldn't be at my side. I wanted the students to know I had a partner so there'd be no misunderstanding. I wanted Sam to know that I was unavailable.

On his part, Michel played the part of the generous mentor and introduced me to all the new students, some of whom I would be teaching during my stay. I felt Kate's eyes on me from across the room, and tried to make a face of regret but Claire had pulled Kate away before our eyes could meet.

Of course, at that moment, who should walk up but Sam. She had a huge smile plastered on her face as if she was so glad to see me. Still very attractive as a woman, tall and fair haired, she reminded me of Lara. Without the kink. Dominant. Assertive. I wasn't as glad to see her, but I'd do my best to be chivalrous and professional. She'd be a student. I'd make sure to treat her as one.

"Drake, you must remember Sam Cuttington from the last time you were here," Michael said and ushered her over.

She extended her hand. "Dr. Morgan," she said, a gleam in her eyes and a smile curving her lips.

"Hello, Sam," I said, trying to hide my lack of enthusiasm about her presence without appearing too interested.

"You came back," she said.

"I did," I said, taking my hand out of hers. At that moment, another young woman joined us.

"This is Camille Johannsen," Sam said. "She's also doing her residency."

We shook and the four of us stood together, me feeling incredibly awkward, wishing Michael would pull us away to another group of students so I wouldn't have to make small talk with them. Instead, Michael seemed intent on talking.

"Drake brought along his fiancée," Michael said and smiled at me. I turned to watch Sam's response. If she was shocked, she didn't show it and I wondered if Claire hadn't said something.

"You did?" she said and smiled perfunctorily.

"I did," I said. We spoke briefly about Kate and I told the three of them about her, proud of her accomplishments. It was then Kate walked over to where we stood.

I smiled when I saw her, glad that she took the opportunity to join me. "And here she is," I said, holding out my arm. Kate stepped into my embrace. I pulled her closer and kissed her squarely on the mouth, wanting there to be no doubt about how I felt.

"Kate, may I introduce Sam Cuttington and Camille ..." I said, but had forgotten the last name of the dark haired woman beside Sam.

"Johannsen," Camille said, smiling.

"Camille Johannsen," I said. "I was telling Sam and Camille that you're an artist and won the Columbia School of Journalism Medal for your thesis work on Mangaize."

Camille and Sam turned to Kate and smiled, but I could almost feel the tension in the air.

"Nice to meet you both." Kate smiled at each of them and then she turned to me. "When you get a chance, can you come speak to me?"

"What is it?" I asked, concerned that she was upset or not feeling well.

"Nothing urgent," she said and shook her head. "When you get a moment."

Kate smiled at everyone and I was surprised when she

15

stood on her tiptoes and kissed me. I obliged happily, wanting to reassure her that I only had eyes for her, that my heart belonged to her and her alone. She left us and went back to Claire, who stood at a table of canapés and glasses of wine, watching us, her expression intense.

I spent the next half hour or so tagging along with Michael as we made our rounds of the new students and faculty. I kept my eye on Kate and Claire, but Claire seemed to be taking good care of Kate.

Sam came over during a break in the conversation with Hans Bribeck, a new faculty member from Germany.

"Drake, I was hoping you'd have time to consult on a case."

I frowned, for the last thing I wanted to do that night was go to the hospital and spend time in the OR. I leaned against the couch as she gave me the particulars of the patient's history. The patient had an open skull fracture and was unstable. The young boy been in a motor vehicle collision and had been airlifted to the hospital earlier in the day. Initial stabilization and surgery had kept him from death, but his vitals were everywhere but where they should have been.

"Let's go speak with Michael," I said and Sam nodded. I led the way to where Michael stood talking with a student.

"Sorry to interrupt, but Sam wanted us to consult on a case."

The three of us discussed the case and Michael turned to me, laying his hand on my shoulder.

"Sorry to do this to you on your first evening in Nairobi, but we could use your expertise and you can count the case towards your accreditation. I'm sure Claire will be happy to escort Kate back to the hotel and we'll have you in and out of the ICU in no time."

I agreed and then made my way to where Kate sat with Claire, wanting to break the news to her as soon as possible.

"Hey," I said and leaned down to kiss her on the cheek. "How are you two doing? Bored out of your minds?"

"Pretty much," Kate said, an edge to her voice.

"Sorry about that. Listen," I said and sat beside her, one arm around her on the back of the sofa. I turned to Claire. "I hate to have to do this, but could you take Kate back to the hotel? Sam has a patient who came in this afternoon that she'd like us to check on. A motor vehicle accident, open skull fracture. Really unstable. Pediatric, so Michael's needed. Michael wants me to come as well."

Kate frowned, clearly unhappy with the turn of events. "Isn't that more for trauma surgeons to deal with?"

I shook my head. "They work on the rest of the body. We work on the brain. We'll check in and make sure everything's OK. Michael's on call this weekend, so…"

Claire stood up. "I'll leave the two of you alone. I'll go speak with Michael."

I stood when Claire did but then sat back down beside Kate.

"I'm sorry to do this," I said. "I know you're tired."

"She's beautiful, isn't she? She reminds me of Maureen," Kate said, her voice definitely sour. "Definitely not a mousy little thing…"

"Mousy?" I said and frowned, for it was unlike Kate to be openly jealous. "Who's mousy?" I glanced at her glass of wine. "How many of those have you had?"

"Two, but who's counting?"

Kate's tone belied the fact that she was very jealous. And a bit drunk.

I shook my head, smiling. Then I looked in her eyes. "Ms. Bennet, I do believe you're *tipsy*." I reached to take her glass of wine away. "I think you've had enough."

"*I* decide if I've had enough," she said, cradling the glass

17

against her body. "We're not Total Power Exchange, in case you forgot."

"How could I *ever* forget?" I said, amused. "I'm flattered that you're jealous, but *Katie*," I said, leaning in close to nuzzle her neck, "you have no reason to be. It's you I want to ravish when I get back to the hotel tonight. It's you I want to tie up and torture with pleasure."

I let that sink in, grazing the skin beneath her ear with my lips.

"I'm *sorry*," she said finally. She pulled away and looked in my eyes. "She's very attractive."

"*Kate*," I said, barely able to keep from laughing out loud. "There's nothing to be jealous of. It's you I want. It's you I *love*."

"She's going to be your student?" Kate said, her voice doubtful. "You'll work with her every day?"

I shook my head. "She came here to learn robotic surgery. That's what I'm teaching."

"So, you'll work with her."

"*Kate*…" I rubbed my eyes and exhaled heavily. Although I understood the reason for her jealousy, I wanted her to understand that I had absolutely no interest in Sam. I had no interest in any other woman. "This isn't like you."

"I've never been face to face with one of your former lovers before. My green eyes got the better of me."

"I love your green eyes," I whispered. "But you have no reason to be jealous. What happened to make you feel so insecure?"

She shook her head. "It's nothing. I'm sorry," she said.

"No, tell me. Complete openness, remember?"

She sighed. "When I was in the washroom, she came in with Camille and I overhead them talking about you. Sam said I was a mousy little thing and that you could do a lot better. *That's* what happened."

"What?" I said, shaking my head, amazed that Sam had already thrown a monkey wrench into things so quickly. "You are *not* mousy. You've got chestnut brown hair with gold highlights. You've got wide green eyes. A hot little body and make-me-delirious breasts. And I *couldn't* do a lot better. You're the best. The *crème de la crème*. Seriously. This is the wine talking."

"*In vino veritas*," she said, holding up her glass. "In wine there is truth. Isn't that how the saying goes?" She took a long slurp.

I knew I had to do something to stop this self-doubt of hers. Right now.

"You want the truth?" I said, my voice quiet so that none of the students or faculty around us could hear.

Kate nodded and leaned in closer. "The honest truth, yes. Tell me, Drake. What is the *truth*?"

"The *truth*, Ms. Bennet," I said and leaned even closer. I stroked her cheek, then touched the scar on her bottom lip. "The unadorned truth is that I was thunderstruck that night I met you and found out who you were."

"Thunderstruck?"

"Yes. When I bumped into you at the bar, I wished that you were a sub because I thought you were perfect. Petite. Lovely. So sexy in your little black dress. Nice rack."

I remembered that night vividly. I believe it was the best night of my life up till that point because it meant the start of our love affair.

I grinned lasciviously and she couldn't help but smile back.

"Then, when I found you at your father's apartment with your knees all bloody, I thought you were a lovely little thing, one of the hired help, who coincidentally happened to have been at the same bar as me. Ethan always kept *Katherine* away

19

from everyone so I didn't think you'd be at the fundraiser. I didn't know you were *her*."

Kate frowned. "What does that mean? Thunderstruck?"

"I was *struck*," I said, smiling wolfishly. "By the lightning bolt, as the Sicilians call it."

"The lightning bolt?" she repeated.

"If you read Puzo's *The Godfather*, you'd know that word. Michael Corleone was struck by the lightning bolt when he first saw Apollonia, his future wife. That's how I felt when Dave introduced you. I thought you were delicious looking when I first saw you, but when I learned you were *Katherine*... Thunderstruck. Completely infatuated. I felt actual physical despair because I couldn't imagine that you'd be a sub and so we'd never be able to get together. Then it was *you* with Lara... I was smitten, Kate, and it's only become more intense the longer we're together."

Kate stared off into the distance for a moment and then I saw her face change as she took my meaning in.

"Thunderstruck, *hmm*?" she said, a slow smile spreading on her mouth.

"Yes, thunderstruck," I said, wanting her to know how much she had affected me. I had been unable to think of anything or anyone else after that moment. "I still *see* women, of course, but to me they're pale shades in comparison to you. You're *Katherine*. My delightfully disobedient and un-submissive sub-in-training. My delicious little morsel of womanhood. Who," I said when she turned her face away, her cheeks flushing so deliciously. "*Who* understands my love for Africa. Who cries during musical performances. Whose heart I'm still trying to win completely." I took hold of her chin so that she had to look into my eyes. "The love of my life."

"Oh, *Drake*..." Tears brimmed in her eyes. "You *have* won it."

"No, I haven't," I said, realizing it at that precise moment. "If I had, someone's cruel and incorrect words wouldn't matter. You wouldn't be jealous."

Kate slipped her arms around my neck and squeezed.

"I was worried you'd grow bored with me and she'd be there, waiting..."

"What?" I pulled back and frowned, then shook my head slowly. "How could I grow bored with you when I've barely trained you? You've barely submitted to me. I didn't think you really wanted it, so I haven't pushed."

I hadn't pushed. I didn't want to scare her off. She was like a young doe, fearful, ready to bolt at any loud noise. I knew I'd have to go slow with her. I wanted to win her completely—body, mind and soul.

"I've totally indulged you, Kate. If I wasn't in love with you, you'd be regularly on your knees to me, saying nothing, complying immediately with my smallest demand – unless you wanted a good barehanded spanking."

"If I did want to submit more, would that make you happier?" she asked, her face slightly fearful.

"No, *no*," I said, inhaling deeply. "I'm happy with you the way you are. I don't *want* to change you. I want to know what you need, and then I want to give it to you exactly the way you want it. I still haven't determined how much of a submissive you are. How much dominance you need from me to be completely fulfilled. It'll take time but we have the rest of our lives."

She smiled and brushed a strand of hair from my eyes. "You really need a haircut, but I think I prefer you with your hair a bit longer."

I smiled back. "If you like it longer, that's the way it's staying. We aim to please." I let that sink in. "You have no reason to be insecure. I'm yours completely, Ms. Bennet. What more must I do to do to prove it?"

"Nothing. Forget it." She sighed. "I'm tired and excited and feeling a bit vulnerable. That's all."

"We have the entire weekend to spend together," I said and touched her cheek. "Once we find a house, we can spend some time alone or we can do some furniture shopping. Whatever you want. I promise. Tomorrow, I'm all yours. Every single *inch* of me." I grinned, knowing where her mind would go.

She seemed to finally give in and leaned her head against my shoulder. I pulled her more deeply into my embrace and I felt her start to relax a bit. Then I kissed her, slipping my tongue between her lips briefly before leaving her to rejoin Michael. Claire was quick to return and sat beside Kate. I was happy that Claire was so willing to take care of Kate while I left her to go to the hospital with Michael and Sam.

"Shall we go?" I said, my hand on Michael's shoulder. He nodded and I glanced back at Kate, touching my lips briefly in a kiss. She smiled back but her smile was quite wistful and I knew she still wasn't secure in our relationship. As we walked out of the Faculty Club to Michael's car, I resolved to do everything in my power to remove Kate's sense of insecurity.

She had to know what there were no other women in the world for me. Only her.

I was surprised how comfortable I felt in the Aga Khan hospital ICU. It had been several years since I'd been there and I was certain I'd feel out of my element at first, but everything came flooding back once I crossed the threshold and entered my old haunts.

A huge complex of red-brick buildings surrounded by palm trees, the hospital was Michael's pride and joy. He'd spent most of his career there. We entered the ICU and the three of us put on lab coats and washed up hastily so we could go on the ward and check on Sam's patient. A young boy with a brain injury who was showing signs of a subdural hematoma.

We checked scans and sure enough, it was as we thought.

"What do you think?" Michael said to me.

"CT is positive. Scored low on the Glasgow Coma Scale," I said. "I'd say its imperative to get in quickly."

"Baptism of fire?" Michael asked as we convened at the nursing station to discuss the case. "Care to scrub in and assist? It would count towards your accreditation, if that's the way you want to go in the future..."

I wanted to get back to the hotel and to Kate, but Michael seemed really interested in having me in the OR with him and I was seriously thinking of doing a fellowship in pediatric neurosurgery. The case would go towards the hours I would need for accreditation.

"How could I say no?"

We scrubbed up and the procedure was pretty routine for me as an acute subdural hematoma was one of the biggest causes of traumatic brain injury, but I knew it was an exciting event for Sam, who was assisting.

Everything went as well as could be expected. We finished up and then left the OR to speak with the patient's family. After delivering the news of a successful surgery, the four of us went to Michael's office for a debrief. Sam gave the report, and I remembered how bright she was, how eager she was to do well. She was a surgeon. That came with the territory. You couldn't cut into a person's brain and not have a huge set of balls – or ovaries, as the case may be.

After we finished the debrief, I removed my scrubs and changed back into my street clothes. On my way out of the hospital, Sam ran to my side.

"So glad you decided to teach this semester," she said as she caught up with me.

"I'm glad to finally have the opportunity to return."

I smiled perfunctorily, hoping she'd get the message that we weren't going to be all cozy again like before, but she didn't seem to get it.

"Want to go out for a drink at Murphy's for old time's sake?"

I shook my head. "I have a very new fiancée waiting for me back at the hotel and I hated to have to leave her on our first night in Kenya. I have to go."

I smiled once more and waved to her as I got into a taxi.

"See you soon," she said and I could hear the disappointment in her voice.

She had to realize that nothing could happen between us. If not, I'd be sure to drive that fact home again if need be. I didn't want anything complicating my life and especially my relationship with Kate.

When I arrived back at the hotel room, Kate was in bed reading.

"There you are," she said when our eyes met. I went over to the bed and leaned down for a kiss.

"Sorry I'm so late on our first night in Nairobi," I said as I started to undress. "The patient decompensated and we had to go in and operate to remove a subdural hematoma to relieve pressure on his brain. Poor kid. Don't know why parents don't put their kids in proper car seats. If they saw what I saw on a regular basis, they'd never get in a car without one."

Kate put down her book. "That's so sad. Will he be OK?"

I shrugged. "If he survives the night, his chances are good. The next few hours will be critical. It was nice to be in surgery again, but I was exhausted, so I was glad I was only watching." I finished undressing down to my boxer briefs and then went to the bathroom to wash up before bed.

After I was done, I stripped and turned off the lights in the rest of the suite. Then I slid into bed beside Kate.

"I'm exhausted. Go ahead and keep reading if you want, but I have to crash."

"No, that's fine," Kate said and put down her book. She turned off the light and we snuggled in the darkness.

I slipped my arm around her waist. "You know I wish I could fuck you, Ms. Bennet," I said. "But I'm afraid I'd fall asleep in the middle and since I'm such a deep sleeper, you'd be trapped beneath me all night and suffocate…"

"Don't worry," she said, and I could hear the resignation in her voice. "I can wait. I went a whole year without sex before I met you. What's one night?"

"Oh, *God*, one night is far too long…" I said, unable to comprehend how she could go so long without a sexual relationship.

I pulled her against my body and kissed her neck, her jaw and then her lips.

"Tomorrow," I said. "I promise. I'm going to make you come four times. You're going to be sore, and so satiated that you beg me to give you a break."

She snuggled more closely against me, hiding her face in the crook of my neck. I stroked her cheek. "Goodnight, my love," he said.

"Goodnight."

Kate was probably disappointed that we wouldn't make love, but I wanted to focus completely on her when we had sex and I could already feel my eyelids getting heavy. Glad that she understood, I closed my eyes, exhausted from the day's events, warm in Kate's arms.

CHAPTER 3

I woke to the sight of Kate's back and shoulders, her hair spilled out on the pillow like silk. I slipped my arm around her and pulled her against my body.

"Good morning, future Mrs. Drake Morgan."

Kate turned over and looked at me, a coy smile on her lips. "You mean Ms. Katherine McDermott, future wife of Drake Morgan, M.D."

"You're not going to take my name?" I said, keeping my voice light. I was a bit surprised, but she was a feminist from a wealthy family, so I expected she might want to keep her own last name. I was happy that she wanted to marry me. Her choice of taking my name was just a detail.

"We never really talked about it," she said hesitantly. "I always swore as a modern feminist that I'd never take on a man's name if I married."

I smiled, narrowing my eyes. "You don't appreciate patriarchal traditions?"

"I'm not a possession," she said, and it was then I realized she was taking me seriously.

I decided to play a bit. Toy with her to see what she thought so I didn't answer.

She frowned. "Do you *want* me to take your name?"

"Of course," I said, keeping my voice formal, frowning back. "As my slave, you must take on your master's name..."

She stared in my eyes as if trying to see if I were serious. Then, I burst out laughing and tickled her. I was delighted when she squirmed and giggled uncontrollably.

"I'm kidding," I said. "I always assumed you'd keep your own name so I was only playing around when I called you Mrs. Drake Morgan. It's the most formal thing I could think of at the time."

I stopped tickling her, enjoying the moment of intimacy.

"I'm serious, Drake," she said and reached out to brush a hank of hair from my eyes. "What do *you* want?"

"I want you to be mine completely," I said and squeezed her, "but that's more a matter of the mind and soul. A name is just a name and if you don't feel it, taking on my name would mean nothing."

"I thought you wanted me to remain my own woman," Kate said, pouting a bit. "Those were your words."

I exhaled, wanting to be truthful but wanting her to choose to take my name rather than feel obligated. "Of course I do. But one who gives herself to me completely. That's what marriage is. Complete and total exclusion of all others. We are each other's property. No one else's."

She nodded. "I will and I do."

"Good. Whatever you decide about taking my name is good, as long as you marry me." I pulled her closer and kissed her softly. When I did, I could taste the minty toothpaste on her tongue. I pulled back. "Hey, no fair! You already showered and brushed your teeth."

She grinned and slipped her arms around my waist,

28

nuzzling my neck, kissing the skin beneath my ear. "Early bird gets the fresh breath."

I tickled her again and she squirmed away from my fingers, laughing. Then I rolled out of bed and strode to the bathroom, very aware of my morning erection. I had to hold it down or else I'd pee all over the wall.

"How often do you work out?" she called from the bed.

I turned to the sink and washed my hands. "Before I met you? Couple times a week. After I met you? Zero. I'll have to use the university weight room and track if I don't want to become a fat old man."

"You'll never be a fat old man, Drake. You're too conscious of your health. Besides, I saw pictures of your father when he was in his fifties. He was still well-built and trim. You'll be like him."

"Hope so," I said and turned on the shower. I stepped in and quickly washed then when I was finished, I dried off before sprinting back to the bed, jumping on it and slipping under the covers. I lay on top of Kate, the touch of her soft flesh under me making me instantly hard once more.

"I hope you're not teasing me, Doctor Morgan," she said, her voice a bit breathless, "coming back here still wet and naked and lying on top of me. I hope you intend to follow through."

I pulled away, frowning in mock affront. "Whatever could you possibly mean, Ms. Bennet? Me tease you? Not follow through? I would never be so cruel...Don't I always finish what I start?"

"You do. You always please me. I hope I always please you as well."

"You do," I said and kissed her shoulder. "But there is one thing I'd *like* to try that I haven't."

Her eyes widened. "And that is?"

I grinned and pressed my lips next to her ear. "Big." I brushed my lips against her cheek, then licked her neck.

Her eyes widened. "Oh, *God...*" She burst out laughing at that.

"Kate, don't laugh at my desires," I said, serious about it. We had to be open about our fantasies.

"I'm sorry," she said quickly and touched my cheek. "I told you already that he won't fit so it would be a waste of time."

I didn't say anything, but I knew that she could fit Big inside of her if she was adequately aroused.

"I tried, believe me," she said, her expression earnest.

"You had orgasms with it," I asked.

"Yes, but that was purely clitoral," she said. "I never got him inside."

I smiled to myself that she called Big 'him' but kept my eyes narrowed. "I could get it inside of you."

"No, I don't think so. You haven't seen it. Waaay too big."

"You want a friendly wager?" I said, aroused at the prospect of proving her wrong. "I'll bet you three free orgasms that I can get Big inside of you and make you come when I do."

She frowned. "That's a win-win for you because you know you'll give those orgasms regardless. Besides, it would hurt."

I shook my head. "No, it wouldn't. I'd have you so worked up that when it was finally inside, you'd come immediately."

She smiled and turned her face away. "I don't know…"

"Is this a *hard* limit, Ms. Bennet?"

"When you call me Ms. Bennet, I can't be a sub."

"I know," I said, smiling guiltily. "*Katherine.* Is it a hard limit?"

Once more, she stared into my eyes like she was trying to read how serious I was. Finally, she shook her head.

"Of course not. If you say I'll enjoy it, I know I will. You've always been right. I trust you completely."

I nodded, pleased that she was willing to give in so easily. "Good. No wager, then. You packed it in the boxes we had sent here before we left?"

"Yes."

"Good," I said again. "Our boxes are already in storage. When I get it, I'll show you just how good it can make you feel."

Then I kissed her and began a slow seduction of her body and mind with kisses on her cheek, down her neck and throat. I kissed her breasts, almost drowning in them they were so lush and full, her nipples hardening beneath my tongue and fingers. She groaned, pressing her breast into my face.

"That's what I want to hear," I murmured against her skin as I traced a line from her nipple to her belly with my tongue, circling her navel. I pressed her thighs apart and Kate exhaled and writhed beneath my mouth.

I pulled away and glanced up. "I'm going to have to restrain you, *Katherine*, if you don't lie still."

"I can't..." She gasped when I flicked my tongue lower, her body jerking in response.

"Hold onto the headboard," I said. "Keep your legs still."

Despite my orders, she didn't stop moving as my tongue swept over her clit again and again, her body shuddering with each touch. I knew it wouldn't take long for her to come.

"*Drake...*"

I didn't stop to build her up again for I wanted to fuck her right away and feel her first orgasm on my cock when I was inside of her. I leaned up over her and entered her with one long smooth thrust, shoving into her fully. I lay on top of her,

31

my arms on either side of her head. I didn't move. I merely lay there, fully inside her body, and kissed her.

She squeezed around me, greedy for more stimulation, but I wanted her to give over control. I stopped, breaking the kiss.

"Stop," I said. "Lie still."

She did. "What are you…"

"Shh," I said and kissed her once more, my tongue finding hers, sucking it into my mouth.

She wrapped her legs around my waist.

"Don't *move*," I said again. She stopped and waited but I knew she was frustrated and in need of release. I wanted to teach her patience.

We lay still, locked in each other's embrace, my cock deep inside of her. Finally, when I was certain she was truly giving over control, I began to thrust slowly, deliberately slowly, my face over hers, watching her closely.

"Drake—" she started to say but I covered her mouth with mine, drowning out her words. I thrust hard and deep and she went over the edge, her breathing erratic, her eyes almost rolling up into her head. I felt her muscles clench around me as I thrust harder and faster. Then I came, pleasure shooting from deep in my groin, my balls, and the head of my cock as I ejaculated into her.

We lay with our limbs entwined for a few moments, both of us breathing heavily.

Finally, I slipped out of her, but I remained on top of her, her legs around my waist, her arms around my neck.

"We've become very vanilla," she said.

I pulled back, one eyebrow quirked. "Not enough kink for you, Ms. Bennet? It sure felt and sounded like you enjoyed it."

"I did," she said and bit her bottom lip. "But is it good enough for you?"

"Being with you, any way I can be with you, is good

enough for me. But I'll make a special trip to the hardware store next weekend so we can play a bit once we get our own place. I *promise...*" I glanced around the room. "This bed is no good for bondage, and I don't want the butler to find any spreader bars or other implements of pleasure so we'll have to make do with plain old dominance. But you have to learn to obey, Katherine, or I'll have to stop being so indulgent and smack that pretty pink ass of yours."

"Am I bad sub?" she said, batting her eyelashes playfully.

"*You* are very bad," I said and kissed her neck. "I'd deny you an orgasm in punishment but you're far too responsive and would come despite my best efforts."

Kate sighed and squeezed me more tightly. "Do you think there are dungeon parties in Nairobi?"

"I happen to *know* there are dungeon parties here because I went to one when I was here before. There are dungeon parties wherever there are enough kinky people. Do you want me to find out when the next event is scheduled?"

"I want you to be happy, Drake. If you need more kink, more D/s, I'm game."

"I *am* happy," I said and kissed her. "I have everything I could want. You're here with me. I have a teaching job and a surgical slate. I'm working with an old friend. Being able to help out here in Africa." I shook my head slowly. "You don't have to worry about that. The only thing that would make me happier would be to know that you couldn't be happier."

Kate smiled but it took her a bit longer to say it. "*You* make me happy," she said finally, and I was a bit disappointed. Was she worried that it wouldn't be enough?

"It's only six months," I said and kissed her chin. "Before you know it, we'll be returning to Manhattan and will start planning our wedding."

She smiled at that. Perhaps she was just anxious about being so far away from everything that she knew and loved.

I'd have to ensure I spent as much quality time with her as I could, given my soon-to-be very busy schedule of teaching and surgery.

Her happiness was my happiness.

WE SHOWERED TOGETHER AFTERWARDS and I felt as if my life had finally come together. It had been years since I had done intimate day-to-day activities with a woman. Eat breakfast, read the papers, shower, talk about the weather, plan for the afternoon, think about dinner. These were things I avoided for years, not wanting to get tangled up in someone else's life only to be untangled painfully as I had with Maureen.

Now, I relished the small things Kate and I did together as a couple.

While we were sitting enjoying our breakfast, I called Jan, our real estate broker to set up appointments to see houses for rent.

When I finished talking to him, I slipped my cell into a pocket. "Jan has three lined up for this afternoon. I thought we might spend the day in bed, but I'd like to jump on this, get a place as soon as possible. Michael wants me to start at the hospital on Monday. Classes start the following week and I have lots of work to do to get ready."

Kate smiled and a pleasant silence passed between us as we finished our meal.

I glanced at Kate, who sat smiling at me. "What are you thinking about?"

"About the open studio courses at the Institute that Claire mentioned to me. I want to check it out, see if they have space. I have that series of paintings to finish that I started in Manhattan. Plus, they have studio space for students. "

I made a face, wanting to tease her about the nude paint-

34

ings she'd done of me. "Not more nudes of me sleeping I hope."

"No," she said with a grin. "You naked in the bath. You naked sitting on the couch. You naked standing at the window, drinking a coffee..."

I laughed. "Can't I be wearing some boxers or something? Not everyone wants to see my *parts*."

"The collection will be for me. And maybe I'll let you wear some boxer briefs. No tighty whities for you."

"*Never*," I said, making a face of mock horror and holding up my fingers, crossed as if to ward off a vampire. "But I thought we'd find a house with space for a studio. You wouldn't have to worry about finding space anywhere or working out a schedule."

Kate smiled. "That would be nice, but part of the reason you work at a studio is to meet other artists. Be inspired by their work."

"You mean like the three stooges at the studio in Chelsea?" I said, only half meaning it. I had been jealous of their time with Kate, I admitted to myself. They shared something with her that I never would.

"They *weren't* stooges!" she said and pouted. "Well, maybe *Jules*..."

"I must confess I didn't really feel comfortable with you being alone with three men," I said, hating to admit it but wanting to be open with Kate so she could trust me.

"*Drake*," she said, chidingly. "I have to have a life outside of you like you have. Maybe I should be jealous of you with all those pretty young OR nurses, not to mention young aspiring female brain surgeons..."

"Ha!" I shook my head. "Skilled OR nurses are hard to find. They tend to be very bossy. They run the OR, in case you didn't realize it. We surgeons come in when they're all ready and do our bit and then leave. As to the surgical residents, most of the time they're far too exhausted to have affairs. Don't let the television shows fool you." I took her hand in mine and stroked her skin. "You have no reason to be jealous."

She smiled. "Neither do you. I doubt there are many gorgeous brilliant talented and sexually dominant artists who could hope to hold a candle to you, Dr. Delish. You don't have to worry, either."

"Well," I said, making a sad face. "If you really want to explore the local artist hangouts, if you *really* want studio time somewhere, I won't stop you. But I reserve the right to be jealous if your fellow artists are too attractive."

"I reserve the right if the OR nurses and residents are sexy young things."

"Agreed."

We both forced a smile. Kate had to understand that there was no one else who could hold a candle to her in my heart and mind.

I'd gladly spend the rest of my life proving it to her.

ONCE OUR MEAL was finished and we'd had a coffee, we took a walk around the hotel grounds. My cell rang and when I checked the display, it was Jan.

"I'm on my way to pick you up," he said, the sounds of traffic on the line. "Expect me in a quarter of an hour."

"We'll meet you in the lobby in fifteen."

I ended the call and turned to Kate. "Jan will be here in fifteen to take us to our first appointment. A place in Kihingo Village."

"Where's that?"

"North and west of Nairobi's city center in Kitusuru," I said, remembering it from my time before. "Gated, walled and really upscale. He has five houses available there, but we'll only see three today."

Kate nodded, and I could tell from her wide eyes and flushed cheeks that she was eager to start finding our new home together.

We walked back to the hotel and freshened up, then went to the lobby to wait for Jan. He arrived in a late model BMW and we met him at the door. After introductions all around, he escorted us to the car and opened the door for Kate.

Jan moved to Kenya from Denmark a decade earlier, and quickly became familiar with the real estate market in Nairobi. He was sought-after because he catered to foreign visitors needing short-term housing. Jan spent the first few moments of the trip explaining the community that we would be visiting first. Made up primarily of rich expat Americans working at the University, area hospitals, or for one of the corporations located in Nairobi, it was secure and quiet. After traveling north from the hotel, we arrived at Kitusuru Estates in the Kihingo Village where the first house was located. There was a gate with a guardhouse at the entrance to the estate. The estate itself was lush and green.

The houses were very upscale and the community resembled any you might find in the big cities in the southern region of the US. It was a family neighborhood, with a soccer field, a lake and wide streets with little traffic.

The first house was a red brick four bedroom with a pool.

Jan stopped the car on the street and turned to us. "This one has four bedrooms and four bathrooms, a huge lot with a swimming pool, and there's a community tennis court, a track and shopping all within the compound."

Kate turned to me, her expression doubtful. "Do we really need a place so big?"

I took her hand. "No, but we can invite people to come

and stay with us. Plus, you can use a room as a studio. I'll have an office and we could have a guest room."

She nodded, and followed me into the house.

It was impressive. A large foyer led to a living room and dining room with vaulted ceilings and huge windows looking out over a large yard. The master bedroom was as large as Kate's apartment and the bathroom off the master was marble with golden faucets and a two-person glass and tile shower. I immediately thought of having sex with Kate in the shower and I smiled to myself when I saw her examining it, wondering if she was thinking the same thing.

"This would be my office," I said when we poked our head into a smaller bedroom. The next bedroom was just as small and we decided it would be a guest bedroom. The final bedroom was almost as large as the master.

"This could be your studio," I said, smiling indulgently at her.

I watched as Kate walked around and examined the space. "It's amazing," she said, standing in the center of the room.

"It is, isn't it?" I glanced around and then turned back to her. "So much better than the studio in Chelsea and that tiny room you had."

She nodded. "I'd still want to get some studio space in the city," she said as she examined the closet. "Otherwise, I'll get really lonely with you gone all day."

"Of course," I said, but I felt a twinge of jealousy. *Damn*. I had to fight it. She had to have her own life if she was to be happy in Nairobi.

Kate came to me and slid her arms around my waist. "You don't sound very certain."

I shook my head and put my arms around her shoulders.

"Of course I am. I can't keep you hidden away like some priceless jewel, now, can I? What kind of future-husband would I be? Typical masculine jealousy creeping in. Ignore

38

it." I bent down and kissed her. "I can't wait for us to make one of these places our home. Buying groceries, cooking meals together, swimming in the pool, walking the streets, sleeping in late on the weekends. Using the shower stall. I can think of a thousand things to do once we're moved in and all alone."

She smiled up at me. "You can? What could you possibly mean?"

I grinned. "I'll have to make a pit stop at the local hardware store for some rope and maybe a few hooks and padlocks. I can't wait to tie you up and keep you so sexually satisfied, you'll never want to leave the grounds."

"I can't wait either," she said, her voice a whisper. "But I'll still have to go out now and then..."

"Now and then." I squeezed her once more and then led her back to the kitchen where Jan stood waiting.

"Well? What did you think?" Jan turned to Kate as if she was the one to decide.

"I can't imagine seeing anything more wonderful than this house."

"It is the nicest." Jan admitted. "But there are a few others I've arranged, so if you're ready, we can go."

We saw two other houses but they couldn't compare to the first house. I could tell from the way Kate commented on the amenities that she preferred the first one, the red brick house.

"Properties are really scarce this time of year," Jan said when we left the final house. "These three are all I have in this area. We can see others tomorrow, but this is by far the nicest community in the city."

We drove back the way we came and ended up driving past the first house once more. I wondered if that wasn't done on purpose, to tempt us even more.

I took Kate's hand and kissed her knuckles.

"What did you think?"

"I loved the first house," Kate said wistfully. "I'd take it now, if it was up to me."

"My thoughts exactly," I said and smiled. "Jan, I think our minds are made up. We like the first house."

Jan laughed. "I thought you'd like it. Consider it done. I'm the renting agent on that one and if you give me the deposit, it's yours. The current renters have moved out, but it has to be cleaned. You can have it in ten days once the paperwork goes through."

SUNDAY WENT by all to quickly. The two of us were lazy, so we spent our time in bed. I arranged for room service and we had breakfast brought in so we didn't have to go out. We read the local English papers and even caught a newscast. I relished every moment with Kate, making very vanilla love to her twice, thinking that I'd probably be exhausted after my first week at the hospital and would likely not have much energy.

I was right.

I started at the hospital on Monday, doing rounds with Michael and meeting with prospective patients and was late getting home my very first full day at work.

On her part, Kate spent the day alone but she texted me to say that she and Claire were going to do some shopping for our house.

I had to stay late to work with Michael, and didn't arrive back at the hotel until midnight. I was extremely tired so I was ready to get to bed. Kate was asleep so I did my best not to disturb her, although I would have liked to have spoken with her a bit before going to sleep. It wouldn't be fair to wake her up just to go back to sleep so I crept into bed and slipped next to her, being careful not to touch her.

I knew that there would be very many similar nights for us in the future. Such was the life of a surgeon, especially one who was in high demand as neurosurgeon were. As one of the vanishingly small number of pediatric neurosurgeons in Africa, Michael was in very high demand and I wanted to soak up every bit of his knowledge because I was hoping to specialize in pediatric neurosurgery. It was still just a thought but my time with Michael would help me decide.

I barely remembered my head hitting the pillow before I was asleep.

CHAPTER 4

THE WEEK PASSED QUICKLY. I was so busy doing rounds with Michael, scrubbing in on cases with him and his residents, that I barely had time to think. I was home late every night and was exhausted. It was quite different from my practice in Manhattan where I chose only the most interesting cases. Here, we were always busy because the hospital was a center for neurosurgery and there were never enough surgeons to meet the demand.

Michael insisted we take Friday night off and wanted Kate and I to join him and Claire for dinner.

"You need some real Kenyan food," Michael said and poked my stomach. "You need to take that pretty young fiancée of yours out or she'll be too bored with life here."

I agreed and texted Kate so she knew to expect me around five instead of later. Once I finished at the hospital, I made a special trip to the storage facility where our belongings were being held until we moved into our house. I sorted through boxes until I found what I was looking for – *Big*. The flesh colored dildo that was bigger than me by about half again. I knew I could fit it inside of Kate, having

43

fit my hand inside of a pregnant woman to deliver her breech twin, but I would have to ensure Kate was completely prepared, aroused and dying for it before I would try.

I intended to try tonight after dinner when Kate and I were alone. It wasn't just the thought of using a sex toy with Kate that turned me on, although it did. I wanted to show Kate that she could trust me with her body and her mind.

I knew what she could enjoy and if she let me, I would ensure she did.

I arrived home and while Kate was in the bathroom, I hid Big in a box in the closet. I'd bring it out later when Kate was already bound and blindfolded and ready.

Once I was certain that it was well-hidden, I had a quick shower and changed my clothes. Then, Michael and Claire picked us up shortly before seven for our night on the town.

The restaurant was called *'Ranalo's'* and was known for its home-cooked food, using fresh local food and recipes.

"You should try the tilapia," Michael said "It's great and very fresh."

Despite the restaurant being busy, we found a table on the patio, which has open to the night sky.

"So Miss Katherine," Michael said to Kate after we ordered our meal. "Tell us what your plans are while you're in Nairobi. As you can see from this first full week, I'm afraid I'm going to be keeping Drake very busy with surgery and teaching. I've been working on him for years to come and help out here at the college, and now that I have him, I'm not letting go easily."

"I understand," Kate said and turned to me, squeezing my hand. "I'm going to spend time painting."

"Kate's an artist and plans on doing some wildlife art while she's here," I said, smiling at her, incredibly proud of her talent and mind.

"I've always wanted to focus on my art," Kate said, "but have been so busy with school I haven't had the chance."

Claire turned to her. "I can take you out on safari if you like. I know some great outfitters and tour guides. Once you get settled, let me know and I'll arrange things."

"Thank you," Kate said. "I'd like that."

Kate looked at me and smiled and I could see real excitement in her eyes.

It was at that moment that Sam and Camille showed up, walking into the restaurant together.

When I saw her, I couldn't help but frown in annoyance. Michael turned when Sam came over.

"Hello," Sam said. "Fancy meeting all of you here."

Claire turned around, her face all surprised. Michael and I stood, pushing back our chairs to be polite.

"What a coincidence," Michael said, extending his hand to Sam. Then he shook the other young woman's hand. "Camille."

"Someone mentioned Ranalo's the other day and I remembered how good their fish is," Sam said. "We finished up with a case and decided some fresh fish was on order."

Then, she turned to me. "Drake, you know Camille Johannsen, from my hometown in South Africa. You met her at the faculty mixer."

I forced a smile. "Of course," I said and shook her hand. I fastened the button on my suit jacket. "You remember Kate, my fiancée," I said, trying to keep my voice light but wanting to reinforce that I was taken.

Kate smiled but I could tell she was uncomfortable.

"Nice to see you again, Claire," Sam said to Claire, who smiled back.

Sam turned back to Michael and me. "Well, we won't keep you. There's a table over in the corner we better snag if we want to eat."

I sat back down once they left and adjusted my jacket, unhappy that she showed up. It couldn't be a coincidence that Sam showed up at Ranalo's on the same night that I was there with Michael. I tried to remember if Michael had said anything in front of Sam, but couldn't recall.

"Camille is an outstanding new doctor from South Africa," Michael said. "She did her MD there and is here to specialize."

I nodded then turned to Kate, leaning over to kiss her on the cheek.

If Sam thought she'd disrupt our meal, she succeeded but I was going to salvage it as best I could. I did not want Sam to be a constant reminder to Kate that we had a sexual relationship when I was in Nairobi before. I would prefer that Sam had never come to Kenya, but there was nothing I could do about it now except give her a very cold shoulder.

Our food arrived and the mood changed back to more relaxed. We ate with gusto, commenting on how delicious the meal was, how fresh the ingredients. Michael and I caught up on our lives, not really having a chance to speak on a more personal level since I started working.

"Tell me about your father," Michael said, his face somber. "I know he died on a trip to Somalia. It must have been such a shock."

I nodded, my mood changing back from festive to reflective. "Even knowing he was putting himself in danger, I didn't expect him to die in a plane crash. I thought he'd get shot in an attack."

I said nothing for a moment, pushing my food around on my plate, trying to think of the right words to say.

"Tell me what happened," Michael said, his voice soft. "I read an article in a newsletter, but don't know the details."

I sighed. "He was flying with a nurse and a local physician to work in a field hospital with the Red Cross. The engine of

46

their small plane failed and they crashed about ten miles from the runway. It took a few days to find the crash site. Luckily, they were still in the cabin or there might be nothing left of them due to scavengers."

"He's buried in Ethiopia?"

I nodded. "Before the accident, we talked about what might happen to him if he was killed in the fighting. He said he wanted to be cremated and his ashes spread in Ethiopia, which was his favorite place. Told me to find a really big Baobab tree and spread his ashes beneath it so that his carbon would feed the tree. He was such a romantic at heart. I did that last year when I visited."

"Where was I?" Michael said. "I would have liked to go with you."

"You were at a conference in London."

Michael nodded and took a long sip of his beer.

Claire turned to Kate. "You wouldn't think to meet Liam that he had such a soft heart, but he did. He was so calm in an emergency, as if chaos made him feel in control. Many people panic when there's an emergency, but not Liam. He always thrived under those conditions."

"You knew him well?" Kate asked.

"I met him through Doctors Without Borders," Claire said. "We invited Liam to stay with us when he was in Nairobi."

"Liam made sure Drake came to Africa with him one year. We hit it off right away," Michael said, turning to me. "I've been trying to get him to come to teach at the college for years. I sure miss Liam, though. He'd stop in whenever he was in Africa. Made a point of visiting even though we have no wars going on, other than on the streets."

The reference to recent violence in Nairobi had us all silent for a moment.

"I tried to talk Liam into working here in our trauma center, but he preferred the battlefield."

"His first medical experiences were on the battlefield in Vietnam," I said. "The streets of Baltimore were too tame for him. That's why he volunteered to come to Somalia. He went the way he would have wanted," I replied. "Flying over Africa on his way to the battlefield. He was more afraid of dying an old man."

"Still, he had many good years left in him."

I nodded and thought about my father, the wild man who thrived in chaos and could never stay too long in one place without getting bored.

After a moment, Claire changed the subject, as if she was trying to lighten the conversation. "We see Drake as the son we never had," Claire told Kate, then looked at me, a smile on her face. "We had four girls, so Michael felt quite indulgent towards Drake."

I smiled back at Claire. She had been very protective when I was in Africa before. She was like a mother to me, fussing over me and always checking on how I was doing. I wasn't used to it, but I enjoyed the attention, having been denied a real mother all my childhood.

We finished our meal and as we left the restaurant, past the line of patrons waiting to get inside, I saw Sam and Camille sitting together at a table. I hoped that she wouldn't be a problem.

Michael and Claire drove us back to the hotel, and after we thanked them for a delicious meal, Michael invited us to their home on the weekend. I glanced at Kate to make sure she was in agreement and she smiled, nodding to me as if she was happy to go to their home. I realized that she might take comfort in having Claire's friendship and I was pleased that Claire had taken on the role happily.

48

"And now, Ms. Bennet, let's go to our room," I said and took Kate's hand. "I want a swim in the pool and then you."

Kate smiled and let me lead her into the hotel and down the hallways to our suite. While I went to the washroom, Kate stood on the balcony. When I was finished, I went to her, slipping my arms around her waist, my cheek pressed against hers. I kissed her neck.

"I missed you all week."

She turned and faced me, her arms threading around my neck. "I missed *you* all week."

"I'll be away a lot at first," I said, pulling her hips against mine so she could feel my growing erection. "I promise I'll do my best to make it up to you when I'm home."

"I can't wait to go on safari and see the sky in real darkness." She leaned her head against my chest.

"Once we get settled, we'll go, but right now, I can't wait to blindfold you and restrain you," I said to her. "I have all kinds of plans for you, *Katherine*."

"You still want to swim first?" she asked, while I kissed her neck.

"Yes," I said. "I can wait a few more minutes to ravish you."

She laughed and we finally ended the embrace. We changed into our bathing suits and when I saw her in the little white bikini she wore in the Bahamas, a surge of desire flooded through me.

"Oh, I *like* it," I said, taking in her deliciously curvy body. "I seem to recall trying to take it off one afternoon and being rudely interrupted by your father..."

Kate laughed and tied the top, her arms behind her back. "No fear of that here."

"When you stand like that, I lose all interest in swimming, Ms. Bennet..."

"I can't help it," she said. "I have to tie up my top."

"I may have to untie it if you keep it up."

Kate turned away almost demurely. We grabbed our towels and went to the outdoor pool. Luckily, there was no one else there. I dove in, preferring to get wet all at once, but Kate sat on the side of the pool with just her legs in the water.

"Come on in," I said as I treaded water in front of her. "It's heated."

She slipped in and ducked under. I swam over and took her into my arms, and we floated together for a moment. "The view is nice," Kate said, slipping out of my arms and lying back, floating, her eyes on the sky.

The water was warm and the night air cool, and while I watched, Kate's nipples hardened in the cold.

"Yes, it *is* nice," I said, barely able to keep a grin off my face.

"You get to see *that* view any time you want," Kate said in meek protest. "Look at the sky for a change. The night's really clear."

I relented and floated beside her for a while, trying to match her mood, but she had to know I wanted her.

"This is like heaven," she said with a sigh of contentment.

"It is."

We floated in a pleasant silence, the stars bright above us. I tried to be patient with her, let her take the lead for when our swim was finished.

She spoke after a while, her voice soft. "Quite the coincidence meeting Sam there. Nairobi's a pretty big city."

I said nothing for a moment, for I was sure it wasn't an accident that she showed up at the same restaurant where we were dining. "I doubt it was a coincidence. Michael must have mentioned it and she decided to show up."

Kate sighed. "Is she going to be a problem?"

"I hope not." I was determined not to let Sam become a problem. I took Kate into my arms so that she sat on my lap in the water. "I don't need any complications right now. I'll be busy at work, teaching and trying to keep you happy."

"Don't worry about keeping me happy," she said. "As long as you're happy and we have time together, I'll be happy as well."

I hoped that was the case. I felt nothing for Sam, but that wouldn't stop Kate from feeling jealous of any time I would have to spend with Sam out of necessity. I wish Sam would just go away, but *that* wasn't going to happen. I'd have to work hard to keep things professional with her because I had a feeling that Sam was here precisely because she hoped to rekindle our former relationship.

I would *not* let that happen.

WHEN WE WERE BACK in the room, I undressed Kate slowly, enjoying seeing her all wet and goosebumpy and naked.

"You're so nice and smooth," I said and wrapped my arms around her from behind, kissing my way down her neck to her shoulder. I was already hard, and had been since we left the pool in anticipation of what I had planned for her. When I lifted her thigh and slid my erection between her legs, rubbing it against her clit, she sighed and leaned back, giving herself over to me.

"I found something," I said softly, my lips brushing her cheek.

"What?"

"You'll see," I said and kissed her. "*Katherine*."

I left her on the bed and then returned a few moments later with cuffs and a blindfold in my hand.

"Lie across the bed, and close your eyes."

Kate complied, barely able to keep a smile off her face. She was a naughty girl, but it was good that she was so eager to be bound and blindfolded. When she was finally all ready,

I stared down at her with pleasure, her body naked and open, her thighs spread, her hands fastened to the bed frame, and her eyes blindfolded.

Then, I went to the closet and retrieved Big and went to the bathroom, immersing the cold latex dildo in a hot water bath to warm it up before use. I went back to the bed where I had Kate positioned across it sideways and leaned between her thighs.

I stroked her clit, my thumb moving over it slowly, alternating between my fingers and the head of my cock. She moaned when I pressed the tip against her, teasing her with the pressure but not entering fully at first. I slowly built up to it, first an inch, then two then four then all of me, keeping my fingers stroking slowly over her clit.

She groaned when I pulled out completely and I knew she was close and was almost ready.

I left her briefly and returned with Big and the bottle of lube, which was also warm. I returned to my position between her thighs, drizzled some lube over her pussy and then began teasing her with it, stroking it over her clit.

She gasped and bit her lip, for she recognized what it was.

"Don't be afraid," I said, keeping my voice calm and soft. "Relax."

She took in a deep breath and I saw her body relax as she gave herself over to me. I stroked Big over her once more, focusing on her clit. Then I slipped my cock inside of her, hoping that I could substitute Big when the time was just right and she was already stretched and ready. I worked her up, watching her breathing, the tension in her body, until I knew she was almost there.

"You want it, *Katherine*?"

"Yes," she said, her voice filled with need. "Please."

"Please, what?"

"Please, *Sir*."

I slipped out of her, keeping my thumb on her clit and then pressed Big at the entrance to her body. Big was too large at first, so I continued to alternate my cock with the tip of Big until I managed to push it a bit farther inside. Kate panted, and when I resumed stroking her clit, it sent her over and she came hard, crying out loud from the pleasure.

"*That's* what I want to hear."

I withdrew Big and entered her, fucking her hard and fast, until my own release, which came more quickly than I anticipated, but seeing Kate like that, watching her willing submission to me, made me rock hard and ready. I collapsed on top of her, our hands entwined as we recovered, both of us breathing hard.

Finally, I unfastened the cuffs and removed the blindfold. Then I lay on top of her, my lips next to her ear.

"Told you."

Kate smiled.

I rolled off her and lay on the bed, unable to keep my hands off her delicious body. I tweaked a nipple, enjoying how it hardened under my touch.

"You came really hard."

"I did," she said, smiling when I cupped her breast. "I've been denied for quite a while."

"Not denied," I said, a bit hurt that she put it that way. "Kate, I've been busy…"

She turned to me and cupped my face with her hands. "I didn't mean it that way. I was kidding."

"No, you weren't," I said and shook my head. "I feel like I'm neglecting you, and that's the last thing in this world I want to do, Kate. Even when I'm at work and busy, you creep into my thoughts and I think of your enticing smile, your green eyes, your incredible breasts, the way you moan when you come… Don't feel like I'm not thinking of you, wanting you, wishing I could be with you. I am."

"I know," she said. "I'm sorry. I didn't mean to hurt your feelings. I think of you, too. Probably more than you think of me, because you're so busy. But soon, I'll be busy and I won't miss you as much."

"I don't want that," I said, grinning. "I want you panting with unmet desire for me when I come home." Then I kissed her.

"When we go back to Manhattan, will you be as busy as you are here?" she asked and turned over to face me.

I sighed and pulled her closer. "I'll probably play with the band a few times a week, but I won't be as busy with surgery. At NYP I only do the really specialized surgeries so my load is a lot lighter. I do more here because Michael needs someone to help with the cases he gets in from areas where there are few neurosurgeons. I probably will teach a class a year though. You know that I love to teach."

Kate and I lay in silence for a few moments. I kissed her shoulder and leaned over her, not wanting her to feel bad about being truthful.

"Let's have a shower. I don't know about you but I'm exhausted."

She smiled and followed me to the bathroom. We had a quick shower and then dried each other off before returning to the bed and lying with our legs and arms around each other.

I fell asleep so quickly, I barely remember closing my eyes.

CHAPTER 5

THE REST of the weekend was spent indulging in each other's bodies, lying in bed late, eating late, lazing around on the couch reading the English newspapers or watching television.

I enjoyed the quiet and seclusion. The week had been very busy—busier than I had been since my own residency years earlier. I touched Kate and kissed Kate and fucked Kate as much as I could, hoping it would get us through another busy week and that she wouldn't feel neglected.

I knew I'd be busy all week and too tired at the end of the evening to do much more than eat a late supper, have a shower, and go to bed. Although I was away from her twelve hours of the day, I made sure to call or text her frequently so she knew I was thinking of her and that I wanted her.

So tired, and was hoping to come home early tonight, but we have some critically ill pediatric patients flown in from a war zone who need surgery and so I'm staying with Michael late again. I love you. Don't wait up.

We finished morning rounds. It's a great hospital but I wish I

55

had my surgical suite in NYP here. Will have to call Dave Mills and get him to donate capital funds to renovate.

Taking a short break after a long delicate surgery on a very sick child. I think I might do a sub-specialty in pediatric neurosurgery. Would mean another year training but after Liam's illness, I realized I really feel happiest when I'm working on children.

Great OR staff – all the brightest and best students work here after they graduate. A group of really professional nurses have been working in the OR for years. They're showing me how it's done. Reminding me in no uncertain terms who really runs this operating theater...

UGH. Hospital cafeteria food is the same all over the world. Consistently tasteless and flavorless. How is that possible? I thought in Kenya they'd have more flavorful food but I guess Americans have been here teaching the cooks. They must go to the same conventions... I can't wait for us to move into our place and cook fresh food...

Speaking of eating, I am very much missing eating my favorite dish... YOU.

GOD I miss you, Ms. Bennet...

Don't hate me, but I have to stay late again tonight... I'll make it up to you on the weekend. After I sleep for 14 hours straight!

When the week was over, this one even busier than the previous, we took Friday evening off. Earlier in the week, I'd called the contact I had in the local BDSM community and asked about any upcoming dungeon parties. As luck would have it, there was one coming up on Friday.

I decided to take Kate. I wanted to make up for all the time I spent away from her and was sure she'd be excited about going.

When I arrived back at the hotel, Kate and I decided to go to the restaurant in the hotel instead of going out with Claire and Michael. It was going to be a special night and so I picked the black leather dress with a zipper up the front for

Kate to wear. She slipped it on while I watched and I unzipped it a bit so I could enjoy her delicious cleavage. She wore her black lace garter belt and black hose with the seam, a pair of simple black leather pumps, and her black diamond 'collar'.

"Wear your hair up," I said, watching in the mirror as she finished her makeup. "I want to see your collar whenever I feel like it. I feel so deprived, I need to remind myself that you really are all mine. But I have a special surprise for you tonight."

She smiled and styled her hair while I watched, perched on the edge of the tub. When she was done, she caught my eye in the mirror.

"You look *beautiful*," I said as I stood behind her. "I've been so busy this week, we haven't even made love once since the weekend. I imagine you're feeling quite neglected, because I know I am."

"You've been late every night and have been exhausted when you get home. I understand."

"I need you *all* the time, Kate, but you know I don't like quickies. I'd rather save it up for a very sensual, very long, slow scene when we have time."

On my part, I wore black leather pants and white linen shirt, untucked.

"You look delicious," she said. "Entirely lickable. What's up with the leather pants?"

"*Lickable*, Ms. Bennet?" I said, quirking an eyebrow. "You like them, do you?" I said and lifted my shirt to show my belt.

"I like *very* much…" she said, and turned back to her hair. "What's the occasion?"

I smiled and pulled on a black tuxedo jacket with satin lapels.

"You'll see."

57

OUR MEAL WAS delicious and when we were finished, I took her hand and led her out of the hotel and to a waiting limousine, which I arranged earlier.

"Where are we going?" she asked as she got in the back. I slid in beside her, my arm around her shoulders.

"Shh," I said. "*Katherine*. You'll see." I kissed the top of her head, signaling that she was to fall into sub-mode. We were in scene.

I reached into a pocket in my jacket and took out Kate's first collar. It had thick black leather and metal adornments.

"Here," I said. "Wear this above your public collar. It's appropriate where we're going."

"Where—'" she started, but I stopped her with a finger against her lips.

"Patience, *Katherine*. Be a good girl tonight or I'll have to spank your lovely tush and this time, it won't be for pleasure." I frowned down at her, but she couldn't help but smile with excitement. I couldn't keep from smiling back. Despite my best efforts, I couldn't maintain a strict Dom persona with her when she was so happy.

"Oh, *you*..." I said and kissed her. "I'll never be able to control you completely, will I? Not until you're tied up and helpless..."

"Promise?" she said, grinning. I tried to ignore her insolence and instead, focused on fastening the thicker collar around her neck so that it sat above the choker.

"If you were anyone but *you*, I'd have to punish you for daring to anticipate and even ask for anything. You know you're supposed to submit to *my* will, which, of course," I said with a grin, "is focused entirely on fulfilling yours." I wagged my eyebrows at her, unable to keep a straight face.

"I'm sorry," she said, her voice contrite. "I'll be perfectly well-behaved wherever we're going."

"Good girl." I kissed her and then turned back to the

window and watched the streets pass, smiling despite myself.

"Where *are* we going?" she said, touching the thick leather of the slave collar and then the diamond of the choker. "I mean, what's the venue?"

"It's a dungeon party that's held once a month in a private club," I said, knowing she'd be happy to be going to the local dungeon. "I went once when I was here before. It's a kind of public service event to help introduce kink to the curious and novices. The other dungeon parties are private, by invitation only. Very exclusive. This one is very mild. It's mostly the leather and Goth crowd. A few of the more hardcore kinksters do demonstrations. That kind of thing. There is public sex, though."

She smiled. "Will we," she asked, her voice a bit breathless. "*Do* anything?"

"*Katherine…*" I said, and this time, I wasn't smiling. "Submit."

She sighed and turned her face away, muttering under her breath. "I want to be prepared."

"I *heard* that," I said without looking at her. Then I grabbed her and pulled her over my knee, hiking up her dress, exposing her bare buttocks. Without a word, I gave her three quick smacks on her butt. I stroked each cheek for a moment and then kissed each one before slipping a finger between her thighs.

"Already wet," I whispered, pleased that she was so excited. Then I pulled her up, helping her to adjust her leather dress.

"Yes, *Sir*," she said.

"Good girl," I replied, ignoring the insolence in her voice. I glanced out the window, barely able to keep a straight face as we drove through the city to a warehouse in the central part of downtown.

The limo dropped us off and we went to the entry, which

was located at the back of the building in a back alley. I spoke with the doorman, who admitted us.

"Remember to wear a mask," he said as we entered the club. "If you don't, you have to sign a waiver."

I nodded and took Kate's hand, leading her inside the darkened hallway to an open dance floor and bar, with tables and chairs. Dozens of people danced and most all wore simple little black masks. We each took a mask from a table at the entrance and slipped them on. I adjusted Kate's so that it didn't ruin her hair and then we entered the cavernous room. I surveyed the room, while beside me, Kate began to sway to the music.

"So, Katherine," I said when I leaned in close, my mouth next to her ear. "You feel like dancing a bit?"

I wrapped my arms around her and led her over to the dance floor where we danced close, moving our bodies together in a very sensual manner. Kate held her hands above her head like she was restrained while I held her hips, pressing myself against her, my mouth moving over her neck to her ear, which I bit softly. She was so beautiful like that, her eyes half-closed, her lips parted. I was already semi-erect just from dancing with her.

We left the dance floor once the music changed to hip hop and went to one of the tables where we stood and watched the dance floor once more.

Kate stood on her tiptoes and whispered in my ear.

"Where's the dungeon?"

"*Katherine*," I said, trying my best to look stern, but I smiled at the look of excitement in her eyes. "So impatient for the main event?"

She bit her lip. "Sorry, Sir," she said, and shrugged, smiling.

"In the back," I said and took her hand. "Let's go."

The dungeon was as big as the bar and dance floor.

Painted black, the interior had a series of black wrought-iron cages. The music inside the dungeon was dub step and metal, grinding guitars and serious bass drops. A scream of pain ended in a groan of pleasure, and when I glanced at Kate, I saw her eyes widen.

In one cage, a man dressed in black leather flogged his almost naked sub, who was lying over a pommel horse, while a Dom applied nipple clamps to his sub in another. Someone else was being pussy whipped with a riding crop against an iron cross, and in one, two men were suspended by a series of ropes and pulleys, their bodies wrapped in a thin film of saran-like material. There was a mix of leather, lace and latex. Typical BDSM crowd you'd find anywhere in a big city.

When I left Kate to get us a drink, I watched as a young sub in black leather pants and a white t-shirt went over to her and spoke with her.

She rebuffed him without any discomfort and he moved off to try another woman. I returned with two vodka tonics with lime. We toasted each other and took a drink.

"See anything you like?" I asked.

Kate glanced around. "I like to watch," she said and smiled up at me. "Even if I don't want to do."

"Voyeur, Ms. Bennet?" I asked but I already suspected that she liked to watch people have sex. She might even want to have sex in front of people, if she was brave enough. It wasn't a kink of mine, but I didn't mind performing in a small group. I often did demonstrations of technique at local dungeon parties in Manhattan and had topped many subs in front of other practitioners. I would never encourage Kate unless I knew for certain that it turned her on.

She nodded and turned back to watch the man who spoke to her earlier bending down to massage a woman's foot.

"That looks OK," she said and motioned the man. "My feet

are killing me in these heels."

I laughed, amused by her naiveté. "If she doesn't watch out, he'll ejaculate right there."

Kate's eyes widened. "Really? I thought he was a sub, wanting to do submissive things, like service women."

"No," I said and shook my head. "He's a foot fetishist. He's turned on by women's feet. He's probably going to come in his pants."

Then, as I predicted, the foot fetishist suddenly fell forward, his face slack.

"Yep," I said, and turned to face Kate, taking her by the arm and leading her away. "Like I said."

"Oh my *God*," she whispered. "I can't imagine it being so arousing to touch someone's foot that you would actually *come*." She looked up at me in disbelief. "I mean, without his genitals actually being involved in any physical contact…"

"His pants are probably very tight," I said. "Some people claim to be able to make their subs come on command but I always believed that was wishful thinking."

"You never tried?" she asked, as if the idea intrigued her.

I shook my head.

"I come in my sleep sometimes," she said. "And I'm not being touched."

"That's the power of your brain," I said. "I guess it could be taught, but I actually like to make someone orgasm by contact. The no-touching thing never appealed to me."

Kate nodded. I ran a hand up her arm and across the tops of her breasts, enjoying when she shivered. I touched her collar, then the choker, and finally ran my fingers over the tops of her breasts again, watching as her skin went all gooseflesh.

"I wish you were wearing spandex so I could see your nipples," I said.

"Everyone else could see them, too."

"That's the idea."

She inhaled deeply and then bit her lip. "You like the idea that other people would see my nipples?"

"I'd feel very proud that you're mine," I said, leering at her. "Every man in the place would be jealous, wanting to be the one with you."

I examined her and then placed two fingers against her neck to check her pulse.

"That excites you," I said, quietly.

"It scares me."

"Sometimes, you misinterpret arousal for fear," I said. "I suspect that's what happened with Flyboy. You thought you were afraid, but you were really aroused and perhaps too self-judging to recognize it. Plus, he was a novice and didn't know how to properly introduce kink into a relationship."

"Whereas you're an expert," she said and leaned closer.

I smiled. "Not an expert, but more experienced." I finished my drink, took her glass and put it on a railing, and took her hand. "Let's go explore. Besides the demonstrations inside the cages, there are both public and private rooms for people to use."

We took a tour of the dungeon and stopped in front of a room to watch a man and woman having sex while the woman was in a sling. She was blindfolded, her hands restrained above her head.

I stood behind Kate and pulled her against my body so she could feel my erection. Then I slipped one hand around her waist and bent down, pressing my mouth over her carotid so I could take her pulse.

She shivered from my touch.

The woman in the window groaned, her voice audible over a speaker. The man thrust even harder, then pulled some chain that was attached to nipple clamps and she screamed out loud, her muscles all tightened, her body arcing, her thighs shaking. Next we watched a man flog a woman who was bent over a padded bench. I stood behind Kate, my arms around her waist.

"Do you trust me?" I asked, my mouth at her ear.

She inhaled deeply. "Yes."

"You hesitated."

She turned and faced me. "Only for a moment. I wasn't expecting the question. Of course I trust you."

"This is your chance to back out." I held out my hand.

Kate took it, offering herself to me willingly. I raised her hand to my mouth and pressed my lips against her knuckles.

"I'm going to blindfold you and take you into a room," I said, matter of fact. It wasn't a request. I was telling her what I was going to do. She nodded without any hesitation, although I could see anticipation in her eyes and perhaps a touch of fear.

I led her through a set of doors and into a hallway giving patrons access to the rooms. On one side were private rooms and on the other, public. Those rooms had windows that were open to the dungeon with speakers that conveyed every sound that took place in the room.

I reached into my pocket and removed a black handkerchief that I often used as a blindfold. I took her shoulders in my hands and bent down to look her squarely in the eyes.

"On one side, the rooms are private. On the other, there's a large two-way mirror that points out into the dungeon so people can watch. I'm going to tie you up, and I'm going to fuck you."

Kate nodded but said nothing.

I removed her mask and tied the blindfold around her eyes. Then I led her down the hall, turned her around several times so she became disoriented. Finally, I led her into a room and closed the door. I left her standing alone, while I arranged the furniture.

I took her hands and fastened them together behind her back, using cuffs that were lined with lambswool. Then, I kissed her, my mouth covering hers, my tongue penetrating her mouth, searching out her tongue.

I pulled back and ran my fingers over her cheek and down her chin to her throat. I touched the collar and then trailed my fingers lower to the zipper of her dress, which I pulled down slowly until it was down to her waist. Kate shivered when the cool air touched her skin.

I kissed her throat and then pulled the neck of her dress down, exposing her shoulder, which I kissed. I repeated this with the other shoulder and then her breasts were completely exposed to the air, her nipples puckering.

"You are so fucking beautiful, Katherine," I said, my cock rock hard and straining at my leather pants. Several people had gathered around outside our window and were watching, their faces hungry.

I took one nipple between my lips, sucking it into my mouth, swirling my tongue around the areola.

"You have the most beautiful breasts," I said. "And they're all mine. If we were in a public room, other men would see you like this, see me sucking your beautiful nipples like this, and they'd be aroused, wishing they were the one touching you instead."

I took her breasts in my hands and squeezed while I sucked, moving from one nipple to another. She groaned and thrust her breast at my mouth, greedy for the sensations.

"You like that idea, do you, Katherine?"

"Yes, Sir," she said, barely able to speak.

"I thought so. I thought there was a bit of an exhibitionist inside of you. You want me to touch you, to kiss you, to suck you, to eat you, to fuck you, but the thought of other men, nameless, faceless men, watching us arouses you, doesn't it?"

"Yes, Sir," she said and licked her lips.

I finished unzipping her dress and it fell open, exposing her black lace garter belt and silky hose. I unfastened her cuffs, moving her hands in front of her body, then refastening them together before guiding her to her knees. I attached the cuffs to a chain that hung from the ceiling and raised it with a winch so that her hands were above her head.

Then I unzipped my fly and pulled out my rock hard dick.

"Open your mouth."

She complied so I slipped my finger inside her lips. She closed her mouth on it and sucked, rolling her tongue around the tip the way she would if it was my cock. I removed my finger and slid my cock over her open lips.

"*Lick* me," I commanded, and she complied, slowly running her tongue under the head, then licked my length, running along the rim, before tonguing the slit.

"All over," I said. "Suck me."

She did, running her wet lips over my length from the base to the head before sucking the thick head into her mouth. I groaned with pleasure.

"Take as much as you can," I said, knowing she needed encouragement.

She did, taking more and more of my length until the head pressed against the back of her throat.

"Oh, *God*, that feels so good..." I began to thrust slowly, pulling out of her mouth completely and then pressing past her lips once more. She gagged a bit when I went too deep and so I pulled back, taking care not to push too hard.

"I'm sorry," she said. "I don't want to disappoint you."

"*Au contraire, ma petite chérie*," I said. "You could never disappoint me. Only yourself."

I pulled out completely and left her on her knees so I could now position her on the padded bench. I hoisted the chains higher and her arms lifted above her head so that they

66

were taut. Then I spread her thighs and stood between her legs. She was breathing fast and so I knew she was enjoying this, and while she thought it might have taken place in a private room, I wouldn't ever tell her. When she was ready emotionally to have sex in public, she'd suggest it. Then, I'd tell her the truth.

I wanted her to relax enough to enjoy what we were doing, and I knew that however much she wanted to perform in public, it would be better to ease her into it.

I took each foot and lifted it so that it rested on my shoulders and began to rub my erection against her shaved pussy, slowly, teasing her clit with each thrust. It didn't take long before the sensations built up and she came from the external stimulation alone, crying out, her body arcing in pleasure.

"That's so good, Katherine," I said and entered her before her orgasm finished, and the added stimulation prolonged everything so that she came again, shuddering around my length. She gasped as I thrust harder and faster, and then I came as well, ramming into her as I ejaculated, my hands gripping her hips.

I collapsed against her, my mouth by her cheek, panting in her ear.

When I was recovered, I kissed her cheek, her chin, her forehead and finally her mouth.

"That was *amazing*..." I whispered in her ear. "I needed that."

Finally, I pulled out, slipping out of her body with reluctance. I zipped up and stood in admiration of how beautiful she looked, bound and blindfolded, her chest and neck mottled with a sexual flush, my come leaking out of her pussy.

We were perfect together.

CHAPTER 6

I KEPT the blindfold on until we were in the washroom where I provided her with aftercare. The scene we played out was pretty vanilla except for the bindings and blindfold—and public sex—but Kate still needed to be cared for. I cleaned her off with wet paper towels, watching her face while I did to detect her emotional state. She seemed elated.

"You were magnificent, Katherine," I said, smiling at her. "You never protested once or failed to comply or showed hesitancy."

She smiled back. "I'm surprised I didn't run away."

I shook my head slowly. "The fact you responded to the public sex the way you did suggested to me that you'd secretly enjoy it, but that you could never do it on your own volition. That's why you have me," I said as I smoothed her hair back from her face.

"I have you for more than just pushing my limits," she said. "But you're right. I could never suggest it myself."

I grinned. "So I'm more than merely a bone to you?"

"That and much more," she replied and ran her fingers

69

through my hair. "You're not going to tell me whether it was public or private, are you?"

"Nope." I zipped up her dress when I was finished cleaning her off, leaving the zipper low enough to show her delicious cleavage.

"You are so mean..."

I laughed out loud. "I know what you need, Kate. Let's leave it at that."

"Damn you!" she said and pounded my shoulder. "I want to know!"

"You'll never know," I said coyly. "I'm very good at keeping secrets."

"I'll deprive you of sex until you tell me," she said and gave a fake pout.

"Ha!" I tickled her until she squealed, twisting out of my arms in a vain attempt to avoid me. "You'll deprive yourself then. You're as horny as me."

She laughed, trying to shield herself. "All right, all right. Stop!" She giggled when I ran my fingers down her ribs. "I won't ask. You'll tell me if and when you think I should know."

I stopped ticking, then pulled her against my body and kissed her tenderly.

"Oh, Ms. Bennet," I said and brushed an errant strand of hair from her cheek. "How happy you make me."

I pulled her into my arms, her softness warm against me.

During the drive back to the hotel, we sat together with our arms around each other, her head on my shoulder.

"I'm so surprised that I got off on the possibility we were being watched," she said, her voice soft. "I'm so inexperienced."

"I knew it was possible that first time we were at the dungeon party in Yonkers," I said, remembering how she responded to watching people fuck.

"Did you like that I had little experience or was it a drawback?"

I smiled and brushed the tops of her breasts, which bulged deliciously out of her dress.

"Don't kid yourself. Every man wants to be the first to introduce his lover to something pleasurable," I admitted. "I enjoy your inexperience. Your response when you enjoy something you didn't expect is a real turn-on for me."

She said nothing for a moment and stared out the window at the passing scenery.

"And once we've done everything and tried everything?" she said, her voice almost a whisper. "You won't get bored?"

I turned to face her. "*Kate*," I said, shaking my head. "After we've tried everything you want and I want, then we perfect it. Believe me, it takes an awful lot of practice to perfect any one thing. *And*," I said, leaning closer, touching her bottom lip with a finger. "And once we perfect something, then we enjoy the perfection. Stop worrying."

She sighed. "I *know*," she said, frowning. "I'm sorry. I should enjoy, right? No analysis?"

I nodded and kissed her softly before turning back to watch the streets outside the limo.

"I'm that girl, aren't I?" she said, her voice soft.

I turned back to her. "What girl?"

"The girl who thinks too much."

I couldn't hold back a grin. "That's my girl. D/s is intense. Everything feels much more significant. It's hard not to over respond." I watched her face, smiling internally at her intensity. "It'll pass. It's the high from the orgasms. I've read that the testosterone in semen gives the woman a bit of an energy boost, and drains it from men so it makes women wake up, their minds race while men fall asleep. ..."

She smiled at me, clearly amused at my conversation.

"*That's* what I wanted to see." I took her in my arms and

kissed her forehead. "You can't resist me. I don't want you to. I like when you comply with me, Kate, so tonight I feel like you and I passed a threshold in our relationship."

"Really?" she said, sounding surprised.

"Yes. Once you gave in, you allowed me to make all the decisions about what we'd do. No questions."

"It's not really fair," she said, smiling.

"What's not fair?" I pulled back a bit.

"You *know*," she said and put a hand on my chest. "You know my mind. Sometimes, I think you know me better than I know myself."

I smiled and trailed my fingers down her cheek to her throat, and then her collar. "I know you, Kate. I told you that the first night we were together. I meant it."

"*How* do you know me?"

"Your father talked a lot about you. He described you to a 'T'. He understands you far more than you realize."

Then I wrapped my arms around her for the rest of the drive.

"I missed you all week, Katie," I said, emotion filling me.

She said nothing for a moment, and together, we enjoyed the mood.

"I missed you, too." She tried to pull away but I held her firmly.

"No, stay like this," I said, pulling her closer. "What made you so insecure, Kate? What happened to you to make you doubt how much a man would desire you?"

She hesitated, considering my question. "I don't know," she said and sighed. "Daddy issues?"

I pulled back and looked in her eyes. "Your father loves you so much, Kate."

"I know that now," she said quietly, "but I guess I always felt like second best next to Heath. Like I was of no conse- quence. My father was always doing things with Heath,

72

taking him to games, playing ball with him, showing him off like he was his little clone. I felt like nothing."

I shook my head and then pulled her back against me. From what Ethan had said, he found it hard to know how to treat Kate, once she reached a certain age. She became a beautiful young girl and he didn't want to embarrass her by being too affectionate.

"I'm sure he never meant to make you feel that way. He's very proud of you. He kept you away from us bachelors because he knew you were worth more than being arm candy on some hungry dog's arm the way you could have been."

"Arm candy? Me?" she said and laughed. "Hardly."

"You don't think you qualify as arm candy?" I said in disbelief. "You are the definition of arm candy to me, with the delicious advantage of being brain candy and heart candy. I wish you knew that. I'm going to spend the rest of my life making sure you do."

She smiled and laid her head against my shoulder. I squeezed her a bit tighter, my chest tightening from emotion. I was going to spend the rest of my life with her, making her happy the way I promised Ethan.

It was entirely selfish of me for that was the surest way to my own happiness.

I TOOK a day off later in the week so we could do some shopping. After a breakfast and coffee, we sat on the patio and enjoyed the morning. It was clear except for a few high clouds. In the distance, the Ngong Hills were dark against a bright blue sky.

I turned to Kate. "We get the place next week. What do you say we ask Jan if we can go to the house and take some measurements? We could go shopping for furniture."

"That sounds nice," Kate said, smiling. "Where do Kenyan's shop for furniture in Nairobi?"

I shrugged. "I have no idea."

She picked up her cell. "Claire will know. I'll call her." While she made the call, I read the local papers, listening to her speak to Claire, pleased that they had become friendly so Kate felt comfortable enough to call her for advice.

"Drake and I chose a house and want to do some shopping for furniture. We get possession next weekend so we want the furniture to be delivered before we move in."

Claire spoke for a while and then Kate wrote something down on a piece of paper.

"Thanks so much," she said and listened some more. "That sounds great. Drake will be working tomorrow, so I'm as free as a bird. I'd love to."

She ended the call and turned to me.

"Well?" I said, putting my paper down. "What did Claire say?"

"She gave me a few ideas of where to shop." She handed me the list of stores.

"What else did she say? It sounded like you two were going to get together."

Kate shrugged. "She suggested that I register in a studio art class through the Institute. That way I'll meet some students. Maybe make a few new friends who share my love of art."

I nodded, but said nothing, for of course a stab of jealousy went through me at the thought she'd be taking art classes and meeting new people. I tried hard to fight it for it was juvenile. I knew Kate had to have a life outside of what we had together but it still made me envious of those who would be sharing that part of her life.

"You don't mind, do you?" she said and sat beside me, her thigh pressed against my knee.

I opened my paper to another section, and didn't meet her eye for I felt incredibly guilty for being so petty. "Why would I mind? You love art. You should do art."

She sighed audibly. "You seemed, I don't know, a little hesitant."

I exhaled, and turned to her. "I thought having a studio in our home would allow you to paint as much as you want. That's all."

"It will, but we'll be here for six months," she said. "You'll be away all day every day and on call every three weekends. I need to make a life here for myself apart from you. If I take a class, I might meet a few students I can have coffee with now and then, when you're busy at the hospital or teaching. With Dawn and me on the outs, I have no one else but you."

"Sure," I said and put my paper down, reaching out to take her hand. I squeezed it. "I *will* be very busy, especially at first. But I want us to be together when I'm not working. I don't want to compete with anyone for your time and attention. When you agreed to come with me to Africa, I had visions of you waiting for me in our house, pining away for me, dressed in something revealing, nice and wet for when I returned home at night... You know, typical male fantasies..."

She laughed at that. "Don't worry," she said, grinning. "When we've been apart, I'm always ready for you."

I kissed her knuckles.

"When you're free, I *want* to be with you." She squeezed my hand back. "At your beck and call." She wagged her eyebrows suggestively.

"At my beck and call, *hmm*?" I said and grinned, trying to look as rakish as possible. "I like that. Reminds me of your slave-girl persona. I'll hold you to that, Ms. Bennet."

She smiled coyly.

We hired a taxi and went to the first of several furniture stores that Claire recommended and spent the day choosing furniture for the house. I wasn't interested in furniture usually, preferring to hire someone to decorate my apartment in Chelsea, but I tried to be engaged with the whole process because it was important to Kate and I wanted her to feel this was important to me as well. Because it really wasn't that important to me, I encouraged Kate to choose what she preferred and was pleased by her choices. We were worn out by the time we'd visited all the stores on Claire's list and needed to relax once we were back at the hotel.

"Let's have a swim, and then a drink before dinner," I said on our way back to the hotel. "I'd love it if a certain slave-girl gave me a nice full body massage tonight. All that shopping used muscles I haven't used for a long time."

"Your wish is my command," Kate said, smiling and bowing in mock servitude. "The hotel has a spa shop with lots of essential oils and lotions. I'll stop in and get a nice massage oil on our way to the room."

"Sounds amazing," I said as we drove up to the hotel's entrance.

Our butler arranged to have our packages delivered to our room and while I sorted that out, Kate went to the spa to get the massage oils. It was after the butler left that I received a call from the hospital. I checked my cell and it was from Michael.

Kate arrived back in the room just as I received the call. She put down her bag and came to my side, a frown on her face.

I looked in her eyes and shrugged while I listened to Michael describe the trauma patient that was being flown to the hospital.

"I know it's the weekend, but can you assist?"

"Sure," I said, not really pleased that my plans for the evening were ruined. "When should I be there?"

"Helicopter will be here in fifteen. Can you come right away?"

"OK, fine. See you then." I ended the call and exhaled heavily. "Sorry about this, but we have a patient…"

"Let me guess," she said, disappointment clear on her face. "A pediatric trauma case."

"You got it. I'm meeting Michael at the hospital. The child's being air lifted in from a car accident and we're meeting the helicopter. I'm sorry," I said and pulled her into my arms. "Sorrier than you can imagine. I'm exhausted already. Can you manage until I get back?"

"Isn't someone else on call this weekend?"

"Cardoso's sick. Michael's taking his call."

She sighed. "How long will you be?"

I shook my head. "I have no idea, but depending on what we find, surgery could be a few hours. We'll probably stay at the hospital until the child stabilizes. You should go ahead and order dinner in. I'll grab something at the hospital with Michael."

She nodded and squeezed me. "Will his resident be operating with you?"

"Sam?" I said, keeping my voice light. "Yes, of course. She scrubs in on all his cases."

Kate turned away, but said nothing.

"*Kate…*" I turned her to face me, because I needed to make her understand. "We already talked about this. How can you still be jealous after last night?"

She shook her head. "Ignore me."

"You have no reason to be insecure. Sam's a resident. A fellow surgeon. Female surgeons are almost *never* submissive, so even if I was looking, she wouldn't be on my radar." I pulled her hard against my body. "And I'm not looking, so you can relax. No one but you is on my radar. I'm all yours. Every inch of me."

77

She smiled up at me. "I love every inch of you, Dr. Delish," she said. "It's just that I know other women would love you as well."

"Other men would love you, too, *Katherine*," I said, my voice firm. "Admit it, we're both catches. We caught each other. It's settled." I grinned, trying to lighten her mood.

She smiled back and leaned in closer. I kissed her deeply, warmly, trying to impart every ounce of emotion inside of me so she'd understand.

There was no one else. There could never be.

I gathered up my things and kissed her firmly before I left the hotel.

"Make sure you have that massage oil on hand when I get back. I have a feeling I'm going to need it."

I MADE my way to the hospital and arrived just moments before the chopper landed with the trauma patient. Michael was waiting on the helipad and I rushed out after hastily pulling on a set of scrubs and mask.

"Just in time," he said and patted me on the back.

We examined the patient in the OR for we already knew we had to go in and work on the skull fracture and damage to the child's spinal cord. It was an intense and extremely critical injury and the next hour would determine if the child would survive.

Before I knew it, an hour had passed as we worked away to put the child's skull back together and deal with the spinal fracture. Finally stabilized, the patient would be taken to recovery and then to the ICU. Michael and I left Sam to finish dealing with the patient, ferrying him to the ICU once he was ready, where he'd be under constant surveillance and care for the first few days post-op.

Michael and I went to the waiting room where the family

78

had gathered and delivered the news that the boy had survived the surgery and now it was a matter of how damaged the boy's brain was and whether he would recover with any loss of function. The spinal cord had been compressed but was not severed so he would likely get the full use of his limbs back.

Whether his brain would be unaffected was another thing altogether and only time would tell.

We went to the break room once we finished answering the family's questions and slumped down on the sofa after getting a coffee.

"That was intense," I said when Michael sat across from me. "I think he'll be okay if his brain swelling isn't too severe."

"I think you're right. I was glad to have you here," Michael said. "If you're serious about pediatric surgery, you'll see a good share of cases working with me."

I nodded. I did want to work with children. They were a special challenge as their developing brains were more elastic and able to deal with trauma but at the same time, required real skill working with robotic implements because of their small size.

My experiences with pediatric patients had all been so rewarding and my time with Liam during his illness and treatment encouraged me to specialize in pediatric neurosurgery.

Being here with Michael now was a great career decision.

Sam arrived in the coffee room a few moments later and poured her own cup of coffee. She came up behind me and relayed a status update on the patient, who was stabilizing. Michael got a page and excused himself to use the hospital phone.

After he left, Sam laid a hand on my shoulder and squeezed. "Feels like old times," she said and leaned down, her mouth next to my ear. "I'm so glad we're together again."

I frowned and craned my neck to look at her. "You know I brought my fiancée with me."

She shrugged. "Of course," she said lightly. "I didn't mean anything. All I meant is that the three of us used to work together on cases."

I nodded, kicking myself mentally for jumping to conclusions. "I don't want there to be any misunderstanding about us," I said, wanting to make it clear.

"I understand, Drake. It's just that you told me back when we were together that you didn't plan on getting married again or doing the whole 'relationship' thing. What happened?"

"Kate happened," I said and stood up, wanting to end the conversation. I went to the counter to dispose of my paper coffee cup. "Now, if you'll excuse me, I'm going to check on the patient and I have to get back to the hotel."

"It was great watching you and Michael in the OR," she said. "I know I'll learn a lot from you."

With that, she left the room and I felt as if she didn't really take me seriously. I had told her back when we were together that I had no plans to enter into a typical relationship. It wasn't for me and at the time, that was true. Meeting Kate changed all that.

With her, I wanted a typical relationship. Marriage. Children. Family.

I wanted it all.

MICHAEL RETURNED to the break room after Sam left, his phone in his hand.

"I've been trying to get ahold of Claire, but her cell is off. A colleague of mine is in town for the week and wanted to get together for a drink. You might like to meet him – head of pediatric neurosurgery at the University of Cape Town. You should come along."

I shook my head. "This was supposed to be my night with Kate," I said and went to the door. "I'm going to stop off and check on the patient and then head back to the hotel."

Michael nodded. "I've forgotten what it's like to be young and in love," he said with a smile. "Go to her. We can get together for coffee later this week."

"Sounds great," I said and ducked out, taking the stairs to the critical care unit. On my way to visit the patient, I sent Kate a text.

I'LL BE HOME *a bit earlier than we first thought because our patient has stabilized. I hope you're waiting for me, all hot and bothered, Ms. Bennet. I want to take advantage of every spare moment we have because the way Michael works, it's only going to get busier...*

I WENT to the unit and spoke briefly with the nurse in charge of the patient's care and then stopped in to see how he was doing. It was still very early in his recovery, so it would be a while before we knew if he'd regain function.

When finished, I checked my cell but there was no response from Kate, so I sent another text, expecting that she might have been in the shower, or perhaps the pool and missed the first one.

I'M *on my way back to the hotel. I hope you get this and are waiting for me, eager as I am. Text me when you get this.*

I WENT to my office and sat down to dictate some notes on the case and check over reports on the patients I'd cared for that week. When Kate still hadn't responded to my text, I left and drove back to the hotel. Once back in the room, I sat on the couch and when she still hadn't responded, I texted her once more.

WHERE ARE YOU? Did you and Claire go out? I called Michael but he's not answering. I'm at the hotel waiting...

I WAITED BUT NO RESPONSE. It was so unlike Kate not to answer me that all kinds of terrible scenarios passed through my mind – abduction and rape, an accident while she was out with Claire...

KATE, where are you?

FINALLY, a few moments later, I received a text from her.

I'M SORRY. Claire and I went to a faculty art exhibit at the Institute for Art. We're out with a group from the function for dinner. Our meal is almost finished so as soon as we're done, I'll get Claire to drop me off. So sorry I missed your texts and phone calls but my cell died. I can't wait to see you and see what you have planned...

AT THAT MOMENT I was so relieved that she was okay that I didn't feel any anger at her not letting me know where she was. The more I thought about it, though, the more upset I became. Kate was out with Claire for dinner with faculty members from the Institute for Art and hadn't bothered to send me a text because her cell died.

That disappointed me.

I shouldn't have been angry, but I was. It showed a lack of consideration for me as her partner. Yes, Kate probably thought I'd be in the OR for a long time and would be late, but she could have sent me a text or email letting me know she would be out with Claire. That way, I wouldn't be worried when she wasn't at home or didn't answer my texts.

It was a sign that she didn't think of me and my needs.

While I waited for her to return, I tried to decide what to do. I needed a shower, so I slipped in for a quick one and then put on the hotel's plush white robe and waited in the sitting area in the dark facing the patio so I could watch the moon make its way across the sky.

CHAPTER 7

KATE ARRIVED ABOUT HALF an hour later.

"There you are," she said and stood in front of me.

Despite being upset, my heart softened when I saw her looking so lovely, her green eyes wide.

"I wish you'd texted me that you were going out with Claire," I said, trying not to sound too upset. "I was worried something happened to you."

"I'm sorry," she said. "Claire was supposed to phone Michael. He was supposed to tell you."

"You could have texted me."

She shrugged helplessly. "My phone's battery was dead because I forgot to charge it. We let it charge in Claire's car. Then I forgot..."

She forgot. I didn't say anything for a moment, trying not to over-react.

"So you went out to the Institute? You're out pretty late."

"I told you we went for dinner after. I thought we'd be back before you and Michael got finished at the hospital."

I nodded. "You look lovely."

"Thank you," she said and turned in a circle, holding out

85

the skirt of her dress. "I wish you could have been there with us. Claire's fun, but she's quite a social butterfly so I spent a lot of time alone, looking at pictures by myself. But at the dinner, I did show some of the faculty my painting of you and got a few nice comments."

"Which picture of me? Not the full-frontal…"

"No," she said and sat on the couch beside me, leaning in close. "The more respectable one. I wouldn't want to make the male faculty jealous or the female faculty interested."

I couldn't help but laugh at that. I brushed a strand of her hair back, then touched her collar.

"I was upset that you were gone when I got back here. I was really looking forward to seeing you."

Kate sighed audibly as if she were getting impatient with me. "Drake, I'm so *sorry*. I thought Michael was going to tell you I was out with Claire. I *thought* you two would be really late. Besides, I have to make a life for myself while you're busy at work."

"I want you to have your own life," I said and I meant it. I did want her to have her own life, but when we were a couple, we had to put each other first. "But how would you feel if the tables were turned and it was me who never called or texted you when I was going to be late? If you waited for hours to hear from me?"

She shook her head and I could see real regret in her eyes. "It was thoughtless of me. I was a bit intimidated by Claire. She has this way…"

I nodded. Claire was an alpha female. She liked to be in control. "When I'm free, I want you to be here," I said and touched her cheek. "I don't want to wonder where you are. When I want you, I don't want to have to wait while you're out partying with people I don't even know."

"Drake…" she said, her voice trailing off. "It won't happen

again. I'll make sure to send you a text if I'm going anywhere from now on so you'll know. My phone…"

I nodded and brushed my fingers over the tops of her breasts. "I feel like I should punish you," I said softly.

She bit her lip and I could tell she didn't like that idea. Subs didn't like being punished but that was the whole point.

"It wasn't my fault that Claire forgot to call Michael…" Kate said hesitantly.

"You could have called using the hotel phone and left a voicemail," I said. "Or used your laptop before you left the room. You could have called me as soon as your phone was charged."

She exhaled. "Claire called and I was rushed…"

"It would have saved me worrying. I had these images of you having been abducted, raped, or in a car accident somewhere on the Mombasso Road."

"I'm *sorry*," she said again and cupped my cheek, leaning in to kiss me. I didn't kiss her back. "I didn't even want to go, but Claire has this way about her."

I nodded, for Kate was often submissive in social situations. "Sometimes, your submissive side extends beyond sex."

She sighed. "With really dominant people, yes. Sometimes it does."

"Maybe I should exert more control outside the bedroom."

She shook her head. "No," she said, adamantly. "I don't want that. You don't want that."

"I want us to work as a couple," I said, calmly. "Maybe you *need* me to take more control. Especially in a new place where nothing's familiar."

She stood up, and I could tell she wanted to escape this confrontation.

"I don't *want* TPE." She went to the patio doors and stood staring out at the sky. I didn't get up, although I knew I

87

should have gone to her. I wanted to see how this played out between us. We hadn't had many tiffs and I needed to see how she responded.

"Our relationship can be anything we want it to be," I said. "It doesn't have to be total. It could be partial power exchange, in some situations and settings. Or only in the bedroom. It's whatever makes us both happiest. Maybe you need me to be more in control. Not totally, but more. I feel like you should have thought about me first when you decided to go out. You should have called me. Left a message. Even if you'd left a damn post-it note on the mirror, I wouldn't have been so upset."

"I am *not* O," she said, her voice firm and a little petulant.

I shook my head. "Of course you're not O. You're Katherine Marie McDermott. Very complicated, passionate, talented. You're also turned on by sexual submission to a dominant man. You need it to feel safe and free. You need a strong dominant man who frees you to feel whatever you can without judgment. I won't *judge* you, no matter how much control you need to feel from me."

"You always said you didn't want a submissive woman. You want a woman who submits in the bedroom."

I exhaled. "I want *you*, Kate. Whatever you need." I stood up finally and went to her side, standing close to her so I could touch her. I stroked her hair, ran my hand over it and down her back. "I *want*," I said and pressed against the small of her back, pulling her against me. "I want *you*. *You* need D/s. Tell me it wouldn't make you feel insecure to top me."

She said nothing but sighed heavily. She knew I was right. She didn't want to admit it to herself but that was the most important part of D/s. Honesty about your needs and wants.

"Am I right?"

She nodded but didn't say anything for a moment. She turned around.

"I thought we were doing really well," she said, her voice sounding hurt. "I thought you were getting what you want from the relationship."

"Kate, *this* is what drives me," I said and took her face in my hands. "I want to give you as much dominance and control as you need to be happy. I want to be the man who fulfills you, whatever that means. If you need me to take more control, I will. *Gladly*." I stroked her cheek with a thumb. "Tell me what you need, Kate. I'll give it to you exactly the way you want it."

She inhaled a shaky breath, so emotional. "I don't know what I need. I only know I want you."

"You have me. But I don't feel as if I have you yet. Not completely."

"You *do* have me. I *love* you."

I shook my head. "If I had *you* completely, you would have done everything you could have to let me know you'd be out. You would have thought of me first, and left a note, left a voice mail. You would have called as soon as your phone was charged. Instead, you had excuses for why you didn't."

She frowned. "I didn't even want to go out, but I did because Claire said I had to make my own life apart from you. That you'd be away so much that I'd become sad and feel neglected if I didn't. I went out with her because I felt I *had* to."

I went to the bar fridge in the kitchen area and took out a small bottle of bourbon and poured the contents into a glass. Then, I went back to the sofa and sat on it, my feet up on the coffee table. Kate followed me and stood beside me, waiting for me to say something.

I said nothing for several moments, sipping my drink.

"Say *something*."

"What should I say, Kate?"

"How are you feeling?"

I shot back the bourbon and placed the glass carefully on the coffee table.

"I'm *upset*," I said. "I'm upset that you went somewhere without telling me yourself. That you didn't make the effort. I'm upset that this whole evening has gone to shit and I was looking forward to spending it making you come several times."

"Don't be mad at me," she said, her voice low. "Me not leaving a note was thoughtless, but Claire was outside and I didn't want to keep her waiting. Then she forgot to tell Michael..."

She exhaled and I could feel her frustration from where she stood. "I guess we have to agree to disagree, then."

"I guess we do, but I still think I should punish you."

"*No*," she said, her voice edged with anger. "Our power exchange only extends to the bedroom and I haven't agreed to change it. This has nothing to do with our sex life."

"It *does* have something to do with our sex life," I said firmly. "I wanted to fuck you senseless, Katherine." I stood up and faced her. "I'm *not* fucking you senseless, am I?"

"You *could* if you weren't so mad over nothing."

Then I pulled her against my body, one hand tangling in her hair, gripping it, pulling her mouth against mine, my lips pressing hers open, my tongue finding hers, sucking it into my mouth possessively. With the other hand, I hiked up the hem of her dress, sliding my hand up her thigh to her buttock, squeezing it, pulling her against my groin, my erection caught between our bodies.

When my fingers slipped around under her panties and I found her clit, she moaned into my mouth. At that show of need, I turned her around and pushed her down so that she leaned against the back of the sofa. I spread her thighs roughly with my knee, lifted the skirt of her dress, pushing it up over her back. Then, I pulled off her panties and was inside of her, my cock completely sheathed in her silky wet warmth. I lay over her, my face next to hers, my cheek pressed against hers. I stroked her clit for a moment, letting her adjust to my size but she didn't want to wait, and pushed back against me.

"I'm going to *fuck* you, Katherine," I growled, "and you're not going to come, do you understand?"

"Then why are you touching me?" she protested, her voice breathless. "I *need* to come."

"I like to touch you. You *do* need to come," I said, deciding to deny her orgasm as punishment. "Your clit is nice and hard, and you're so wet. But you're not going to come, *Katherine*. I'm going to punish you for not contacting me yourself so I'd know where you were. I'm going to fuck you until I come inside of you and then, I'm going to deny you release."

She said nothing when I began to thrust, hard and fast. "You're *not* going to let yourself come, Katherine, do you understand?"

Still, she met every thrust with her body, tightening her muscles around me. I groaned, inhaling sharply when I felt her body contract around my shaft, teasing the head.

"*Don't* let yourself come," I said, trying to sound commanding but I was so close, my voice was shaky. Despite everything, she started to climax, her body tensing in that way I had come to know and anticipate when I fucked her.

"Don't come," I said, barely able to speak because I was so close as well.

"I can't stop..."

I could feel her cunt spasm around me and it drove me on, thrusting all the harder, until I felt the white hot pleasure as I began to ejaculate.

I grunted like an animal as I came, my eyes clenched shut,

teeth gritted. When I was finished, I leaned over on top of her, my mouth on her shoulder as both of us recovered.

I had to stop from laughing out loud at what a fool I was, thinking I could deny her an orgasm.

"I'm going to have to find some other way to punish you," I said, smiling against her shoulder. "You're too damn responsive."

I kissed her shoulder and then slipped out of her body. I stood up straight and held her down so I could watch my come drip down her thighs.

She complied, waiting for me to release her. Finally, I let her up and she went to the bathroom to clean up.

When she started to undress, I stopped her and took over. I unzipped her dress and she hung it up in on the back of the door and then removed her bra. Her panties were still on the floor in the living room where I dropped them.

I stood in the doorway to the bathroom and watched her clean up then run a quick bath. She stepped inside the tub and started washing.

"You're not going to say anything?" I said, wondering what her mood was.

"That was *good*," she said rinsed the soap off her body. "I needed that."

I shook my head slowly while she got out of the tub and wrapped a towel around her body.

"What am I going to do with you, Ms. Bennet?"

She grabbed her clothes and brushed past me, smiling. "Anything you want."

I followed her into the bedroom and watched while she hung up her dress in the closet.

"Anything I want, *hmm*?" I said, amused.

"You're the Dom."

She dried off slowly, well aware that I was watching.

Before she could put on her nightgown, I grabbed her and

pulled her over to the bed, then pushed her down onto her back. I lifted her farther up onto the bed so that my mouth was right over her pussy.

"What I *want* is to eat you and make you come again."

She closed her eyes and covered her face with her hands to hide her smile.

I made her come again with my tongue and fingers and it was only when she'd had her second orgasm that I felt relieved.

I was generous like that.

LATER, we lay together naked, our limbs entwined.

I kissed her neck. "So, other than the fact that you should have called me sometime during the night, how did your evening go? Did you meet other students?"

Kate sighed as if she wasn't all that happy with the evening. "It was OK."

"That doesn't sound like much of a ringing endorsement," I said, her response confirming what I thought.

She turned to look in my eyes. "To tell you the truth, it wasn't much fun. I felt uncomfortable a lot of the time."

"Why?" I brushed a finger over her bottom lip. "What happened?"

"Claire went off and was a social butterfly. I was stuck with this man who made a few strange comments and innuendo. I only wanted to come home and wait for you but I was trapped."

"What man?" I said, keeping my voice controlled, but the knowledge some strange man was bothering her upset me and brought out the green-eyed devil in me.

"Sefton deVilliers," she said. "He's the artist in residence at the Institute. He's offering an open studio course and offered me a spot but I don't know if I want to take the class from him."

"Why?"

"He made me uncomfortable. I told him I was engaged to you so he'd stop."

"Was he at the dinner, too?" I asked lightly, not wanting to show her how jealous I was.

"Yes," she said, and bit her lip. "He was a bit suggestive..."

"Suggestive?"

"He asked me if I was a submissive."

"What?" I frowned, tensing. "How did that come up? What did you say to him?"

"*Nothing*," she said defensively. She touched her collar. "He saw my choker and asked me what it meant. Do you think he was at the dungeon the other night and saw me, recognized my choker?"

"I don't know why else he'd think you were a submissive," I said, a rush of adrenaline going through me. "He must have been there." I shook my head and rubbed my eyes. "That was presumptuous of him and not acceptable. People in the lifestyle usually only meet through known contact routes—online websites, personals, or through friends who are in the lifestyle. You don't ask a stranger and even if you've seen someone at an event, you don't mention it unless you're close enough. It's respect for privacy. Besides, we were wearing masks. That means we don't want our participation in the event to be publicly known. He knew that if he was there."

"He's a buffoon," she said dismissively.

"He is." I said nothing for a moment, trying to figure out if he had been at the dungeon and what that might mean. "Did he say anything other than that?"

She shook her head. "No. He made a few comments when he saw my painting of you that at first I thought could be taken two ways." Then she glanced at me. "So I take it we were in a public room."

"Why do you think that?" I said, but of course, that would be her first thought.

"Because if he saw us having sex, he would know you're big."

"I'm neither going to confirm or deny that," I said and shook my head. "He's not going to spoil the experience for you."

I inhaled deeply and stoked her hair as she lay beside me, her arm across my chest, her face pressed against my shoulder. It was such a nice intimate moment, but I felt angry that some other man was the one to reveal the truth to her about having sex in the public room.

"Might want to keep your distance from him," I said. "I'd advise against taking his studio class. Not because I'm worried you'll become involved with him," I said and turned to face her. I tilted up her chin so she had to look in my eyes. "I may get jealous, but I know you love me. Still, you don't want to feel harassed. You want someone to appreciate you for your talent and not because you are the most delicious bit of womanhood around."

I smiled briefly and kissed her. Of course, I figured if this man was a Dom and had been at the dungeon, he'd be interested in her. Of that I had no doubt. A submissive who was an artist? I was certain the man would want to eat her for breakfast.

"I'll check with Nial Mbuno, the Dean of the Institute, about other open studio classes."

I nodded and pulled her against me, glad that she was willing to take a different class. It wasn't only that I was jealous. If this man was at the dungeon and was a Dominant, I felt certain that he would pursue her.

I didn't want that to complicate things between us.

First, Sam showed up to make things difficult between Kate and me. Then this deVilliers fellow shows an interest in Kate. When we came to Kenya, I thought the culture shock and change of lifestyle would be the main challenge we faced. I had no idea it would be from two possible competitors, hoping to get between us.

With Kate in my arms, our bodies warm and relaxed, I soon fell asleep, even the thought of Sefton and Sam unable to keep me awake.

CHAPTER 8

I SPENT the next week shadowing Michael and taught my first classes at the college. It was an exhausting week, for I had to rework my old lecture notes to include new material, recent research and new developments in technology so I was up late every night writing and reading, and then up early every morning to go to the hospital for rounds and surgery.

I often missed supper and only arrived home late, joining Kate for a late swim in the pool and drink of hot tea before bed. Despite wanting her, I was too exhausted to have sex and so the week passed with little in that way. I hoped to make it up to her on the weekend, when I could sleep in and relax, recharge my batteries. They hadn't been worked that hard since I was a new surgical resident.

Kate didn't protest and for that, I was thankful. She understood how much of my energy was taken up with teaching and surgery, and I loved her even more because of it.

Finally, moving day arrived and since I had no classes, I took the day off.

Kate was so eager to see our new place, she was practically bubbling with enthusiasm. I was as well, but was still a bit weary from my week. Her excitement was infectious and I found myself eager to get the keys. We took a taxi to Kitusuru Village and met Jan at the house. The movers came and delivered our furniture and I brought over our luggage and housewares in the taxi so we spent the morning getting settled.

I walked up behind Kate, slipping my arms around her waist.

"We're finally here, Ms. Bennet," I said, kissing her neck. "Our own house. I can't wait to make it our home. Buy some groceries. Cook a meal. Christen the bed."

"Christen the bed, you say?" she said, in mock innocence.

I pulled her more tightly into my arms, kissing her neck.

"What do you say we get a taxi and go for lunch and then hit the market?"

She squeezed her arms around me. "Sounds wonderful."

OUR TAXI DRIVER, Jomo, took us through the streets of Nairobi, talking to us about his time in Manhattan when he attended a Model UN. He was a student at the University of Nairobi, and was a very bright articulate fellow who was pleased to show us around the city. He took us to a local hangout known for its fresh fish and left us with his card so we could call when we were ready to go back to the hotel.

We ate at a small restaurant that was busy with locals—a sign that it had good food. Then we walked through the open-air market and selected fresh produce and meat to stock our refrigerator.

Once we were finished, we sat on a bench and watched the locals while we waited for Jomo to return.

"You didn't haggle over prices like the locals do," Kate said, poking me in the ribs.

"I don't really get the money system yet," I said and laughed. "Maybe we should have asked Jomo to be our agent. We probably overpaid for everything we bought today."

Kate shrugged. "Maybe, but we can afford it."

"Who knows? I may have paid a small fortune for those vegetables," I said with a laugh. "We should probably shop at the mall until we get to know prices and the money a bit better."

As the only Americans in the market at the time, we were quite noticeable and were the object of interest for all the children passing by. One small child called out "*Mzungu*," as her mother pulled her quickly by us.

That meant 'white person' in Swahili.

"We're curiosities," Kate said, waving at one small girl.

"Definitely." I smiled and waved at the girl as well and then she disappeared back into the crowded market.

After about ten minutes, Jomo, our taxi driver, returned and took us to yet another furniture shop where we bought a table for Kate's studio and some shelves for supplies. Our last stop was a computer store at a local mall where I picked up some paper so I could print off handouts for my class.

We arrived back at the house some time later and after I gave Jomo an extra large tip for being so helpful. He promised to be our personal guide whenever we needed one, if he was available.

We brought in our bags and put the food away, collapsing onto the couch.

"I wish we were back in Manhattan," I said. "So we could order delivery from *Marcellus* or go to the bagel shop across the street from your apartment."

"There's that bag of potato chips," Kate said and yawned. "We could eat that. No cooking. No cleaning."

I pulled her into my arms and kissed the top of her head. "What happened to our plans to cook real food?"

"Exhaustion happened," Kate said with a smile. "I think I could go to bed and stay there all night. Like John Lennon and Yoko Ono. Only we wouldn't be protesting anything except sore muscles."

I laughed. "The pool guy was here. Luckily, Jan thought of everything. We could go have a swim, then eat the bag of chips and listen to some music. I doubt I'll be able to stay awake much longer than nine o'clock, the way I feel."

"Sounds like a plan."

And so, that was exactly what we did.

After our swim, we sat on the couch and listened to some music on the new sound system I bought. I looked over some notes for my lectures in the morning and so Kate took out her laptop and worked on a schedule for herself.

"Oh, I completely forgot," I said and reached into my briefcase for the safari brochure I'd tucked away inside. "This is the one," I said, pointing to the third safari option in the brochure. "Claire gave it to me." I handed it to Kate. The safari was for artists, and was scheduled for a weekend at the end of March.

"Our schedule for that week's ER call was posted and Michael and I will be on call but you could go with Claire," I said. It was Claire's suggestion and I was pleased that she had decided to take Kate under her wing. "She's an amateur photographer and wants to go to get some good wildlife photos. Michael promised to arrange it so we can all go together on a regular safari, but Claire would love to go on this one, according to Michael. I know you wouldn't want to miss an artist safari."

Kate smiled eagerly and spent the next hour checking out the safari online.

Once I could no longer keep my eyes focused on my

lecture notes, I yawned and suggested we get ready for bed. We did our usual routine and then fell into bed. I pulled Kate close and she happily snuggled into my arms.

"Good night," she said as we spooned together, my arms around her from behind, one hand beneath her luscious breast.

"Good night my love," I replied, yawning. "Sorry to be so unromantic, but I'm almost asleep with my eyes open."

"It's OK. So am I." Kate turned to face me and we kissed. Then I closed my eyes and the sound of her breathing was the last thing I remembered before falling asleep.

THE NEXT DAY dawned bright and I was up early, showering and getting dressed, a spring in my step. I was eager to start teaching, and then checking my surgical slate so I could take charge of my own patients.

The class went well. The students were all in their last year of their programs and were eager to get into the OR and practice what they were learning. I had a busy surgical slate for the rest of the day once my class was finished and so I called Kate at about seven o'clock to say I probably wouldn't be home until after ten. Michael had gone home with a cold and so I agreed to take over the rest of his slate instead of canceling surgeries. As a result, my final surgeries were done with Sam assisting.

As usual, she took the opportunity to refer often to our past together, reminiscing about cases we worked on while she was a student, and to our intimacy.

I smiled but didn't engage her, and finally, she gave up trying to get me to talk more personally. I tried my best to keep our talk professional and she didn't seem to appreciate it.

When we were finished, she stood beside me at the sinks while we washed up and I could feel her eyes on me.

"So, tell me about this woman you brought along with you. I'm surprised she's not a nurse or a doctor. What does she do? A student?"

"She's doing her Masters in Journalism," I said, irritated because I was sure Sam already knew everything there was to know about Kate from Claire. "She's also an artist and is going to take a studio class while we're here. As to her not being in medicine, I learned my lesson with my ex-wife. I find I need someone outside the field or else it can get too," I said and paused, trying to find the right word. "Too incestuous. You know, knowing each other's business so well, there's nothing to talk about. With Kate, I'm always learning something new. Art. Politics. Completely outside my world."

She shrugged. "Many doctors marry nurses or other doctors. They understand our schedule. They don't feel neglected when we spend every night in the OR or ER."

I finished drying off my hands. "Kate understands."

"Lucky you," Sam said, but I could tell by her slightly patronizing tone that she didn't believe me.

I went to my office and dictated some notes on my cases so I wouldn't forget and then checked on my lecture notes for the next day. Then, I made my way out of the hospital to wait for a taxi to take me home.

As I waited, a small BMW convertible drove up and stopped beside me.

The window rolled down. It was Sam. "Need a ride?"

I considered. "No, thanks," I said. "I've already called for a taxi."

"Save your money," she said and motioned to the door.

"No, really," I said and pointed to the taxi that drove up behind her. It was Jomo. I called earlier to arrange a taxi and was glad that he was working. "Here he is. See you later and thanks for the offer."

I smiled perfunctorily and got into Jomo's cab, glad to see his face.

"Just in time," I said.

Jomo smiled at me. "Glad to be of service," he said and drove off.

By the time I arrived home, it was even later than I thought. I crept into the bedroom as quietly as I could and got ready for bed, doing my best not to wake Kate. When I finally slipped into bed, Kate woke despite my best efforts.

"You're home," she said and turned to face me. "What time is it?"

"Eleven fifteen," I said and kissed her, pulling her into my arms with a sigh. "Sorry to wake you up. I tried to be quiet but I tripped over a box when I turned off the lights."

"Are you all right?" She wrapped her arms around my neck. "I missed you so much. I realized I didn't speak to a single soul today, until now."

"I'm sorry," I said and snuggled closer. "Your first art class is tomorrow. You'll meet some other students there, maybe make a friend." I kissed her again and stroked her hair. I would have loved to fuck her, but I was too exhausted to do anything. I snuggled in closer and kissed her shoulder.

"How was your day?" Kate said.

"Busy. Had my class. Then a demonstration of robotic techniques to some visiting neurosurgeons from Ethiopia. Then OR time. Then, I had to cover for Michael. He went home sick with a cold so I scrubbed in on his cases."

She nodded and ran her fingers through my hair. I knew she felt neglected.

"I'm sorry that you've been alone all day," I said and stroked her cheek. "I promise I'll make it up to you tomorrow."

She said nothing in reply. Instead, she snuggled down into my arms and was silent. I lay awake beside her, despite being exhausted. Late surgeries did that to me. Your reserve had been tapped earlier in the day and you ran on pure adrenaline. Then, once the surgeries were done, you felt sapped of energy.

I lay there exhausted but unable to fall asleep. Kate did, however, and soon she was breathing slowly and deeply.

Finally, I fell asleep, but it was only temporary, for a few hours later, I woke up and could not get my eyes to close. My mind went back to my discussion with Sam about marrying outside of the medical field and how difficult it was for people not used to the hectic schedules and demands of a doctor or nurse's life to deal with the absence. I could only hope that we were able to work things out to each other's satisfaction. I intended to keep some balance between work and my relationship so that I didn't make the same mistake with Kate that I did with Maureen.

Unable to fall back to sleep, and feeling like I needed to do something to take my mind off Sam's words, I slipped out of bed and went to the kitchen where I found my guitar among the boxes of our possessions. I felt like playing but didn't want to bother Kate so I went into the pantry off the kitchen.

I was playing away, some music I'd recently found while listening to a station that wasn't my usual choice, when the door to the pantry opened.

I glanced up and saw Kate.

"Hi," she said and smiled. "Sorry to interrupt."

"No, that's fine," I replied. "Sorry I woke you."

"You couldn't sleep?" She came over to me and laid a hand on my shoulder.

"Nah," I said. " I'm exhausted but at the same time, I can't fall sleep."

"Insomnia," Kate said, and leaned against the wall across from me. "What were you playing? That was nice."

I played a few bars from the piece that I particularly liked. "A song that reminded me of you and of us. It's by a musician from LA I found a while ago when I took a break from my father's music. The song is called *See You Again* by Jason Falkner."

"Keep playing," she said. "It was nice and I hardly ever get to hear you sing or play."

I played for her and sang, but still felt quite uncomfortable. It was strange—I'd played literally hundreds of hours in front of small audiences, but there was something anonymous about it. With Kate here, now, it felt so personal.

When I was finished, I looked up at Kate, whose eyes were brimming.

"That's so sweet," she said and kissed me, her hands on my shoulders.

"I miss you," I said. "I'm so busy now, but I won't be this busy the whole time we're here."

"I know," she said, and ran her fingers through my hair. "I miss you, too, but I'll survive. My first class is tomorrow. I can't wait and expect I'll be busy from now on with my art."

I nodded and strummed the guitar. "Well, I guess I should put this away. My first surgery is early tomorrow." I put the guitar in the case and we went back to bed.

I yawned when we crept back into bed, but I still couldn't sleep. Instead, I tossed and turned, worried about how Kate would handle being so far away from her life while I was extremely busy at the college and hospital.

Sleep was a long time coming.

CHAPTER 9

I ROSE EARLY despite the sleepless night I'd spent worrying about our relationship. Kate got up as well, and while I made coffee, she had a shower. She finished dressing and came to the kitchen in a pretty little sundress covered in flowers. It made me realize how lucky I was to have her – sexy, with a touch of innocence that I found irresistible. She was the kind of woman I wanted to possess, and at the same time, if I had a mother who was involved in my life, I'd want to take Kate home with me to meet her.

I held her at arm's length and looked her up and down. "Ms. Bennet, you make it very hard to leave you all day when you wear that dress."

She held the skirt out and smiled, curtsying. "You like?"

"I *love*. You're not wearing it to your art class are you?"

"Of course not," she said, and turned in a circle. "I put it on to show you what you missed yesterday. I'll wear something more appropriate to an artist's studio. My overalls and a t-shirt."

"Whew," I said and mock wiped my brow. "Thank God, or someone would definitely steal you away from me. But

107

please wear that tonight when I come home. No matter how tired I am, I'll *have* to ravish you if you're wearing that."

She laughed and leaned against me for another kiss. "You ravishing me is my one desire."

I kissed her, lingering over her, touching her face, stroking her hair, wishing I could call in sick and spend the day with her, but I had a class and patients waiting.

Finally, I left, hoping she would have a good day and would be happy now that she was starting her classes.

My day passed quickly, the lecture feeling as if it was over before it started, but that was good. I was immersed in the material, and only yawned once or twice, hiding my yawn by turning to face the chalkboard and writing down a word or line. I usually used my computer and a projector, showing a PowerPoint presentation, but now and then I wrote a word or phrase down on the board for emphasis. It came in handy, for I didn't want my students to think I was bored. I was anything but bored.

After class, I had a coffee and looked over charts for my existing surgical patients and then did rounds with the nurses and residents to discuss the cases. After lunch with a few fellow surgeons, including of course, Sam, I had OR time scheduled and was able to get through my caseload in record time. After I finished scrubbing up, I was on my way to my office when Sam caught up with me. She pulled off her cap and threw it in a trash can as we walked along the hallway.

"Hey, some of us are going to a local dive for supper. Want to come along? They have great food."

I shook my head, annoyed that Sam wasn't going to let up. "I'm done early and will be going home to Kate."

She shrugged. "Okay. Just thought I'd be collegial and ask."

"Thanks," I said, feeling instantly bad for being so anti-social. It was common for the staff to eat a meal together. I would have to find a way to interact with Sam because she wasn't going anywhere. I just wanted her to know with absolute certainty that there was no hope for anything less than professional conduct between us. "Kate had her first art class today and I want to go home and see how it went. Some other time."

She nodded and went to the staff lounge while I went to my office.

Once there, I sent Kate a text before dinner, saying that I hoped to be home a bit early as the hospital was pretty quiet, surgeries were all finished and the patients were out of recovery. After I finished up my charting, I called Jomo and requested his services.

Jomo arrived and I asked him to stop off at the hardware store and then the local liquor store so I could pick up some supplies for the night I had planned. Then, I texted Kate.

I'm on my way now. Have a shower and wait for me. After we eat dinner, I want to eat you.

She texted right back.

Do you want me to wear something special? Do something special?

I considered.

Now that you mention it, I want you to be my slave-girl tonight. I know we're not 24/7 but for tonight, we can pretend that we are. I want you wearing your nylons and garters, but no undies. I want you to wear that sexy little flowered sundress. I want you to have your hair up and your collar – your thick leather collar – on. Be waiting by the sofa on your knees, like a good slave, your eyes downcast. I want dinner ready in the oven, so you can serve me. I bought some flavored vodka at the Junction and picked up some really soft rope that I plan on using to tie you up. And then, I'm going to ravish you, Katherine...

I knew that would get to her. I hoped so.

I was hard imagining it.

109

Just when we were approaching the gate at the entrance to the village, I sent Kate another text.

Katherine, I'm on my way home. I just went through the guardhouse. Be waiting for me. Be ready for me. I'm more than ready for you...

She texted back right away.

I'm very ready for you, Sir.

I smiled to myself, thinking of her waiting for me, a smile on her face in anticipation of our slave scene. It was the first time we would have role-played and I wanted to see how she responded.

I entered the house and kicked off my shoes, throwing my jacket over the back of the chair. I went to the kitchen and took out two glasses and then went to the living room, where she was waiting for me, her head bowed as I expected.

I took her chin in my hand and tilted her head up. She kept her eyes closed, and waited like a good obedient slave. I kissed her, pleased that she was so willing to comply with my wishes. I drank down a shot of green apple vodka and kissed her quickly so she could taste the vodka on my tongue.

"I missed you today, Katherine."

"I missed you, Sir."

"You can open your eyes now."

She did, blinking. I smiled when our eyes met and then lifted her up, my hands under her arms, so that she stood in front of me. Then I inspected her, checking out whether she had complied with my demands.

She had and looked a perfect mixture of innocence and seduction. Her face was youthful, her features soft and young. Her body was curvy and sexual, despite her petite stature. Exactly as I liked it.

"Very nice," I said, running a hand over her shoulder and down over her dress, cupping a breast. "I like the way your breasts look in that. It makes me breathless." I stepped closer. "In fact, it makes me want to do this."

I pulled down one strap, exposing her shoulder. Bending down, I kissed it and ran my tongue over her collarbone and down over the curve of one breast. Kate gave a soft moan when I squeezed it and then pulled the fabric down further to expose the entire breast.

"So perfect," I said, admiring her full heavy breast. "Breasts that demand attention." I guided Kate back onto the couch and leaned over her, leaving a line of kisses down from her cheek to her jaw, then down to her breast once more. I sucked a nipple into my mouth, then pulled on it with gentle teeth. Kate gasped and arched her back, pressing her breast into my face.

I wanted to eat first, because I needed the energy for the evening, so I pulled her up and looked her over approvingly.

"I'm starving. Let's eat."

Kate seemed surprised that I wasn't going to follow through.

"OK..."

I grinned. "A bit worked up are you, Ms. Bennet?"

"A bit," she said, smiling back at me. "Did you intend to work me up and then leave me unsatiated, Sir? Are you so cruel?"

I took her hand and placed it over my erection.

"I'm very cruel," I said. "I'm also too damn hungry to delay any longer."

"Dinner's almost ready. There's salad in the fridge, a fresh baguette, and I only have to turn on the broiler and the shrimp will be cooked in ten minutes."

My stomach rumbled at the mention of the food. "Sounds delicious. Let me pour you a glass of wine."

I led Kate to the kitchen and she seemed a bit taken aback that we weren't fucking right away.

"Am I supposed to stay in submissive mode through dinner?"

"Yes, *Katherine*," I said sternly. "That was the idea so watch that saucy tongue of yours. I'm only tolerating it because I'm so hungry. You do what I tell you, serve me when I tell you, comply without question to what I demand of you. That includes using proper forms of address..."

"Yes, *Master*," she said. "I haven't called you that for a long time and it feels pretty..."

She said nothing for a moment, biting her lip.

"Pretty what?" I said and stopped at the island in the kitchen, turning to face her, my arms crossed.

"Nothing," she said. " Master."

I nodded, but I knew there was resistance in her to submission as much as it titillated her. She wanted it, but she still didn't like what she thought it meant about her. I knew it would be a long road ahead to convince her it meant nothing other than she liked sex that way. Nothing more.

"Good," I said, trying to sound authoritative. "Now, I'm going to sit here at the island and watch you finish dinner. We can eat here. I don't care about eating in the dining room. I want to drink my wine and relax, watch you serve me."

She smiled and continued fixing dinner. I watched her for a while, admiring her in her lovely sundress, her cheeks flushed from the heat of the stove.

"How was your day?" I asked while she cut up the baguette and placed the buttered pieces in a basket. "You had your first class. Did you enjoy it?"

She sighed. "For the most part," she said hesitantly.

"What does that mean?"

She stopped what she was doing and looked in my eyes directly.

"My instructor's great," she said. "Talia's really talented and a good teacher. She said some really nice things about

112

my work. She also said I shouldn't be in that class because it was below my skill level and she wanted me to take a master class she teaches on Thursday nights."

I raised my eyebrows, pleased for her. That must have made her feel great—to have her work seen as at that higher level. I couldn't figure out why she was subdued about the class. "That's *great*. You are talented. Come here," I said and waved her over. I pulled her onto my lap and embraced her, smiling. "I'm so glad for you that it went well." I kissed her, then brushed a strand of hair off her cheek. "What part wasn't so great?"

She hesitated once more and I tried to brace myself for what she was so afraid to admit.

"Sefton deVilliers brought his class into our room for the second part so his students could use the nude model. They're going to share the room with us during every class for a month or so."

"*Oh...*" I said nothing in reply, taking a moment to process this bit of information before I reacted. Sefton would be present for half her class? I frowned in spite of myself. "Did he pester you?"

She nodded and made a face of regret. "He commented on my choker again and then he asked me if we were 24/7."

"What?" A jolt of adrenaline surged through me. "He *asked* if we were 24/7?"

"When I asked him what he meant, he tried to say he meant to ask if I wore my choker 24/7, but I'm pretty sure he really did want to know whether we are a 24/7 couple."

"*Damn...*" I rubbed my eyes, feeling suddenly exhausted. "Did he say anything else?"

"He tried to give me a ride home, but I had already called Jomo and luckily, he arrived and I was able to escape."

Damn that man... He had some nerve. It wasn't enough

that he knew we were in the lifestyle, and it wasn't enough that Kate told him we were engaged. He was persistent.

Was he going to pester Kate until I punched him out?

"Well, maybe you should drop the drawing class like your instructor suggested and take the master class on Thursday nights. I usually work late Thursday anyway, so I won't feel deprived of your attentions."

She bit her bottom lip and looked in my eyes, a guilty expression on her face.

"What?" I said, bracing myself for more bad news.

"Sefton co-teaches the master class..."

"Oh, *no*," I said and glanced away, needing to calm myself down. "No." I turned back to Kate. "I don't want you taking a class from him."

"I don't want to either, but it's either take the day class or night class."

I took in a deep breath. "Maybe you should stay in your day class."

"Or no class at all," she added.

"No," I said and shook my head. "You have to take a class." I paused for a moment. "You said he was only going to share space with your class for a month?"

She nodded and avoided my eyes. "Yes, for a month or so."

I sighed. "I'm sorry this had to happen to you. You see?" I said and bent down to look in her eyes, despite her avoidance. "You're a very delicious woman. Other men will want you. Will hit on you. I can see I'm going to spend a lot of my time away from you being jealous of their attention."

"I don't want their attention, Drake," she said. "I only want yours. Honestly. I wish I'd never met him, he's so pushy and annoying and everything he says has a double meaning. He's so..."

"Dominant?" I said and cracked a rueful grin. "We tend to be

114

a persistent lot, we Doms, but usually only with those already in the lifestyle and only if we are certain of interest. To pursue someone who isn't interested is boorish." I took in a deep breath, and ran a finger over her bottom lip. "So you think he's a Dom?"

She hesitated and glanced away. "There's something else," she said, her voice soft.

"What?" I turned her to me and searched her face. "Tell me."

"He said something."

"What did he say?"

"He called me *ma petite chérie* like you did while we were in scene at the dungeon."

I closed my eyes. "*Christ…*"

"So, that means we were in a public room," she said quietly and I hated deVilliers with a passion at that moment. He'd gone and ruined a perfect evening for us.

I sighed heavily, trying hard to avoid overreacting. "I'm sorry you had to find out like that. I wanted to wait until I felt you were ready to know. What a *bastard* he is… Now, there's no doubt he's a Dom and sees you as a potential conquest. He's a jerk, though, because as soon as he heard you were engaged, he should have backed off and been totally polite and respectful. And letting you know he saw you?" I shook my head in disgust. "You don't ask people if they're in the lifestyle. They tell you if they want you to know. You don't let on that you saw them at a function. Their careers may depend on anonymity. That's why I didn't pursue you when I first met you, despite being absolutely smitten."

"You didn't want to try to tempt me with beguiling tales of bondage and dominance?"

"Not on your life," I said, remembering how torn I was back when I first met Kate and thought she was just a vanilla kind of woman. "Trying went disastrously wrong the first time."

She nodded. "It's lucky for us both that I was interested already."

"If I had any idea you were..." I said and laughed. "I would have been on the case even sooner."

"On the case..." she said and smiled, snuggling into my arms. "The shrimp," she said suddenly and slipped out of my arms. She rushed to the oven and checked.

"You were a project," I said as I watched her turn the shrimp and then prepare a salad. "I had to plan for you, plot my way into your mind and between your thighs."

"Were you so Machiavellian?" she asked, tilting her head to the side.

"Completely." I poured some more wine. "I intended to have you. I intended to take you off the market. I couldn't stand the idea that some other Dom, someone who wasn't quite as gentle as I am, might snag you first."

"I wouldn't be with someone who was a sadist," she said. "Only someone like you."

"You'd be surprised how far someone can take you, Kate, if they're skilled enough," I said, thinking of other submissives I had spoken with over the five years I had been active in the lifestyle. "What if I had wanted to do more than we do now? Did you ever think you'd have sex in public, that you'd be on display for every kinkster in the place to see?"

She shook her head. "I never imagined it."

"What if I wanted to flog you?" I added. "What if I wanted to gag you and do nipple torture or use clothespins on your labia? Would you run?"

She stopped what she was doing and glanced away, not wanting to meet my eyes.

"I probably would let you try, because I trust you enough that you'd stop if I didn't enjoy them."

"But you'd do it at least once," I said. "With someone who is really charismatic, you might do more than you would like to please him and take the pain, especially if you were really submissive."

"I'd like to think I'd run screaming the other way."

"So would I," I said, frowning. "But getting back to Sefton, maybe try to ignore him as much as possible

"I'll try."

Kate took the shrimp out of the oven and placed them on a serving dish and we were ready for our meal.

AFTER DINNER, we took our wine and moved to the living room. I sat down in the center of the couch and stretched my arms over the back.

"Come here," I said and pointed. "On my lap."

Kate smiled, then sat on my lap, her legs on one side and her arms around my neck like that first night.

"I remember this position," I said, catching her eye. "I was so hard that night, hoping that you'd fall. Worried that you wouldn't."

"I'd already fallen," she said, "but I hadn't hit solid ground yet. It wasn't until you kissed me that I did. It was game over at that point."

"It was for both of us," I said, smiling softly.

I pulled her into my arms and remembered that night, how excited I had been and how worried at the same time that I'd go to far too fast with her and scare her off. It almost went disastrously wrong, but she was here now, with me.

Mine.

"I seem to recall you saying something about being a slave-girl," Kate said, "with body lotions and massage oils…"

"We fall out of our roles pretty easily," I said. "I'm such a bad Dom."

"No you aren't." She pulled back and frowned. "You're exactly right for me."

I nodded. "We're right for each other. I should enforce my rules, be a little stricter with discipline though. To make things more enjoyable. Speaking of which, I want you to be my slave-girl for the rest of the night, *Katherine*..."

She smiled back. "Your wish is my command, oh Sultan."

I kissed her, pushing her down on the couch, eager to touch her now that I was fed and mellow from the wine. When our tongues touched, I was hard as rock, and couldn't keep my hands off her lush body. I ran my hand over her hip to the hem of her sundress and felt up her thigh to the garters. Then, I slipped my fingers between her lips to see how wet she was.

She was nice and warm and wet and I ached to be inside of her – that moment when I filled her up completely and we were joined, our arms and legs entwined. It was one of the few things vanilla I still loved.

"I want you to take me into the bedroom, undress me, and then I want a full body massage with some nice oil. I want you naked except for your hose and garters. I want you to do all the work. Ride me like a bull."

"A bull, Sir?" she said, bating her eyelashes.

"That's right," I said, trying hard not to grin. "A bull. I'm going to enjoy watching you make yourself come on my cock."

Her eyes widened at that. Obediently, she stood and took my hand, pulling me behind her to the bedroom. She led me to the side of the bed and began undressing me, biting her lip, trying hard not to smile.

"You can smile," I said, fighting to keep from laughing. "Men like it when their lovers are pleased, excited, enjoying it."

She smiled widely undid the buttons on my shirt,

throwing it on the bench at the foot of the bed. Then, to my delight, she knelt down and ran her lips over my erection. After she unzipped my pants and pulled down my boxer briefs, she ran her tongue all over me, from the base of my cock to the head. When she took me into her mouth for a brief suck, it felt so good that I groaned out loud.

She stood up and removed her sundress but left on her hose and garters.

She knew what I liked. Then, she pushed me on the chest softly. "Lie down, Sir, while I get the massage oil."

I climbed onto the bed and lay back, my hands behind my head, watching as she went to the bathroom to get the massage oils.

"On your stomach, if you please, Sir," she said, twirling her fingers.

"Oh, I please," I said, looking so forward to what would come next.

I lay on my stomach, my head resting on my hands, and waited. Kate crawled over top of me and straddled my hips. I felt cool oil drizzle over my back and then her hands, soft and gentle, rubbing the oil over my skin. She worked at my shoulder muscles, which were tense after my day of surgery. I couldn't help but sigh in contentment. Then she worked my lower back and hips, my upper thighs, and finally my calves. When she began massaging my glutes, I groaned. She slipped her fingers between my thighs and I spread them a bit so she could stroke my balls.

I wasn't used to letting a woman take control, even though I had ordered her to be my slave girl. It was usually me doing and Kate receiving whatever I was doing.

I liked this. I could get used to it.

"Turn over now, if you wish, Sir."

"I wish you'd call me Master instead," I replied, turning over. "Master does rather go with slave-girl after all."

"Yes, *Master*," she said obediently.

She straddled my thighs and then leaned over me, her hands on either side of my shoulders.

"Would you permit this slave to kiss you first, Master?" she asked. I glanced down at her body poised above me, her thighs spread wide, her breasts full and ripe before my eyes.

"I would permit it," I said, amused at this little game we were playing. "Make sure you kiss all of me. Don't neglect the other parts."

"I would never dream of it," she said and bent down to kiss me, pressing my mouth open with her tongue. I groaned when she pressed herself against my erection, sliding along it.

"You *like* that, Master?" she asked in mock surprise, her eyes wide.

"I like it very much. Keep doing what you're doing, slave-girl. You're doing a very good job. Except you forgot about kissing all my parts. And the massage."

She rubbed against me again. "Did I?"

I grinned and then closed my eyes with pleasure when she rubbed her warm wetness against the head of my cock.

She took her massage oil and began working it over my chest and abs, tracing her fingers over my hips and down to my thighs.

"Sit on me now," I said, hungry to feel my cock fill her up.

"But Master..." she said, pouting playfully. "I haven't kissed all your parts yet."

She leaned down and ran her lips over my cock from base to tip, licking the head. Then she kissed it, before sucking the head in her mouth. I groaned and closed my eyes, smiling despite my best attempts to stop.

"Now, *Katherine*."

I held my erection for her and she proceeded to miss my cock on purpose, running her labia over my length.

Several times.

"Shameless slave-girl," I murmured. "Disobeying your Master's command."

"This slave apologizes, Master," she said, a bit breathless as she rubbed against my cock once more. I didn't really try to stop her for I enjoyed the sight of her pleasuring herself with my body. "But she can't help herself…"

She kept rubbing herself against me, her eyes half closed, and I let her for a while. I finally outmaneuvered her and held my cock just so. The next time she went to slide down my length, she sat on me fully.

"Oh, *God*," she cried as the head of my cock plunged inside of her.

"That's what I want to hear," I said, my voice almost a growl. I took her hips in my hands and watched as she rode me. She didn't take long and soon, her body showed signs that she was getting close. Her breathing became faster, and the skin on her neck and chest were mottled with a sexual flush.

"Master I — I'm going to…" she managed.

I leaned up and took one nipple in my mouth, sucking hard and that was enough to send her over. She closed her eyes and groaned with pleasure.

"Look at me," I said, taking her hips in my hands and helping her thrust.

She forced her eyes open and looked in mine when she came.

Then, she collapsed on top of me and lay still, her breathing rough. I let her lie like that, enjoying the sensation as her body convulsed around my cock. Then, it was my turn and I rolled her over, still inside of her while I did. I kissed her hungrily, sucking her tongue into my mouth while I started to thrust. Slowly at first, I took my time, making sure to withdraw fully then sliding over her clit before entering her again in a measured pace.

I wanted her to come again, and kept that up until I could see she was reaching another climax.

"Come again for me," I said, breathing fast as I increased my pace.

When she cried out, I thrust harder and finally went over, both our bodies shuddering in pleasure.

"*God*, that was good," I said, kissing her neck while I tried to catch my breath.

"You *are* good," she replied, smiling, her eyes closed. "*Master*."

I chuckled, and lay on top of her, completely fulfilled.

CHAPTER 10

I DIDN'T EVEN GET a chance to see Kate the next day except in the morning before I left. I bent down to kiss her goodbye while she stayed under the covers and hoped to come home by eight so we could do a later dinner and sit together on the sofa, listen to some music and talk. Unfortunately, my plans for a quiet evening together were thrown by the wayside when one of my patients decompensated and I stayed late, almost to midnight, to make sure he was getting proper care, waiting in case we had to do emergency surgery.

Of course, Sam took the opportunity to spend as much time as she could with me, every chance she got. I was in the staff room, taking a break from cases, a cup of coffee helping to get me through the afternoon when she plopped onto the old leather sofa beside me.

"That was an intense case," she said after we worked on a pediatric trauma case. It was entirely normal for physicians who work a case together to relax together afterwards, especially if you are working with residents or students, and if it had been anyone other than Sam, I wouldn't have cared. But it was her. I didn't want there to be any chance that

123

rumors might start about us so I merely nodded and got up from the sofa and threw out my empty coffee cup. I left the staff room without a word, planning on going to my office and dictate some notes, but she followed me out of the room.

"Hey," she said and took my arm.

I stopped and looked pointedly at her hand on my bicep.

"Don't be like that," she said and frowned.

"I have some work to do, if you'll excuse me…"

I pulled away but she persisted.

"Drake, we have to work together."

"We are," I said simply, not stopping to engage her.

"No, I mean, we have to get along. I feel this," she said and caught up with me, walking briskly to keep up. "This animosity from you. I don't want you to get the wrong idea about us. I just want to be friends. We do have a history…"

"We do," I said and stopped, facing her. "That was in the past. This is now. I'm in love with my partner and we're getting married. I can't flirt with you and be your confidant. I hope you understand."

She had a hurt expression on her face and I hoped I hadn't made an enemy. "Who said I was flirting with you? Who said I want to be your confidant?"

I shook my head. "Sorry. Just want to make things plain."

I turned and continued down the hall, hoping she left it at that.

She didn't.

"Claire said she broke your heart. If she did it once, she could do it again."

I stopped once more and turned to face her, angry now.

"Claire said *what*?"

Sam came closer, and lowered her voice. "When I first learned you were coming back, Claire told me that you were running away from a broken heart. That Kate had broken up with you and you were escaping, coming here to lick your wounds."

I shook my head.

What the hell, Claire?

I had told Michael that I had just broken up with a woman with whom I was serious, and coming to Africa would be a good escape and change of scene, but I never said Kate had broken my heart…

"Look, this is none of anyone's business, but just to set things straight, Kate and I broke up but it was over a total misunderstanding. Once things were clarified, we were back together and made a commitment to each other. There was never any change in how we felt for each other—just a mistake due to a meddling person. So, Claire misunderstood what happened between us."

Sam stood quietly and said nothing, but I could see that she was still upset.

"You and I are colleagues and we will work together," I said, my tone firm, "but I'm not interested in anything more. I'd like to avoid the appearance that we are anything more than that. Is that clear?" I said, impatient to get this over with.

"Perfectly clear," she said and turned on her heel, stomping away down the hall in the opposite direction.

I spent an hour in my office, cooling off, distracting myself with dictation of my case notes. I hoped that Sam didn't become a problem. There would be enough challenges for us being in a new country and away from friends and family. We didn't need more people meddling in our relationship.

When I got home that night, it was very late and as much as I wanted to speak with Kate and snuggle with her, she was fast asleep when I arrived and I didn't want to wake her. So I went the whole day having said very little to her. I spoke more with Sam than Kate—a fact that irritated me, especially after my run in with Sam earlier in the day.

THE NEXT DAY was almost a repeat of the previous day, except Sam kept her distance—thankfully. I was up at six thirty that morning due to an early surgery and after I'd showered and dressed, I bent down and kissed Kate's cheek, my arms on either side of her. I nuzzled her neck, regretting that my day started so early.

"Ms. Bennet, I look forward to the weekend when I can stay in bed with you and wake you up with a slow fuck."

She hid her face from me, and smiled. I kissed her cheek, her chin, and then her forehead before stroking her jaw.

Then I was gone, leaving her alone once more.

MY DAY WENT QUICKLY and luckily, there were no more problems with Sam. She kept a polite distance and so I was satisfied that our little chat in the hallway had some effect.

When I looked up from dictating notes on my previous procedure, I saw that I had at least an hour off. Kate would be in her class so I decided to pop by and surprise her. I called Jomo and asked him to take me and he showed up at the rear entrance to the hospital. I just purchased a coffee from the cafeteria and sipped it on the way to the Institute. I didn't have a lot of time due to the time it took to travel to and from the hospital and didn't even take off my lab coat.

I found the building where Kate's class was being held and popped my head inside the open door. I glanced around and my eyes came to rest on Kate, who was seated at a bench with an easel in front. Standing over her, bending over closely and speaking to her, was a tall blond man dressed in khaki slacks and white shirt. He looked rather like someone you'd find on safari rather than an art class.

It had to be the deVilliers guy.

The man said something to Kate, a conspiratorial smile on his face. She glanced over to where I stood just inside the door.

Our eyes met and I wanted to smile at her, but I couldn't help but feel jealous that the bastard was there, looming over her possessively.

In truth, I wanted to punch his face.

Kate got up, saying something to deVilliers and then came to me, her cheeks flushed.

"Ms. *Bennet*," I said, trying desperately to control my emotions. I took a sip of my coffee, hoping to appear calm. "I thought I'd pop in and see what it is you artists do when you're not being watched. I take it that's your other suitor?"

"He's *not* a suitor," she said breathlessly. "How long have you been here?" She put a hand on my shoulder, touching me like she wanted to show everyone—deVilliers included—that we were a couple. It pleased me, but I was still on edge.

"Long enough."

She frowned. "What do you mean, long enough?"

"Long enough to know that he's got his eye set on you, Kate."

She forced a laugh, but it sounded hollow. She knew I was right.

"He promised to be a complete gentleman and apologized for being improper."

"I'll bet he did."

"*Drake...*"

I exhaled loudly. "Kate, if you can't see his behavior for what it is, let me enlighten you. He *wants* you. He's probably decided to lay on the charm so he doesn't scare you off."

"He admitted as much." She shook her head. "He promised to be entirely professional."

"Of *course* he did. I did, too, if I remember correctly, and we all know how that turned out." I wanted to smile, make light of it, but my heart wouldn't let me.

"What are you saying?"

I shook my head and glanced over her shoulder. deVilliers leaned against the wall by the huge bank of windows, his arms crossed. He stared across the room at us.

Then Kate put her hands on my shoulders, leaning up to kiss me. I didn't bend down to meet her for a kiss so Kate had to stand on her tiptoes in order to reach me. I kissed her back, wanting deVilliers to see me kissing her.

At that moment, Kate's instructor came over.

"Kate, is there a problem? We're about to finish up."

Kate turned to the woman. "I'm sorry. This is my fiancé, Drake Morgan. He popped in for a moment."

The woman nodded, her expression one of polite impatience. "If you could wait outside, I find visitors tend to disrupt the class."

I nodded. "I apologize," I said. "Of course."

I glanced at Kate briefly, then went out the door, closing it softly behind me.

I left the building and went out to sit on the curb, my heart pounding just a bit faster than it should have. I was far too upset about this but I knew that deVilliers was probably exactly what Kate should have been attracted to. He was obviously a Dominant if he was attending the dungeon party, and was so forward with Kate. He was an artist. He was younger than me and good looking. Even I had to admit that.

I bit back my jealousy and had to remember Kate wanted me.

She chose *me*.

Jomo arrived back at the appointed time and got out of his car while I waited for Kate.

"How is Miss Katherine?" Jomo said while we waited.

"She's fine. The class wasn't completely finished when I arrived."

We spoke briefly about his classes. Then, Kate finally came out of the building with the other students. I stood and took her art portfolio while Jomo reached out to take her art kit.

The drive to the house was quiet, and luckily, the traffic sounds were loud. We arrived at the house and Jomo handed Kate her things. Kate came to my side of the taxi and I rolled down the window.

"I have to get back and scrub in for a surgery at 1:00."

Kate checked her cell as if checking to see if I had time, but I didn't.

"I wish you wouldn't leave like this," she said and glanced at Jomo, who was busy putting in his earphones as if he wanted to give us privacy. "I don't like to see you upset because of a misunderstanding."

"I understood perfectly, Kate," I said, not looking at her. "It's you who doesn't understand."

"Drake, don't leave things like this."

I shook my head. "We'll talk later. Be waiting for me. In proper position."

"What do you mean?" she said, but she knew.

"You know what I mean." Then, I kissed her briefly but intensely, one hand tangled in her hair, pulling her against my mouth. "I need to do a scene with you tonight to wipe his memory from both our minds. What do you think, Katherine?"

"Whatever you want," she said, frustration in her voice.

"I *want*," I said. "I'll let you know later when I'll be home. That rope is still unused."

She smiled at me, but I could tell it was as forced as my smile.

I kissed her again and then tapped Jomo on the shoulder.

We drove away, my gut in a knot that things had not gone as I hoped.

THE ROPE REMAINED UNUSED, despite my best intentions. I texted Kate at seven to say I'd be late again because of an emergency head injury from a collision on the Mombasso Road.

I know I intended to do a scene with you tonight, but once again, we have multiple patients and I have to stay until Michael is convinced they're stable.

She texted me back.

Drake, please don't take what happened at the Institute the wrong way. Sefton was apologizing for being improper with me and promised to be completely professional from now on.

I responded immediately.

You're very naïve, Kate. But this is something I should have known I'd have to deal with. You're young and inexperienced in the ways of men, especially Dominant men. I'm sorry to have been so busy lately and that you feel neglected. I swear I haven't been worked like this since I was a resident. I don't know where Michael gets the energy but he beats me in that department. He thrives on work, according to him. Says he feels 'alive' when he's working a trauma case.

Don't think this is how our life together will be. It won't. You're everything to me, and if you don't feel that, I've failed.

She texted back right away.

Please don't worry about Sefton. He's <u>nothing</u> to me. He's an art instructor who might help me improve. That's all. I love you.

I sat and stared at her response, trying to sort through my feelings. I knew I had to trust Kate. Trust was the foundation of a relationship. Especially one that involved D/s. Part of me held out—the jealous part of me that couldn't stand the thought that another Dom was involved in Kate's life—especially that part of her life that I could never be part of, other than encouraging her.

I tried to formulate a response that would be fair and understanding and big, but I was at a loss for words. I tried again and again to gather my thoughts but before I could finish typing a line, a code came over the intercom and I knew I had to run. Code Blue on neurosurgery. One of our patients had decompensated. Badly.

I ran to the ward, my cell tucked into my lab coat pocket, my message to Kate left unsent.

After the patient stabilized, I went back to my office and sat down at my desk, dictating notes on the patient. When I was finishing up, Michael ducked his head inside my office, an expression of concern on his face.

"Multicar pileup on the Mombasso Road. Multiple casualties."

"Christ," I said, shaking my head. "That road is insane. I thought Manhattan had bad traffic."

"Get used to it. We see a lot of head trauma cases as a result. Be prepared for a busy weekend. Keith is sick and so I'm on call for him."

"That means I'm on call with you," I said, regretting it, but it was part of the job.

"Afraid so."

I followed Michael down the hall to the ORs where we scrubbed in, waiting for our first case.

Hours later, I was up to my elbows in blood, totally absorbed in the cases, one after the other, that came to me. I felt like a trauma surgeon in a battle zone. The head traumas were complicated by fractures and internal injuries. A dozen surgeons worked together feverishly to try to save life and limb.

When the last of the cases was finished, I spoke with anxious families and spent the rest of the evening watching my patients, wanting to be there during the first few hours in case anything critical happened. When I checked my watch, it was past midnight and so I decided to sleep at the hospital rather than take a taxi home only to come back again, as I would lose at least forty minutes if I did.

Instead, I made one last check on my patients and bunked down in the resident's lounge. Luckily, I was the only one trying to sleep as the usual residents were all busy. I was alone in the darkened room, a pillow over my head while I lay on the couch with a hospital blanket thrown over me. I tried to sleep, but thoughts of Kate alone with deVilliers plagued my thoughts. When I was still awake an hour later, I cursed myself because I should have just gone home to Kate, given how much time I wasted lying awake thinking of her.

I slept for about four hours and took a taxi home for a shower and change of clothes.

And to see Kate.

CHAPTER 11

I DIDN'T WANT to wake her until I'd had my shower, so I tiptoed into the house and was as quiet as possible, slipping into the bathroom and taking a shower without any noise. I finished and pulled a towel around my waist and went into the bedroom only to find Kate sitting up in bed, rubbing her eyes. I went to my chest of drawers and chose some boxer briefs.

"What time did you get in?" Kate said from the bedroom. "I didn't even know you'd come to bed."

I dropped my towel and slipped on a pair of navy boxer briefs. "That's because I slept at the hospital."

"Drake…" she said, sounding horrified "Not because of what happened?"

I shook my head. "There was a seven car pile up on the Mombasso Road and we had a multiple casualty event. I was in charge of three patients and had to watch them until they were stable so I stayed and caught up with some paperwork. I fell asleep in the resident's room and came home to shower and change clothes."

"That's too bad," she said. She watched me dress for a few

133

moments in silence. "Why are you up so early? You have this weekend off."

"We're on call for Keith."

She sighed audibly. "I hope you got some sleep at least or your day will be a pain."

"A few hours."

I went to the bed and leaned over her, my hands on either side of her body. I stared at her for a few moments, and then took in a deep breath.

"I'm sorry I wasn't home last night," I said. "I can't really promise to make it up to you tonight, but I'll try."

She forced a smile and pressed her fingers against my lips. "Don't promise me anything. I know you have to do this. I'll have to learn to amuse myself when you're working late."

I sat beside her on the bed and leaned over her possessively.

"I'm sure this wasn't what you expected when you came with me. I'm sorry. This is important to me, helping Michael, teaching. But *you* are my love."

"It's all right," she said, sounding nonchalant but her voice wavered just a bit. "Things will get better soon enough once you're no longer Michael's shadow."

I leaned down closer and kissed her cheek, then her chin and then the tops of her breasts, pressing my nose between them and inhaling.

"You smell so warm and delicious," I murmured. "I better go quickly or I won't be able to drag myself away from you."

She smiled when I kissed her breasts once more and then I was off, grabbing my suit jacket from the hanger in the closet. I stopped at the door before leaving and looked back at her.

"If I can't make it up to you tonight, tomorrow night for sure," I said, raising my eyebrows.

She shook her head. "No promises, Drake. We'll do what we can when we can. That's good enough for me."

I stood for a moment longer trying to take her in, so I could imagine her later when I had some spare moments in my day.

Then I left her alone once more.

THE DAY WENT FAST, for we were busy with the patients from the Mombasso Road crash as well as incidental head traumas that came in through the ER. A worker fell off a ladder down two stories onto his head. Of course, he didn't wear any safety harness.

A teenager dove into the shallow end of a swimming pool in one of the gated communities and broke his spine. An elderly woman came in with a hemorrhagic stroke.

When I finally caught a minute of respite, I decided to text Kate.

How are you, Ms. Bennet? Missing me much? I miss you...

She texted back right away.

I miss you so much, you wouldn't believe. When will you be home?

I checked my watch.

Home... I like the sound of that. Not sure yet when I'll be home. We're working through the supper hour due to an emergency that came in and threw off our schedule. Michael wants to take the residents out for dinner and then I'll be home. Don't wait up if you're tired.

There was a brief hesitation before she replied and then I realized why. She'd be thinking of Sam...

I'll try to stay up, but if I'm not awake when you get home, wake me up so we can at least talk a bit. I miss you so much.

I responded right away.

135

I miss you too. Think of me kissing you, you lying in my arms. I'll wake you up for at least a bit of affection before bed. I love you.

Her reply was immediate this time.

I love you, too.

As luck would have it, everything settled down later in the evening, and Michael took us all out for a dinner at The Butler's Pantry, a British pub that was a regular haunt of hospital staff. Of course, Sam was there, but she behaved herself for the most part, although I felt her eyes on me throughout the meal. I deliberately held off sitting down at the table so I could pick the seat farthest from Sam. I didn't want to feel obligated to make conversation with her.

After several beers and some tasty food, I caught a ride home with Michael, who was going back to the hospital to spend the night.

"Claire is busy and so I'd rather stay there and be close, in case anything develops in the night."

I thanked him for excusing me from duty, and went inside the house, making my way to the office to charge my cell before going to the bedroom. I went right over to the bed and bent down to kiss Kate, whose eyes were sleepy.

"You smell almost good enough to eat and drink," she said when I pulled away. "Where did you take your residents for a meal?"

"This pub called The Butler's Pantry not far from the hospital. A lot of the staff go there when they get off shift. I had Guinness and bangers and mash, I think they call it. It's one of Michael's favorite places to eat after work. Reminds him of his days in London as a med student."

I went to my closet and undressed quickly.

"I ate some popcorn and drank Earl Grey Tea for supper."

I turned to her and shook my head. "I'm so sorry. I felt bad going out for a meal when you were here all by yourself, but it's a bit of a tradition to take the residents out when you work them through supper. I *had* to go…"

"Don't even think of it," she said softly. "You're a staff member now. You have to follow the traditions. I was fine."

She forced a big smile.

I went over and sat on the bed beside her. "No, you weren't fine. You got by, but you weren't fine. I promise I won't neglect you this weekend. It's free and clear and I won't set foot in the hospital until Monday morning."

She put her arms around my neck and I pressed my forehead against hers.

"I won't kiss you because I probably taste like Guinness. But wait for me. I'll go brush my teeth."

I left Kate on the bed and brushed my teeth, standing in the doorway to the en-suite bathroom. "How was your day?" I managed around the toothbrush.

"Fine," she said. "Claire took me to lunch."

"How did that go?"

She shrugged. "The food was good. I ate too much. Sefton was there."

I stopped brushing and frowned. "He had lunch with you?"

"No," she said quickly. "He was there with his girlfriend."

I made a face of disbelief. "Awfully coincidental. Nairobi is a big city."

"But the expat crowd is pretty incestuous, according to Claire."

I shook my head and went back to the sink. After I finished rinsing, I went to bed and crawled under the covers, snuggling close to her.

"And did he pester you? Or was he busy with his woman?"

"He was so polite when he came up to speak to us, I almost thought he was a different person."

137

"I may have to duel with him," I said, nuzzling her neck. "Rapiers at Dawn. Set him straight."

"He was *fine*, Drake," she said. "I told him to lay off, and it seems that he has."

"Good. But I'll still sharpen my sword."

She gasped when I kissed a trail along her collarbone. Then I sighed heavily and laid my head on her shoulder, my arm around her waist, one thigh thrown over her legs. "I have to crash."

"I know," she said and stroked my hair. "You've had a long day."

"I promise I'm all yours tomorrow night," I said, wanting her to feel some hope for the weekend. "I feel so guilty leaving you alone all day."

"Don't feel guilty," she said softly. "This is your life. I want to be a part of it, whatever tiny little sliver of it you give me."

I sat up at that. "Kate, you aren't merely a tiny little sliver in my life. You *are* my life. The surgery and teaching?" I said and leaned down so that our eyes met. "They're my calling. I do both because neurosurgeons, especially those with a specialization in robotics, are in short supply. I'm *needed*. I feel like I can't say no when the need is so great."

"My *need* is so great, too," she said, coyly. "Maybe I'll have to find a substitute. One named Robert, perhaps."

I frowned. "Robert?"

"You know, B-O-B." She smiled again. "Battery Operated Boyfriend."

I nodded. "I always think of it as Big. For a minute, I thought you were serious and was wracking my brain for someone named Robert."

"Drake, how could you even imagine?" she said, her voice horrified.

"I can imagine a great deal, Kate. You have to remember Maureen left me for Chris."

I bent down to kiss her before reaching over and turning off the bedside light. Then, I sighed heavily. "I know it's hard, Kate. Bear with me. I'm doing the best I can. Things are really busy right now."

"I know. I'm doing the best I can right now, too."

I snuggled against her, my arm around her waist, hand under her breast. Despite my earlier concern about that deVilliers bastard, I was so exhausted, I fell asleep almost immediately.

I woke up in the morning, the sun filtering in under the curtains and wanted nothing more than to wake Kate up with a kiss to the nape of her neck. I pressed my erection against her butt, and slipped my hand around her body to find her pussy. I felt her move and bit her shoulder playfully.

She craned her neck to look at me and opened her mouth, but I stopped her.

"*Don't* say anything," I whispered, rolling her over in bed. I wanted to finally use the rope I'd bought and had been too busy to use, which was squirreled away in the drawer in the bedside table. I took her hands and raised them above her head. "I *need* you. I need *this*," I said, my voice a bit shaky from lust. "I don't want you using Big, Bob or your fingers when you have me."

Then I tied her hands to the headboard before blind-folding her with a black handkerchief.

I bent her knees, spread her thighs, propping up her hips with a pillow.

Then I began to stroke the head of my cock against her pussy, teasing the entrance to her body, then rubbing the tip against her clit. I bent forward and sucked her nipple hard, my teeth grazing the hard bud, and her body arched with pleasure in response.

Perfect," I said. "I want to try something." I left her alone on the bed, bound and blindfolded and went to my gym bag where I had hidden a pair of nipple clamps. I didn't know if I would ever use them, but Kate had responded enough to my teeth on her nipples during sex play that I suspected she might enjoy them if she gave them a chance. But I also knew it was best not to let her know what I had planned for she would become anxious and not enjoy it as much as she might otherwise.

When I returned to the bed, I began to suck her nipples again, preparing her. When I thought she was ready, her hips thrusting up against me, searching out stimulation, I clipped the nipple clamp against one of her nipples.

She gasped. She didn't stop me, so I sucked her other nipple and then I attached a clamp on it as well.

"There," I said, examining them. "How does that feel? Not too painful? They're not very tight."

"They're fine," she said, but her voice was a little hesitant. "I didn't know you had any."

"I picked them up on the way home one day. You enjoy my teeth so I thought you might enjoy these. Now, shh."

I licked and kissed my way down her body to her pussy and flicked my tongue over her clit. Her hips jerked involuntarily in response. I worked her up until she was breathing heavily and then removed the clamps. Blood would rush back into vessels and nerves and sensation from her nipples would compete with those of her clit, mixing up the two. When I slipped my fingers inside of her, she groaned.

I moved up and licked her nipples, sucking on them gently until she was writhing beneath me. When I thought she was almost at the edge of her orgasm, I entered her completely, my thumb on her clit.

She gasped out loud.

"That's what I love to hear," I said, moving her body, gripping her hips. "You gasping with pleasure."

I fucked her, stimulating her all the while, watching for a

sign that she was close. When I saw the mottling start on her chest, I knew she was ready and pulled off the blindfold.

I bent over her while I thrust. "Open your eyes when you come for me."

She complied, her eyes half-lidded and heavy with pleasure.

"Tell me when you're going to come."

She licked her lips, her eyes wandering, then almost closing. "I'm going to..."

Then she closed her eyes tightly as her body went rigid and I knew she was over the edge.

"Keep your eyes open," I commanded, but she struggled with it, her eyes open just a slit.

I began to thrust faster, harder, my hands grabbing her hips, pulling her body to meet mine with each thrust.

"Oh, *God*," I groaned when pleasure exploded inside of me. "So fucking *good*. Oh, *God*..."

When I was finished, I collapsed on top of her, my arms on either side of hers, my hands covering hers, which were still tied above her head.

I panted for a few moments, catching my breath.

"I'd like to take longer for this," I said, once I had recovered. I nuzzled her neck. "But I have to run. Next time, we'll play for much longer."

She smiled, her eyes closed and that was all the encouragement I needed.

She came into the shower with me and we washed each other, our soapy hands sliding over each other tenderly. I shampooed her hair, lathering it and running my fingers through it while she ran her slippery hands over my abs.

"I could get hard again with those hands of yours touching me like that, Ms. Bennet," I said while she washed me, soapy hands slipping between my thighs.

"You don't have time," she said. "I want you home for a

141

nice dinner and then maybe a bath. I want to play slave-girl again and lick you all over. I'll be so hungry for you, I'll want to wash every *inch* of you."

"You talk like that and I won't be able to concentrate in the ER," I said with a leer.

"Keep that thought for later tonight. What would you like for supper?"

"You mean, after I eat you?" I said, grinning. "I might like a nice piece of steak. We should christen that barbecue on the lanai."

"Your wish is my command." She kissed my wet shoulder as I turned off the faucet.

We dried each other off and I dressed quickly, for I was running late. When I was dressed, I returned to the bathroom and brushed my teeth beside Kate, watching her brush her hair in the mirror beside me.

"Enjoy yourself today," I said after I finished rinsing. "I hope he won't bother you."

"I'll try," she said, making a face. "I won't let him. I'll think of coming home to you, enjoying you."

I smiled and brushed hair from her cheek, but no matter how hard I tried, I couldn't shake the jealousy and worried that the time they spent together would eat away at her resolve.

She followed me to the living room and watched as I slipped on my shoes. I noticed her glancing at the car I brought home.

"I got a rental," I said as I stood beside her. "I'm going to brave the streets of Nairobi myself." I bent down to kiss her. "You look so delicious, naked underneath that towel, your hair wet, I may have a hard time leaving you."

She smiled. "I doubt that very much. You enjoy teaching too much to be distracted. I'm sure you have a few surgical patients with complicated cases to focus on."

I did and knew that they would keep me busy all day so that I barely noticed the time passing. Still, I felt bad leaving her alone once more.

"I'll be thinking of you all day," I said, catching her eye, wanting to show her how serious I was. "Keep reminding yourself it's only for a few more weeks. Besides, you have the safari next weekend. That's something to look forward to."

She leaned up and kissed me and then I left.

CHAPTER 12

I WAS RIGHT.

The day went by very quickly. After my class, I had office hours so I could meet with my students and answer questions. Then, I had some clinic hours, seeing patients post op who needed follow up. Finally, I covered the ER with Michael, and had to respond to an early evening crash that meant another traumatic brain injury.

I texted Kate and apologized that I'd be staying later than planned once more.

When I finally arrived back home, Kate was asleep and the light was off. I slipped into bed, trying hard not to wake her.

I wanted to go right to sleep because I had to work early Monday, despite working all weekend on call.

One more day and evening that I didn't spend any time with Kate.

The next morning, I rose early once more and showered, dressed and was ready to leave before Kate even woke. Not wanting to leave without speaking with her, I went to the bed once I was ready and sat on the edge. She blinked awake and stretched, a smile on her face.

"Are you going to take the night off?"

"I told Michael if I didn't, you'd divorce me before we were even married," I said, bending down to kiss her goodbye.

"I'd never do that," she said. "Don't make me out to be the bad guy with Michael. If you need to stay, you need to stay. I know this isn't trivial."

It wasn't trivial, but neither was my relationship with Kate. "I'll do my best to be home at six."

"Do what you can," she said and tucked my hair behind my ear. "I'll be here either way, missing you."

I kissed her warmly and then left, intending to leave as early as I could so that we could spend the evening together, try to make up for lost time.

Fate, or circumstance, didn't allow that to happen.

My young patient, a boy with a rare brain tumor that pressed on motor nerves and gave him seizures and tremors, died despite all our efforts to save him. The inoperable tumor responded to chemo and shrank in size so that it no longer pressed on the nerves. I performed deep brain stimulation to offset the tremor so the boy could at least eat and speak.

He was in for another round of deep brain stimulation when he died of a rare side effect, leaving me to console the parents. It brought up everything with Liam and I felt particularly helpless and even hopeless about prospects for having a child of my own.

It hit me particularly hard for I had been used to treating grown patients, older patients with Parkinson's or epilepsy. Losing them was hard for there was so much hope in the procedures I employed to help with movement disorders. I lost so few of the patients I treated.

Losing a child was especially hard.

I sat on the sofa in the staff lounge, my head in my hands, and tried to gather my thoughts before going to speak with the family. I felt a hand on my shoulder and turned.

It was Sam.

"That was hard," she said. "The nurses are crying."

I nodded. "I'm not used to this," I said and all I could think of was Liam back in the USA. I wondered how he was and if he would survive. All I wanted was to go to Kate and hug her, lie with her on the couch and listen to some music.

Lose myself in her.

Michael came into the room and stood, his hands on his hips, his head bowed.

"I need a drink." He turned to Sam. "What do you say I take the team out for a drink? We're officially off at six and I don't feel like going home."

Michael turned to me and as much as I wanted to go home and be with Kate, I thought it would be good for team building to go for at least one drink.

"Sure," I said. "I could use a shot of something hard."

So, despite my promise the morning when I left, I texted Kate at about five forty-five PM, with the news.

PARTICULARLY HARD DAY AT WORK. *I'm going to be a bit late for supper as Michael is taking the residents out for a drink to help us all unwind. I'll be home around seven. I hope you're wearing that pretty little sundress I like so much... I need to get lost in you tonight.*

SHE TEXTED BACK A SIMPLE RESPONSE.

I AM, and I'm all yours.

THAT PLEASED me so I texted her right back.

MMM...

WE DROVE to the Pint and Post, a favorite of the residents and students, and sat around a couple of tables pushed together and proceeded to get drunk.

Sam sat across from me, watching me, but thankfully, she didn't try to talk to me and behaved herself all evening. On my part, I shot back several vodka shooters and then drank a few bottles of beer as we recounted the case and what went wrong. By the time I checked my watch, I saw that it was almost nine o'clock and I said I'd be home at seven. I felt like a cad, but I really needed to get drunk after the events earlier in the day.

"I have to go," I said to Michael, who was sitting next to me, regaling the residents with tales of past cases.

"Of course," Michael said. "Are you able to drive?"

I shook my head, for I could tell I had too much to drink. "I'll take a taxi," I said, planning on leaving my car at the pub and picking it up the next day.

"You can't leave your car here overnight!" He turned to the residents. "Who's sober enough to drive Drake's car to his house?"

The residents glanced at each other and Sam nodded. "I am. I've only had two beers."

I didn't like the idea that Sam would be the one driving my car home, for I was sure it would upset Kate, but I was more interested in getting home. So the three of us set off to my house, driving in tandem. I rode with Michael, and Sam took the Mercedes. We offered to drop a couple of students off at the dormitory where they were living and so they rode with Sam. Finally, we drove up to the house around ten. Michael helped me inside for I was a little wobbly on my feet.

I smiled when I saw Kate at the door.

"Hi, Katie," I said, my mouth feeling like cotton. "Sorry I'm so late but we had a few more than I thought."

Kate frowned and turned to Michael. "I hope Drake didn't drive home like that."

Michael smiled. "No," he said and pointed to the Mercedes behind him. Sam was getting out. "Sam was kind enough to drive Drake's car back."

Sam walked up the driveway and handed the keys to me.

"Here you go, Doctor *Dizzy*," Sam turned to Kate. "At least he's a fun drunk," she said, smiling in a condescending way. "It's good to let your hair down now and then."

"Thank you so much for driving my car back," I said, before turning back to Kate. "Don't be mad," I said. "I forgot to eat lunch we were so busy and then I drank a bit too much…"

Michael assisted me into the house and sat me on the sofa. Before he left, Michael turned to Kate, laying one arm on her shoulder. "Don't be too hard on him, Kate. He had a really rough day. Lost a pediatric patient he'd been caring for. It hit him hard. I think the boy reminded him of Liam. He needed to unwind."

Then Sam and Michael left Kate and me alone.

Kate closed the door and turned to face me. I could tell by the expression on her face that she wasn't very happy.

"I'm so sorry, Katie," I said, feeling very bad for being so late. "I know I'm really late. I didn't mean to be."

"I know," she said and nodded. "Do you want me to grill you a steak?"

I shook my head. "Save them for tomorrow. I had a burger at the pub. I really need to crash."

I struggled up to my feet and swayed for a moment so Kate took my arm and led me to the bedroom. I went to the en-suite bathroom and leaned on the countertop for a moment. Then, I brushed my teeth, watching Kate who was leaning against the doorjamb, watching me.

"Don't be mad at me," I said, my mouth filled with white foam. "I had a bad day."

"I know," she said quietly. "Michael told me you lost a young patient."

I nodded and closed my eyes, the memory of trying to revive him in the OR flooding back.

"He made me think of Liam. Kate, I want a son but I'm afraid…"

She nodded and came to me, threading her arms around my waist, pressing her cheek to my back.

"Just because Liam had cancer doesn't mean all your children will."

"I couldn't take it," I said. "It was hard enough with Liam. What would I do if it was *our* son that we raised? Or our *daughter*?" I shook my head, my eyes tightly closed.

"It won't happen," Kate said, so certain that lightning couldn't strike twice. I wasn't so certain.

I rinsed my mouth, then turned to embrace Kate. We stood in each other's embrace for several long moments. Losing that young boy hit me hard but I now regretted drinking so much in response.

Kate started to take off my clothes, and I let her, watching her while she did.

"You're so good to me," I whispered. "I spent the entire evening with Sam and you aren't even mad."

"You were also with Michael and the other residents, right?" she said, her voice light. "Why would I be mad?"

I shook my head. "I wish she wasn't here doing her residency. I didn't want her to come. You have to know that."

"I do," she said softly and forced a smile.

"Did Mr. deVilliers hit on you today?" I asked, my eyes half-hooded while she removed my belt.

"Not really," she said, but her expression said otherwise.

"What does that mean, not really? Half-heartedly? I don't like to think of him pestering you, Katie. I'd like to punch his lights out."

She laughed at that. "That's the booze talking. What was it this time? Guinness or vodka?"

"Both." I smiled a crooked smile at her. Then, I closed my eyes and swayed a bit, a wave of nausea striking from out of the blue. "Oh, God. Please leave, Katie. I think I'm going to puke..."

She put an arm around me and turned me towards the toilet. "I'll help you."

"No, no. Please go..." I leaned over the toilet and waved Kate away, not wanting her to see me puking. She left, closing the door behind her.

"Let me know if you need me," she called through the door.

I retched and gagged when another wave of nausea struck, then emptied my stomach contents into the toilet. When I was finished, I went to the sink and washed my face off and then rinsed my mouth with mouthwash.

"Oh, *God*," I muttered, cursing myself for drinking too much.

"Can I get you anything?" Kate called through the bathroom door.

"A time machine so I can go back to before I drank those vodka shooters?"

"No can do," she said, a touch of humor in her voice. "How does sympathy and a cold cloth on your forehead sound?"

"That sounds good," I said and opened the door. I rubbed my forehead. "What an idiot. You'd think as a medical man I'd know enough not to mix booze."

"You're also a human, underneath the godlike-persona of a highly specialized neurosurgeon. Come to bed," she said and put her arm around my waist. I threw an arm over her shoulder and together, we walked to the bed.

"Not so godlike when I'm puking."

"Not so much." She steered me to my side of the bed.

Then, she finished undressing me, removing my clothes until I had only my boxer briefs on.

"I promised you several orgasms tonight, I seem to recall..."

"You can take care of that promise tomorrow," she said and went back to the washroom for a wet washcloth. "Right now," she said and draped it across my brow. "You should try to sleep. I'll bring a trash can so you can use it in the night if you need it."

"Not very romantic, when your fiancé is too sick to make love," I murmured, my eyes closing as she covered me up.

She kissed my cheek and I made a kissing motion with my mouth but didn't try to kiss her. She turned off the light and went to the bathroom to do her own nightly ablutions. I lay in a haze, my head spinning, regretting that I went to the pub and drank too much instead of coming right home as I originally planned.

The child was still dead.

I felt no better.

And Kate had been alone again.

THE NEXT MORNING, I called Michael early and asked for the day off.

"I hate doing it," I said as I lay in bed beside Kate. "But I'm pretty much good for nothing."

I spent the morning lying in the shade by the pool with sunglasses on, drinking copious amounts of water and juice and generally taking it very easy. Kate joined me after her shower and a quick breakfast.

"So tell me what an asshole I was last night," I said, making a face of regret.

"You weren't an asshole at all," she replied. "You were a polite drunk, apologizing profusely for puking and otherwise ruining my Friday night."

"I'm sorry, Kate. I hate having to say sorry about something like that. Asinine."

I told her about my patient, who we all thought would pull through since his cancer responded to the chemo and how a rare side effect and not the cancer killed him.

"After Liam, I'd hate to have another child with cancer," I said to her, taking her hand in mine, our fingers entwining.

"Is it likely that another child of yours would have the same cancer?" Kate asked softly.

I shrugged. "Probably not, but stranger things have happened. I've seen so many rare and unexpected things in my career, I've learned not to count out any possibility, however remote."

She squeezed my hand and I looked into her eyes, then kissed her knuckles.

"We'll cross that bridge when we come to it," she said.

I sighed and turned back to the view, rubbing my thumb over her knuckles.

KATE LEFT me by the pool and went inside to work on her painting. I lounged outside in the shade for a while, waiting for the coffee and painkillers to kick in and take away my headache. When I felt better, I got up and went in the house, then stood just outside the door to her studio and watched her paint.

When she looked up and caught my eye, I stepped inside. "Can I come in?"

She smiled. "Of course. I'm used to having other students around when I work so no worries. But no peeking."

"Aww, that's no fair. Let me see it!"

"You know the rules."

She stood up and stopped me from coming around to see the canvas, her fingers threading through mine, pressing me back.

"When you're on the safari, will you be standing around painting live tigers and lions?"

She laughed and kissed me, trying to restrain me when I glanced over to try to see the canvas.

"From what I've read, we'll be painting from a safe position and won't be in any real danger."

"Good." I nodded, trying do dodge around her.

"Stop," she said, her voice firm. "You can't see it until it's finished. That's the rule…"

"No fair," I said and pretended to fight with her. "The three stooges got to see your work in Chelsea. Why not me?"

"Because," she said and stood in between me and the canvas. "You're the subject matter. You can wait until I'm finished."

"Oh, all *right*," I said and gave in. "If you insist."

"I insist."

Kate frowned, and took in a deep breath, as if she had something to say.

"What's that look for, Ms. Bennet? Something bothering you?"

She sighed and put her hands on my shoulders, looking in my eyes.

"Drake, I have something to tell you…"

CHAPTER 13

I FROWNED at the tone of her voice. Hesitant. Guilty. "I'm afraid to ask what it is."

She sighed and ran her fingers over my shoulders and down my arms to my hands, which she took in hers. "It's really not that important. Sefton deVilliers is coming along on the safari."

"What?" I glanced away, trying hard to compose myself before I looked her in the eyes. "This is too much, Kate. I could tolerate him being in your class because he's an instructor, but this?"

She frowned. "It's one of the few art safaris in the area. I can't control whether he goes or not."

"There's no doubt he's going in the hopes that he can seduce you while you're alone out on the savannah," I said and shook my head.

"The way Sam tries to get you drunk so she can take advantage of you?"

I frowned at that. She was right, of course.

"Drake, he has a girlfriend. Besides, if he is hoping to

157

seduce me, he's going to be sorely disappointed, since I have absolutely no interest in him."

I exhaled and pulled her into my arms. "Christ, and here I thought the safari would be a great chance for you to get away from it all, enjoy yourself when I'd be busy all weekend. Now, I don't want you to go but I also don't want you to cancel because of a buffoon."

"Maybe I *should* cancel. I can make up an excuse about being sick, or something," she said, but as much as I didn't want her to be on safari with deVilliers, I wanted her to go. The fact this was an art safari made it even more important and desirable for her.

"I don't like the thought of him being there, and I'm not there to get in between you two," I said and stroked her cheek.

"I know," she said and laid her head on my shoulder. "I feel that way about Sam." She stayed like that for a moment, and I wondered what she'd decide.

"I have to live my life, Drake. I can't hide from people I don't like. I don't enjoy the idea that Sefton is going to be there, but he's more of an annoyance than anything else. He's not a threat to me or to us."

I nodded, and ran my hand over her hair and then forced a smile that I didn't feel. "He's a jerk. I'm glad you told me about this. I would have been upset if you hadn't told me."

"I learned my lesson with Kurt. I'll tell you everything, and you'll tell me everything, right?"

"Yes," I said. "Perfect honesty and openness. If you feel something, you tell me. I need to know how you feel, and you need to know how I feel."

She hugged me more closely. We had to trust each other when we were away from each other, and when we were around other people. Trust was everything.

I had no interest in Sam. I had to believe that Kate was being truthful when she said she had no interest in deVilliers.

That didn't mean I couldn't hate him, but I loved Kate.

Her happiness was everything to me.

The next day dawned with a gloomy overcast sky. I snuck out of bed and had a shower, made my coffee and dressed all while Kate slept like a baby. When it was time to leave, I sat beside her on the bed.

"Hey, sleepyhead, I'm going."

I kissed her cheek, and then her shoulder. She rolled onto her back, the sheets pulling back to reveal her naked breasts.

"Mmm," I said, nuzzling first one and then the other. "How can I go to work when you're so warm and delicious looking?"

"I wish you could stay in bed with me all day, but I have my class."

"That bastard deVilliers gets to see you longer than I do," I said, my voice gruff. "It makes me very jealous, Kate."

"You don't need to be," she said. "I tolerate him because he's a good artist and I can learn from him."

I frowned at that, but kissed her cheek, her forehead and her chin. "I don't want him teaching you anything."

"Drake…"

"I'm serious, Kate. Please stay away from him. Ignore him."

She looked in my eyes. "What if he has something helpful to tell me about my work?"

I shook my head slowly, fighting with myself. "I'll be home around eight, if nothing comes in."

I stood and left her on the bed, going to the closet to pull out a jacket. I stopped at the door and glanced back at her. "Have a good day. I love you."

"I love you," she said, waving at me and then blowing a kiss. "Have a good day at work."

159

I left her on the bed, still wrapped up in the sheets

Alone once more.

My week was completely absorbing, with classes and surgery and call. Despite being almost overwhelmed with work, my mind turned often to Kate and her weekend on safari with that bastard deVilliers.

Every morning, I was gone first thing while Kate was still wrapped up all warm in the covers and I arrived back home at night for a late supper and then bed. Friday was fast arriving and I was not looking forward to saying goodbye to Kate. I hated that she'd be spending the weekend with him.

On Thursday night, I made a point to come home early and we had a nice warm bubble bath before I shaved her and tied her up with the soft rope I bought at the hardware store. After blindfolding her, I made her come several times before I did. If she was going to spend a special weekend with deVilliers, another Dominant, I wanted to reinforce in Kate's mind my own D/s relationship with her.

Kate was meeting Claire on a bus after lunch on Friday, so we said goodbye in the morning when I was getting ready for work.

Instead of staying in bed as usual, Kate got up when I did, and we fucked in the shower. I wanted to tie her up first, and left Kate in the shower to get one of my ties, but before I could wrap it around her head, she stopped me.

"It'll be ruined. We don't need one."

"I'll buy another one."

She put her hand on mine. "You don't have to do a scene," she said, her voice soft.

"Yes, I do." I wrapped the tie around her eyes. "I can't tie you up in the shower, but I want you on your knees."

I helped her down to her knees, guiding her with my hands under her arms.

"Put your hands behind you, and clasp them. Imagine that they're bound."

She did, waiting for me to command her. I pressed the tip of my erection against her lips, and she licked me before taking the head in her mouth. She sucked the head, her tongue swirling around the rim, and I began to thrust softly, sliding in and out of her willing lips. I grasped her head and guided her while I thrust, giving her a bit more each time. When I was close, I withdrew and lifted her up once more, kissing her deeply.

She was being the perfect sub, eager to do what I demanded, no hesitation, no question. Waiting.

I turned her around and spread her thighs, pushing her body down so that she rested her hands on the ledge that ran around the shower enclosure. Then, I entered her from behind, my arm around her waist, my fingers on her clit as I thrust.

I kissed her shoulder as I thrust and soon, she went over, her voice tight as she warned me.

"*Drake...*" she managed, but I didn't say anything or stop and soon, her legs shook as she came. I thrust harder when I felt her shudder and then I bit down on her shoulder as I came. Harder than I intended.

I lost control.

"Oh, God," I said when I saw the mark, touching it with my fingers. "Oh, Kate, I'm sorry..."

I helped her up, kissing the spot, before removing the blindfold from her eyes. She turned to me and I kissed her deeply, brushing the wet hair from her forehead.

"I hurt you," I said, shaking my head, angry with myself. It was like I was some animal marking my territory.

"You did," she said and stepped out of the shower to check the mark in the mirror. My teeth marks were clearly visible.

"Marking your territory, Master D?" she said, catching my eye in the mirror.

"Kate, I didn't mean to bite that hard. I—"

"It's OK." She stopped me, her fingers against my lips. "Forget it."

"It was sloppy of me," I said, hitting my forehead lightly with a fist. "It won't happen again."

I took out a bottle of hydrogen peroxide from the cabinet and cleaned off the bite.

"I hate to see you go away for the weekend," I said, my voice soft. "I'm so jealous right now that the bastard is going to be there instead of me."

Kate smiled. "I wish you were going to be there instead of him, too," she said and kissed me. "But you don't have to be jealous. I plan on studiously ignoring him all weekend."

"Still, this is something I don't share with you," I admitted. "I'm jealous that any man gets to see your work before I do, watch you draw and paint."

She threaded her arms around my neck in a way that was so enticing, I didn't want to let her go. "You have no reason to be jealous. He's my instructor."

WE KISSED long and deep at the door when I was ready to leave for work.

"I'll miss you," I said, kissing her over and over again. "I love you."

"I'll miss you," she replied, her eyes filled with tears. "I love you."

"Oh, Ms. Bennet," I said and squeezed her, lifting her up off the floor. "What would I do without you?"

I brushed my thumb over her bottom lip and gave her a little smile. Then I was gone.

This time, Kate wouldn't be alone. She'd be surrounded

by her fellow artists. She'd be having the experience of a lifetime.

It would be deVilliers and not me experiencing it with her.

I drove to the hospital lacking the usual excitement I felt at the prospect of a busy day of surgeries and teaching.

It made me realize how much of a hole Kate filled in my life and how I would do anything to keep her.

My Friday went on as usual, with teaching, a demonstration of robotic surgery after lunch, and a late call in the ER. It was late when I got a text from Kate.

Hi there. Had a great day drawing elephants – can you believe it? I'm really enjoying myself, and now we're going out to do some star gazing. Sefton is no problem and the only thing that would make this perfect would be if you were here to enjoy it with me. I can't wait for us to go on safari together some weekend when you have time off.

I was glad to hear she was enjoying herself and that deVilliers wasn't being an ass.

That's great! I can't wait either. I'm so glad you're having a good time. I was worried that Mr. deVilliers would be pestering you and would ruin things. So glad things are good on that front.

She texted right back.

They are good. I'm not going to let him ruin things for me. How are things at work?

I responded, thinking about my day and the two trauma cases we were waiting for in the OR.

Hectic, as usual. Typical Friday night in Nairobi, shootings, stabbings, collisions, beatings. There is no risk that I'll be out of a job any time soon, sadly! Looks like I'll be up late tonight as we have a couple of trauma patients who will need emergency surgery. Wish I was looking at stars instead of patient charts...

She knew me too well.

I'm sure you love what you're doing. Tell me the truth – you love having to cut into someone's brain and fix things. :)

I responded right away.

You got me. It's a privilege to be working here, somewhere that I am needed. But I miss you, Ms. Bennet.

Her response made me very happy.

I miss you, too. Have to go now as our bus is leaving. I wish you were here... I love you.

I smiled as I typed my response.

I love you, too. How I miss you in my bed so I could touch you, kiss you...

That was it. I put my cell away and glanced up, heaving a heavy sigh. Although I was glad to help Michael out, and although I knew my skills were in short supply and thus in high demand here in Kenya, I really would rather have been out on safari with Kate.

There was no reason why I couldn't be. I had enough money to never work another day in my life, but I loved neurosurgery. I loved teaching.

Helping Michael out at the hospital, and teaching class, was fulfilling.

If only the workload wasn't so heavy. I worked as hard as a surgeon who relied solely on his income. In contrast, I had more money than I knew what to do with, and had to give it away so it wouldn't be wasted.

Once my six months was up with Michael, I planned to return to a much more manageable schedule back in Manhattan. I'd teach one class a year and lighten my surgical load so that I spent more nights with Kate than with the OR staff.

Our two patients arrived via medevac chopper so Michael and I were busy for the next few hours and I forgot everything but the patient in front of me.

When we were done, and after we spoke to the families, Michael and I went to the staff room and discussed the cases.

"It's been really great having you here, Drake. It's been great having you shadow me. Together, we can get a heck of a lot done and so I'm grateful."

I was only too pleased to be of help to my old friend and mentor.

"Keep letting me assist in your pediatric cases and I'll be a happy man."

"Still thinking of a specialization in pediatric neuro-surgery?"

I nodded. "Even more convinced about it. Maybe next year. Kate and I are going to get married and start our lives together. I want to have a good first year. If I work too hard, she might get frustrated and leave me."

Michael laughed. "No, she won't. She's more likely to do what Claire did—build her own life and focus all her ener-gies there. We're like two ships that pass in the night. It's inevitable."

I nodded, and took a long drink of my water but inside, I knew I didn't want that with Kate. I didn't want us to be strangers to each other. That was the way my own father was and it led to a broken marriage because he was emotionally absent from the family.

I wanted to be like Ethan. Involved. Committed. Engaged in his children's lives.

I went home that night very late and after a shower and a glass of water, I lay in our king sized bed alone and thought about Kate, wondering how her night went. I hoped deVil-liers didn't give her any more trouble.

Somehow, I suspected both Sam and Sefton were not going to give up easily...

CHAPTER 14

SATURDAY WAS SPENT COVERING the ER. Michael and I sat in the staff room talking about our cases and plans for the hospital's neurosurgery program while we waited for trauma cases that might need our expertise.

Since it was Saturday, Sam was supposed to be off but she was hanging around, scrubbing in on Michael's cases so she could get extra credit for different procedures. It irritated me that she was hanging out, apparently more interested in Michael than me, but I suspected the opposite was true.

Despite her feigned disinterest in me, she kept asking me about Kate and what she was doing.

"She's on safari with Claire," I said. "It's an art safari. Kate is a painter."

"That's right," Sam said. "Michael mentioned something about it yesterday. Claire's a photographer. She's there with some art class Kate is taking? I guess she has to keep busy since you work so much and you two barely see each other. It must be hard on a relationship."

"They say absence makes the heart grow fonder," I said, forcing a smile.

"Not in my experience," Sam replied. "In my experience, absence makes people's eyes wander."

I didn't say anything. What could I say? It was true that when couples became distant that infidelity was more likely. That was my concern with being away so much from Kate but I certainly wasn't going to voice any concerns about Kate's fidelity. Of course, Sam's questions and comment brought me right back to the whole issue and I grew morose over the separation from Kate once more.

I returned to my office and found my cell, thinking of her with a touch of sadness, when I saw that she had sent me a text. It indicated she was really having a great time.

I miss you. I drew giraffes this morning, and now we're looking at wildebeests at a watering hole. We ate our lunch at a folding table on the savannah with white tablecloth and china. I feel a bit like a member of the British Raj in Colonial Kenya. I wish so much you were here with me...

I responded immediately, noting that she had texted me hours earlier.

Sorry I didn't respond to your text but I was in a long very complicated surgery and then had to scrub in on another right away due to an industrial accident after a crane collapsed at a construction site. Several serious injuries. I'm exhausted and am crashing at the hospital. Hope you're enjoying yourself. I miss you.

Her response came right away so she must have had the phone close beside her.

I miss you so much. Sefton has been an asshole again. I wish you were here...

I texted right back.

I wish I was there to defend your honor, Ms. Bennet. I'd like to punch him in the face. If he persists, please talk to the tour guide and tell them he's harassing you. Give me the phone number and I'll call if you need me to.

She tried to down play it in her response.

I'll ignore him. Don't worry about me. Sorry I mentioned it. I love you.

I was left with the unsettled feeling that deVilliers was intent on trying to put a wedge between us. It wasn't the first time a man sought to raise doubts in a woman about her partner.

The man was a Dominant, and that meant he was used to getting what he wanted and from the sounds of things, he wanted Kate.

I spent the night at the hospital once more, sleeping in the resident's room, hoping to catch a few hours of rest before the start of the next day. If I couldn't be with Kate, I didn't really want to go home and sleep in our big empty bed.

Of course, I didn't get to sleep the night through. Barely an hour after I fell asleep, I was awoken by a page. When I got to the ER, I found we had a multiple vehicle collision and several patients en route. It was going to be a very long night.

Michael had gone home so I was already scrubbed in and working on the first patient when he arrived, looking bleary eyed. Together, we cared for the four patients who arrived over the next hour. My patients took extra long to complete and so it was morning when I was finally finished in the OR.

I had a whole day of call ahead of me and had no idea how I would get through it. I tried once more to catch some sleep, but got no more than another hour. There were walk-in patients to see at the ER as well as trauma cases brought in via ambulance.

Later on Sunday, after the ER quieted down, I was sitting in the staff room, drinking a cup of coffee when Sam arrived.

"I heard you had a busy night," she said and sat on the sofa across from me.

"Multiple vehicle accident. Michael and I were up all night."

"You must be exhausted."

I nodded and popped a couple of Tylenol for a headache. "Headache."

Sam stood up and came over to me. "Here," she said as I was rubbing my neck. "Let me give you a massage."

"No, that's all right," I said, waving her away.

"I insist," she said and began massaging my shoulders.

It was then I saw motion in the doorway and turned to see Kate and the receptionist from the Information Kiosk.

Before I could say anything, Kate took off down the hallway. I pushed Sam's hands away and followed Kate down the hallway. She was almost running in her haste to get away.

"*Kate*," I said and grabbed hold of her arm. "Why did you leave? What's the matter?"

Her jaw was set and her face flushed with emotion. She avoided my eyes. "You know very well what the matter is."

I frowned and shook my head. "It's not what you think."

"Isn't that what everyone always says when caught in a compromising situation?" she said. "What, exactly, do you *think* I think?"

"Sometimes it really isn't what you think." I sighed. "You saw Sam offering to give me a neck rub because I have a headache. I refused and she insisted but you didn't see or hear that."

"No I didn't," she said. "All I saw was you alone in the staff room with Sam, leaning your head forward, rubbing your neck, and her massaging your shoulders."

I took hold of her arms, trying to catch her eye, but she kept looking away.

"What you *didn't* hear was that she offered to give me a neck massage when I complained of a headache because I was up all night. I said no, but she ignored me. I can't help that she did it anyway."

I took her face in my hands, cupping her cheeks. "*Kate*," I said, my voice soft. "It was nothing. Nothing happened. There's nothing between us."

Kate finally stopped struggling and looked in my eyes.

"You didn't answer any of my texts. I thought you were mad at me."

"I haven't checked my phone for hours," I said, shaking my head. "I didn't *get* your texts."

She stared at me for a moment like she was checking to see if I was telling the truth.

"I'm sorry," she said and hit her head with a fist. "You have to understand how it made me feel to see you like that. I've been away all weekend, missing you so much, and what do I find but you alone with *her*. A woman you had sex with. And she's giving you a massage." Then she took in a deep breath. "And something else. Sefton said and did some things to me this weekend and I..." she said, hesitating. "It looked so intimate I thought you were with her..."

"What did Sefton do?" I said, a jolt of adrenaline coursing through me. "Tell me." I led Kate to a small waiting area and she sat on the sofa beside me.

"I sent you texts about it. I think Claire misinterpreted..."

"Kate, you're not making any sense. Tell me what happened."

She stared in my eyes, and I could see that she was afraid to tell me.

"Sefton was drunk and followed me to my tent after dinner. He tried to kiss me, and Claire came in and saw. She thought we were together. I couldn't talk sense into her. She said she thought you and I were wrong for each other. I figured Claire would have told Michael or even called you or texted you."

I frowned, not at all happy to hear Sefton had hit on Kate. "Go on."

"I had to tell him I was going to scream if he didn't leave me alone. He finally left."

"Did he kiss you?"

"No, *no*," she said. "You have to understand. I did nothing to encourage him. You know how I feel about him. He's pushy and rude."

"I knew you shouldn't have gone when I found out he was going but I didn't want to stop you," I said, regretting that I hadn't put up more of a fight. "I know how much it meant to you."

"I'm sorry," she said and tried to smile past tears. "Claire knows about you."

I frowned. "What do you mean?"

"She said something about your *peculiarities*. Drake, she knows you're into kink."

I exhaled loudly and leaned back, running my hands through my hair. "I don't need this right now. *Goddammit.*" Kate got up and once more started walking away, out of the waiting room and down the hall. I followed her, keeping a few feet behind. She walked aimlessly through the halls, and I knew she was lost, but she needed to calm down.

"You're going in circles," I said finally when we ended up back at the bank of elevators where I first caught up with her. She stopped and stood with her eyes closed, trying to breathe in deeply. "Kate, let me get my things and we'll go home."

She didn't say anything. Finally, I reached out my hand, wanting to connect with her and move past this.

She stared at it, not taking it.

"Let me lead you to safety," I said, trying to be funny. "This place is like the labyrinth in Greece. You could get lost and wander forever. I swear I've seen the Minotaur here once or twice late at night…"

When she looked at me, I smiled and shrugged helplessly.

"Don't do that," she said, frowning, but I could see she was trying hard not to smile.

"Do *what*, Ms. Bennet?"

"Don't try to make me smile."

I stepped closer and ran my hand down her arm. "I don't want you to be upset," I said, my voice soft. "I don't want you to misinterpret what you saw. I want you to listen to me and to believe me when I say not to worry. I'm doing everything in my power not to misinterpret what happened with you and Sefton."

Kate sighed. "When I saw you with her, both of you in scrubs, I thought you belong with her. She's tall and beautiful and a surgeon... And Claire said—"

"Forget what Claire said. I *don't* belong with Sam," I said and pulled her closer, holding her face in my hands. "I know you don't want Sefton. You were ready to stay here because he'd be there, but I encouraged you. This is all my fault." I stroked her cheek and felt such emotion swell up inside of me. "Kate, I belong with *you*. I *am* with you. You have to understand that. Accept that you have nothing to fear from Sam. Or anyone. Do you believe me?"

"I do," she said finally.

"No, you don't." I pulled her into my arms. "If you did, you'd be putting your arms around me and kissing me."

She was stiff, unyielding. Undeterred, I took her hand and led her down the hallways to my office.

"Here," I said and closed the door. I pulled her over to the couch. "Sit with me for a moment."

I sat on the couch, my arms spread out on the back like that first night in her apartment. I wanted to remind her of our relationship.

"*Katherine*," I said, trying to be authoritative. "Sit with me."

She wouldn't look at me. "I've been sitting all morning."

"Poor excuse," I said. "*Sit* on my lap."

"Why?" she said, resistant. "So you can overcome me with your seductive Master D ways?"

"Yes." I grinned despite trying to keep a straight face.

Finally, she straddled my hips and wrapped her arms around my neck. She kissed me, the kiss hesitant at first but then becoming more insistent. She pressed herself against me and kissed me deeply and I kissed her back, my hands slipping around her waist to pull her against me.

I pulled back, breaking our kiss. "I'm so sorry you had to see that," I said. "She means nothing to me. *Nothing*. Only you. You're everything to me."

I pulled her back into my arms, kissing her hungrily, slipping my hands under her shirt to cup her breast through her bra.

"Oh, God, I missed you, Kate. I don't want you going away without me again. It was hell thinking of you alone with him where I should have been. I hated it."

"You seemed fine with me going despite him being there," she said.

"I didn't want to deny you the chance to go on safari." I ran my fingers through her hair. "I wanted to be with you on safari. I wanted to be out looking at stars with you at night in the middle of the savannah. Instead, it was him." I shook my head, realizing how much I hated being apart from her. "I was incredibly jealous, but I knew I couldn't keep you from going, even if he *was* there. You're an artist and you need to do art."

She ran her fingers over my shoulder. "I don't know if I *am* an artist. I don't know if what I do is really art."

"How can you say that? Your teacher invited you to take the master class. It means she sees you as an artist, even if you don't."

"Forget it," she said. "I'm *trying* to be an artist. Let's go home."

I nodded and kissed her once more.

"Oh, Ms. Bennet," I said when the kiss ended. I touched her cheek with the backs of my fingers. "I missed you so much. I didn't want to go home and have to sleep alone in our bed. I couldn't face it so I stayed here and slept on a bunk. Don't leave me ever again."

She smiled and kissed me. "I won't."

"I mean it," I said, and I did mean it. I'd gone so long sleeping alone, but after having Kate to myself, even for so short a time, I couldn't stand the thought of her sleeping away from me. "Promise me we'll never spend another night apart."

"Promise." She leaned down, nestling her face in the crook of my neck. I stood, picking her up and letting her slide down my body with reluctance. Then I went to my jacket and removed my cell. I examined it for a moment, but didn't open any text messages, although I saw several from Claire.

"Claire texted me and left a voice mail. Do you want me to read them?"

Kate sighed but I knew she was hesitant. "If you want."

I held the phone in my hand, trying to decide how to proceed. I was curious about what Claire would say, but I wanted Kate to feel that I trusted her. Finally, I handed the phone to Kate.

"You read. You listen," I said. "Delete both afterwards if you want. I trust you."

She took the phone while I went to the staff washroom.

When I returned, she handed the phone to me.

"I didn't delete anything," she said. "I want you to know what she wrote and what I said."

I checked the text.

Drake, I don't know how to break this to you, but I tell you as someone who has your best interests at heart. I found Kate with Sefton deVilliers, one of the art instructors she's taking a class with,

175

and they were alone in our tent and in each other's arms. You can imagine how shocked I was for we thought that she was so sweet and would be so good for you. I'm sorry to be the one to bear bad news. You can count on Michael and I me to help if you need it at all dealing with this.

I rubbed my eyes, angry and frustrated—and jealous at the thought Kate was alone with Sefton. Angry at Sefton for being such a bastard. Jealous that he was so good looking and a talented artist, when I couldn't draw a stick man. Angry at Claire for being a busybody and a gossip.

Then, I read Kate's text.

Drake, something happened with Sefton and Claire completely misunderstood. Please, if you hear from her, don't believe what she says to you. Nothing happened with Sefton. He came to my tent when I was here alone and grabbed me. He's under some delusion that I'm meant for him, but I sent him away. Unfortunately, Claire came in when he was holding my arms, and she misinterpreted everything. Now, she's sleeping somewhere else, angry at me because she thinks I've cheated on you. I haven't. You know I can barely tolerate Sefton.

Please answer me as soon as you get this. Please call me...

When I finished, I slipped the phone into my pocket, and turned to Kate.

"You said he had hold of your arms. *Were* you embracing?"

She shook her head. "No. He grabbed hold of my arm like this," she said and demonstrated. "It actually hurt. I thought he might force me to kiss him, or worse. He saw your bite mark when I took off my shirt during the mid-day heat, and he thought I was into rough play so there's no telling what he might have done if I hadn't threatened to scream."

I sighed, exhausted from my night of no sleep and from the drama of the past half hour. "I'm so sorry this had to happen to you. I'm sorry Claire had to see it. Michael's a very close friend of mine. I don't want there to be any hard feelings between us. I'm going to have to go in damage control mode with him."

"I'm sorry," she said, tears in her eyes.

"It's not your fault you're so delicious," I said and pulled her into my arms. "I'm so glad you're mine."

We stood together, in each other's arms, and reconnected. After that message, I needed to touch her, I needed to feel her in my arms and I really needed to fuck her and make her come several times.

That would have to wait.

The entire drive home I held her hand, brushing my thumb over her knuckles, not wanting to let go for even a moment. I parked the car and came around to open Kate's door, taking her hand and leading her up the path to the doorway. Once inside, I pushed her back against the wall beside the door, taking her hands in one of mine and raising them over her head so that she was confined and unable to move.

When she opened her mouth to speak, I placed my finger over her lips to stop her.

"Shh," I said firmly. "No talking."

I didn't kiss her. I touched her, squeezing her breast, tweaking her nipple, running my hand down her body to cup her belly and then her buttock before pulling her hips against mine so she could feel my erection.

"Keep your eyes open and on mine."

She rubbed against me and I groaned, rubbing back.

I stripped her top off so that she was in her lacy bra and I squeezed her breasts once more, enjoying their fullness in my hands. Then I pulled down the fabric and took her nipples between my fingers and thumbs. She gasped in response.

I bent down and sucked on first one then the other nipple, while Kate writhed against me. I pulled off the tunic of my scrubs, struggling with the tie at the back of my neck, roughly throwing it on the floor before turning to Kate's jeans, stripping them off her, my thumbs hooking her lace thong and pulling it off so that she stood naked before me. I pressed her roughly against the wall again and kissed her hungrily, one hand slipping between our bodies to brush her nipples, then trailing down to her pussy. I slipped my fingers between her lips and groaned against her throat when I felt how wet she was.

She was ready.

I was hard as rock.

I pulled down my scrub trousers and let them fall around my ankles, followed by my boxer briefs, which I pulled down to my knees. Then, I placed her arms around my neck and picked her up.

In response, she wrapped her legs around my hips, groaning when I pressed the head of my cock against her and rubbed her clit, kissing her, my tongue finding hers, sucking it into my mouth hungrily. I took my cock in hand and move her so that I slid inside of her warm tight wetness. I didn't start thrusting yet. I wanted to feel myself buried deep inside of her. I wanted to feel her muscles clench around my cock.

I kissed her, all my focus on our mouths, one hand squeezing her breast.

She closed her eyes and I knew waiting was driving her crazy.

"Open your eyes," I said and when she did, only then did I begin to thrust, each thrust slow and deep, coming all the way out before thrusting hard back inside, making sure to brush her clit first when I withdrew and when I entered her. I kept this pace, slow and deep, our eyes locked together.

My pace quickened, and Kate responded, her body becoming rigid, a flush spreading over her neck and chest.

She gripped harder onto my shoulders, gritting her teeth as her orgasm neared, her eyes closing.

"Keep your eyes open," I said with a growl, thrusting faster. "*Look* in mine."

She tried but was barely able to open them as she went over. I thrust hard and fast, and soon, I came as well, my own teeth gritted, pleasure ripping through me with each thrust and ejaculation. I gasped, my mouth pressed against her shoulder, kissing my bite mark tenderly.

Finally, I lifted my head, moving my lips along her chin before kissing her deeply. When I pulled away, I stared in her eyes, frowning.

"*Don't* ever doubt me," I said, my voice deep, firm.

"Don't ever doubt *me*."

I nodded, then sighed heavily and leaned back down to her shoulder, kissing the mark there gently once more.

CHAPTER 15

ONCE WE WERE FINISHED, and our breathing was back to normal, we decided to take a bath. While the bathtub filled with warm water, Kate lit candles, which she placed around the sides of the tub. They provided the only light, creating a very mellow mood.

I pulled her into my arms and we lay in the warm water. "Tell me everything he said and did."

"Do you really want me to?" she said, her voice doubtful.

I thought for a moment. Did I really want to torture myself with the details of his attempt to kiss her? I knew if she told me, I'd lie awake and picture it in my mind's eye and would probably have a hard time falling to sleep, despite being exhausted after my weekend of ER hell.

"Tell me, Kate," I said finally. "We need complete openness and honesty. I need to know what he did and how you felt."

Kate smiled. "Most men avoid talking about feelings at all costs."

"They didn't study psychology like I did." I ran a finger over her wet shoulder and down to the curve of her breast. "Men want to *do*, and believe me, I want to *do*. I want to go

181

and punch his lights out. We usually don't want to talk. But I know women talk things out. So talk. Tell me."

She sighed, reluctant to be open. I couldn't have that. She had to learn not to hide anything from me.

"Come on," I said and shook her shoulder gently. "*Tell* me. I won't get mad or upset."

Then she told me.

The bastard had been open about his desire to have her. He'd manhandled her, pulled her into his arms and tried to kiss her. He'd said that my work was more important to me than she was and that she spent more time with him than with me that weekend.

Claire walked in when she was trying to resist him and of course took it all wrong. I frowned as I thought about the kind of man Sefton was. The kind of Dominant he was.

"Sounds passive-aggressive. Or else he thinks you're attracted to a sadistic Dom who likes to humiliate a submissive. Some women respond to that kind of behavior. I know you don't but he doesn't seem too bright if he was treating you like that."

"He actually suggested that he and I would be 24/7 if we were together. That I needed it, even if I didn't want to accept that fact."

I shook my head. "No, and that's how I know he's not a good Dom. You're not the type for TPE. I'm not the type for TPE and that's why we're good together. I might be able to do it for a weekend for fun and games, role playing, but not all the time."

Kate exhaled and sank lower in the water, her hands on my shoulders. "I might like roleplaying TPE for a weekend, too, but not all the time. Pretend I was your slave girl. That kind of thing but it would only be an act for fun. It wouldn't be real. And no humiliation. I do that enough on my own."

"You don't humiliate yourself."

"In my mind I do. Like today, when I walked away. I should have gone in the room and pushed Sam out of the way, put my arms around you and kissed you in front of her. Claimed you as my own," Kate said, biting her bottom lip. "But instead, I ran away like a child because I was afraid you'd read my texts and Claire's and were turning to her for comfort."

I exhaled in frustration. Kate was vulnerable. Sefton tried to take advantage of that for his own gain. He made her feel doubt about our relationship, and then Claire had threatened to tell me that Kate was cheating on me.

"You were vulnerable because we'd been apart all weekend and you'd been assaulted by Sefton. You were emotional and couldn't face a confrontation. You didn't humiliate yourself."

"Sam was probably laughing at me."

"Why would you think that?" I asked. Yes, I knew Sam was disappointed that we wouldn't reignite our relationship, but she had backed off since I had my little talk with her.

"She wants you, and don't you think otherwise. That first night at the student-faculty mixer, she admitted as much."

"What?"

"She said that you weren't married and pretty much indicated you were fair game…"

I made a face at that. The fact that Sam thought I was fair game despite being engaged said everything I needed to know about her. She had no ethics if she felt able to step in between Kate and me. It was the same with Sefton.

"She'd be wrong." I touched her cheek. "I just haven't made you a respectable woman yet."

Kate tried not to smile, but failed. "Drake, no single woman goes up to a single man as good looking as you and offers to give him a massage without wanting more… *You're* very naïve," she said and sighed in a mock-resigned manner.

"She wants to jump your oh-so-desirable bones, Doctor Delish."

I laughed out loud at that. "You think she's still lusting after me after all this time? She *knows* I'm a Dom and that I don't want a purely vanilla relationship. She's far too dominant herself. She has an icicle's chance in hell of ever getting me. *You've* got me, Ms. Bennet, by the mind, heart *and* balls."

Kate smiled at that. When I bent down to kiss her, she reached one hand down, trailing it from my hair to my chest, her hand over my heart and then down over the crest of my hip.

"I do, do I?" she said coyly.

I moaned when she cupped me with her hand. "Most assuredly you do," I said, my dick jumping. "Now, don't touch me there unless you mean serious business and plan on being fucked hard."

I quirked an eyebrow at her, grinning in as evil a manner as I could.

When she ran her hand along my quickly-hardening length, her fingers slipping around the head, I inhaled sharply and leaned down to her, my lips hovering over hers.

"I take that as a yes," I said and kissed her. The touch of her wet skin on mine was enough to chase all the bad thoughts about Sefton and Sam from my mind—for at least a few hours.

We quickly settled back into a routine after the drama of the safari weekend. Unfortunately, I still worked far too many hours and on several occasions, I had to stay late or do call all weekend, and Kate still had to spend most of her day alone or with other people.

On Kate's first day back in the open studio class, I decided once more to stop by and pick her up as I had some time between surgeries and wanted to surprise her. Of course, I also wanted to check up on deVilliers and see if he

184

was still harassing Kate. She said he was being a perfect gentleman, but I didn't believe her. Once a rogue, always a rogue. And I should know. I knew that until he had her, he wouldn't let up.

I knew I wouldn't have, if I met her now and knew she was a submissive looking for a Dominant.

I drove over, still wearing surgical scrubs, and went into the building to the elevator, planning on going up to meet her outside her classroom. I pressed the button and waited for the car to arrive, but heard voices as the elevator made its way to the main floor. The doors started to open and a male voice with a distinctive South African accent spoke.

"Remember what I said. If that boyfriend of yours ever leaves you wanting more, I'm in the wings, waiting. I could teach you so much..."

"Please let me by," Kate said, and when the doors were fully open, I saw that the man was leaning over Kate, blocking her way, a look of clear anger on Kate's face.

That was it.

I'd had enough of deVilliers and his insistence on bothering Kate. Adrenaline kicked in and I barged into the car and knocked him a good one. deVilliers was taken off guard, and I was able to pin him against the elevator wall, my forearm across his throat, my fist at the ready, held in front of his face.

I heard Kate gasp but kept my focus on deVilliers.

"You almost broke my nose," the man said, clearly shocked. He touched his nose and it came back smeared with blood.

"You'll be waiting nowhere near Kate, if you know what's good for you, or you'll have more than a broken nose," I said.

"Is that a threat?" deVilliers said. His face was pale, his teeth gritted.

"It's a promise," I said, surprising myself with a voice that

185

sounded like a growl. "You leave Kate alone or Kate and I will be making a trip to the police to talk about what happened during the safari."

Then I stepped back and adjusted my shirt. I slipped my arm around Kate's shoulders and led her out of the elevator and down the hallway. Despite my show of strength, my heart was pounding.

"*Drake...*" Kate said, her face blanched.

"Let's get out of here," I said, kissing the top of her head. "No arguing. I had the element of surprise going for me, and if I almost broke his nose, it was totally by accident. He's a big fucker and I don't know if I could beat him if he wants to fight."

I heard deVilliers behind us and decided that it was best to pick up the pace.

"I could have you charged with assault for that," he called after us.

"Kate could have *you* charged with assault," I replied.

deVilliers didn't reply.

I took Kate's hand in mine and pulled her, running through the doors and down the walkway to where my car was parked. We both laughed so hard as we tumbled inside.

"That was awfully Bruce Willis of you," Kate said.

I started the engine. "Yippee-ki-yay, *motherfucker!*" I said, grinning widely as I squealed the tires and sped off.

deVilliers stood at the entry to the Institute, watching us, a hand to his bloody nose.

When we got home, I pulled Kate into the house and kissed her deeply, my hands roving over her body, up under her shirt to cup her breast while the other slipped down her pants and under her panties.

"I want a quickie," I said and pushed her over to the couch. Then, I proceeded to bend her over the back, pulled down her pants, untied my scrubs and rammed myself inside of her.

Neither of us took long to come.

When we were done, as I leaned over top of Kate and kissed her neck, panting to catch my breath, she started to giggle.

"What are you laughing at, Ms. Bennet?" I said, smiling despite myself. "Are you laughing at my show of masculine prowess?"

"*Masculine prowess...*" she whispered, and then burst out laughing. I tickled her, enjoying her laughter. "No, I was laughing at Sefton and how shocked he was. You, Dr. Delish, were magnificent."

"I was," I said and nuzzled her neck. "Even if it was totally a cold-cock and he had no idea what was coming."

"Better than rapiers at dusk," Kate said and I could feel her cheek rise in a big smile.

"Much better." I kissed her and pulled out, watching my come drip out of her with satisfaction. "And now I must leave you because I have a surgery in a very short time."

I left her there, backing away, enjoying the carnal scene I'd created.

"Are you going to leave me like this?" she asked, craning her head back to see me.

"I am," I said when I reached the door. "I want your lovely ass and pussy to be the last thing I see before returning to work."

Then I blew her a kiss and was gone.

I was happy the next day after the showdown with deVilliers. I no longer had any concerns about Kate being interested in the man in any way, and figured he'd most likely keep his distance if only to avoid any further drama. So I actually whistled as I wandered through the hallways at the hospital, popping in to check on my patients and make sure all my cases were in order.

I was even polite to Sam when she was in the staff lounge at the same time, for I knew that Kate was also no longer concerned about her. Things were going along well. Kate was taking classes and happy doing her art and I was immersed in my cases.

Then Kate called when I was out on rounds and it all went to shit.

WHEN I ARRIVED BACK in my office to find Sam waiting, I frowned for I thought she'd only be there for a brief moment to get some lecture notes, but she was waiting on my sofa, a cup of coffee in her hand.

"You're still here?" I said, a touch of annoyance creeping into my voice.

"Drake…" Sam said, frowning. "You suggested I use your office to copy notes. I only did what you suggested."

"I thought you'd only be here for a few moments, not an hour." I plopped down behind my desk and pulled out a file, hoping she'd get the message and leave. She remained sitting on the sofa.

"Was there anything else?"

She was still frowning. "Kate called."

I raised my eyebrows. That wouldn't be optimal. Although I felt sure that Kate was more comfortable now with Sam's existence, her answering the phone in my office would not be a good thing.

"Why didn't you say so right away?" I picked up the phone, intending to call her immediately.

"She said something about her father being ill."

I dialed the number, a stab of adrenaline in my gut the moment she said it. "What did Kate say exactly?"

"She said her father had a stroke."

"For Christ's sake, why didn't you come and get me right away? Ethan had a stroke? Is he still alive? What did Kate say?"

Sam shrugged. "I didn't want to interrupt rounds."

"Christ..."

I was so angry. Sam waited until I finished rounds, which was not what I wanted, given the circumstances. She should have come to me right away and told me that Kate called about a family emergency. It was her passive-aggressive way of trying to hurt my relationship with Kate.

I dialed her number and Kate answered on the second ring.

"Drake..." she said but couldn't continue, her voice breaking.

"Kate, I'm so *sorry*..." I said. "Tell me what happened."

"I haven't spoken to Elaine yet but she said he had an intercerebral hemorrhagic stroke and had surgery. I left her a message but she hasn't called back. I have a flight out tonight and will be in Manhattan tomorrow before midnight."

"Did you book two tickets?" I asked, my mind turning immediately to who could cover my cases. "I'm coming with you."

"You have class tomorrow and surgery and I could only get one ticket on the earliest flight out. You can come later. I have to leave right away."

"I want to come with you," I said, adamant that I would not let her go by herself. "Let me find a flight we can take together."

Kate exhaled loudly. "Not if it means I have to wait another day, Drake. I have to go right away. Elaine said I

189

should get back as soon as possible. Just in case." She sobbed out loud.

"Oh, *Katie*..." I said, my voice soft. "Let me check to see if I can find us seats together. I'll cancel class and see if MacMillan can scrub in on my cases tonight. Give me a bit of time to work things out and I'll be home."

"You don't have to come with me," she said tearfully. "I know your patients have been waiting so long for their surgeries. I can go by myself."

"No," I said firmly. "You forget that Ethan is like a father to me. I want to be there to see how he is. I want to be there with you."

"OK," she said and we hung up. When I looked up, Sam was waiting.

"What's up?" she said, her voice sounding so pleasant, like she didn't know what a terrible tragedy this was.

"Kate's father had a stroke and I'm leaving tomorrow," I said, my teeth gritting. "If you'll excuse me, I have some work to do."

I opened a case file on my desk, not looking at Sam, too angry to say anything to her.

"Don't be mad at me," Sam said, her voice pleading and whining at the same time. "I didn't want to interrupt rounds. Your work is important."

I glanced up at her, barely able to keep my cool. She was pouting, her mouth turned down at the corners.

"Kate is the most important thing in the world to me. Her father is like the father I never had."

She shrugged. "You called her. Everything is fine."

"No, it isn't," I said and slammed my file closed in anger. "You should have come and told me right away. You should have done your copying and left. You shouldn't have been waiting in my office."

"I'm sorry," she said, but I could tell she was angry. "For

me, work comes before everything and that's the way it is for pretty much everyone I know in our profession. Kate is going to have to get used to it if you two stay together."

"If we stay together?" I said, my voice louder than it should have been. "We're getting married!"

She shrugged like a teenager. "What's the date?"

I stood up and went to the door, opening it. "If you don't mind," I said and gestured to the hallway. "I have work to do."

"You didn't answer my question. What's the date? Have you even set one?"

I said nothing and waited for her to leave. Of course, Kate and I had not yet set the date, but I didn't want to admit that to Sam. It wasn't even an issue, but I knew Sam would make it one.

"Just as I thought," she said. "You haven't set a date. Why not?" she said, tilting her head. "Can't commit?"

"Out," I said firmly.

Finally, she flounced out of my office. After that, she couldn't imagine that there could be anything between us but if she was dense enough to think I wouldn't be angry at her, she might not get that either.

I went back behind my desk and picked up my phone to call Bob MacMillan to see if he could cover for me in the OR. I'd covered for him when he was sick so I hoped he would return the favor.

Luckily, he had the day off and was willing to pick up some extra OR hours.

I cancelled my surgeries for the day and called Michael to let him know I'd be leaving for at least a week, maybe two.

He understood completely. I knew it would mean hardship for everyone on staff who had to fill in for me in my absence, but I had to put Kate and Ethan first.

Before I left, I called the hospital in Manhattan and spoke to Aaron Clark, Ethan's neurosurgeon. He informed me that

Ethan was critical, but he was hopeful they were able to take the pressure off Ethan's brain to prevent any further damage. Luckily, they caught the stroke early enough that they could treat it before too much damage occurred, but it would be touch and go for the first twenty-four hours.

I left the hospital within the hour and took the car home, rushing along the Mombasso Road, anxious to get to Kate so we could plan our trip.

WHEN I ARRIVED at the house, I went right to Kate. She was sitting in the living room with her laptop, searching the net for articles on Ethan's stroke.

I sat beside her and took the laptop from her lap, putting it on the table and then pulled her into my arms.

She slipped her arms around my neck and I kissed her warmly before pressing my forehead against hers.

"Have you spoken to Elaine?" I asked softly.

"Yes," she said, her voice breaking. "She said he had an AVM."

"I know," I said, nodding. "I called the hospital and spoke with Aaron Clark, Ethan's neurosurgeon. He's still critical, but Aaron's hopeful they were able to take the pressure off and minimize any damage."

Kate buried her face in the crook of my neck and couldn't hold back her tears. She wiped hers eyes, trying to be strong. "Did you get tickets?"

I nodded. "Two. First Class on Swissair with a layover in Zurich. We leave here at 12:20 a.m. and get to La Guardia at about eight thirty tomorrow night. It was that or wait until morning and take a flight to Amsterdam with a shorter layover, but I thought you'd rather get going as soon as possible."

She wiped her cheeks. "I can't stand to sit around, waiting. I couldn't sleep anyway."

"I'll give you a sleeping pill," I said. "You can sleep on the plane. I got us a hotel room for the layover so you can rest if you want."

"Thank you." She kissed me tenderly, and I pulled her into my arms, my heart swelling with love for her, and with sympathy. I knew how much she loved Ethan and how afraid she'd be. I found out that my father was killed in a plane crash only the day after and it had come as a total shock. There was no time to prepare. He was just gone.

I hoped and prayed that Ethan would survive, but there was always the chance he wouldn't. Still, I had to encourage Kate not to despair.

"Most patients with a first AVM stroke survive," I said, my voice soft. She nodded and relaxed a bit in my arms. "Are you hungry?" I asked and ran my hand over her hair. "Can I fix you something to eat?"

She shook her head. "I couldn't eat anything right now." Trying to be brave, she forced a smile. "Go ahead and fix something for yourself. I'll have another cup of tea."

I left her on the sofa and went to the kitchen, warming up some leftover lasagna. When it was done, Kate and I sat and discussed Ethan and I told her about my conversation with Aaron Clark.

We remained like that for the rest of the evening, sitting on the sofa, arms around each other while Kate Googled and searched the internet for information on Ethan's condition.

When the time came for us to leave, after packing hastily, we left our house and drove through the darkened Nairobi streets to the airport. I had no idea whether Kate would be coming back with me, and I felt a twinge of regret as we left our house behind.

CHAPTER 16

KATE SLEPT most of the way from Nairobi to Zurich and then a few hours at the hotel we stayed at during our brief layover. While we waited, Elaine texted Kate with an update.

Ethan had to undergo a second surgery after another bleed, and had lapsed back into a coma after a brief period of consciousness.

I explained why, trying to dispel her fears but at the same time, prepare her in case he didn't wake up. The ruptured vessel was close to the brain stem. One of the most dangerous, strokes like Ethan's often led to death due to the effects on the autonomous nervous system. Ethan's surgeons were hopeful that they had successfully removed the blood and that the vessel was no longer bleeding. All we could do was wait and see.

Once we arrived at La Guardia, Kate was eager to get to the hospital. I grabbed a sandwich at one of the airport delis and handed her a half, insisting that she eat. She complied without arguing. We arrived at the hospital and I led the way to the ICU to Ethan's room. I spoke to the duty nurse, who went to let Elaine know we were there. Elaine came out, her

195

face pale, but happy to see Kate and me. She and Kate hugged for a long time, and she turned to me and we embraced as well.

"I'll take you to the room," Elaine said and took Kate's hand, squeezing it. "Prepare yourself, Kate. He looks pretty bad. Very pale, and his face is paralyzed on the left side. He's still drifting in and out of consciousness but talk to him. Tell him you're here and that you're praying for him. It will comfort him if he can hear you. Be positive. He needs to be encouraged to choose to live."

Kate hugged me once more before going in to the room alone.

I watched through the window as she entered, walking softly into the room, and going to the side of the bed. Ethan's bed was surrounded by a bank of telemetry that monitored his condition. Ethan looked frail, with electrodes attached to his chest, a blood pressure cuff on his arm, an IV in his hand. He was getting oxygen via a nasal cannula, which was a good sign since it meant he was still breathing on his own. One of his hands was bent, and one side of his face was drooping from the effects of the stroke.

As I watched, Kate covered her mouth with a hand.

Then she sat on the chair beside Ethan, his hand in hers and spoke to him.

While we watched, I told Elaine about speaking with Ethan's doctor.

"Dr. Clark is one of the best," I said to Elaine. "He's one of the tops in the field in the US. The world, for that matter."

Elaine nodded. "He's been devoted to Ethan, dropping in frequently to check on him."

I wanted to hear what Kate said to Ethan, but I couldn't snoop like that. It was touching to see her speaking to him, father and daughter. I thought how lucky she was to have developed such a good relationship with Ethan before this happened and it made me regret losing my own father and not having grown as close to him as Kate and Ethan had become.

I went to the coffee machine and got a cup, then sat in the waiting room while Kate visited with Ethan.

Finally, a nurse came over and spoke with us. She wanted to do vitals and so Elaine went to the door and opened it, poking her head inside.

"Honey, they need to do a check of his vitals. Come on out and have some coffee. You must be thirsty."

Kate nodded and leaned down to kiss Ethan. She came out of Ethan's room and right over to me, where I waited with a coffee. I stood up and pulled her into my arms and we embraced, watching as the nurse took Ethan's vitals and checked him over.

"How are you?" I said, rocking her in my arms. I pulled back, brushing hair from her forehead. "Why don't you let me go in and visit him for a while. Have something to eat."

"That's a good idea, Kate," Elaine said. "Let Drake go in for a while."

She nodded and let go of me, following Elaine to a coffee shop on another floor. Now it was my turn to visit Ethan.

I DIDN'T SPENT TOO LONG with Ethan, not wanting to monopolize his time since I was not yet really a family member, but it comforted me to be able to look at him, check his stats myself, and speak to him in a quiet voice. I told him about his condition even though he was unconscious, and I told him not to worry, that most patients with an AVM survived a first stroke. I told him how much we all loved him, and how we would be there with him the entire time that he was in the hospital. That I would look after both Elaine and Kate while he recovered. That I was so glad to have had him in my life. That he was the kind of father I wish I'd had growing up.

After a short time, I turned away and left Ethan alone, satisfied that I had said what I wanted to say to him. I never had the chance to say goodbye to my own father and it still haunted me that we hadn't been close enough before he died so he knew how I felt.

I wiped my eyes and went to Kate, pulling her up from her chair and into my arms. I buried my face in her neck and squeezed her tightly.

"Are you scared, too?" she said, rubbing my shoulder. "I thought you really liked Dr. Clark."

I pulled back and looked in her eyes. "Of course I'm scared, but Aaron's the best for this kind of injury. Ethan's bleed was deep in the brain. It still all depends on whether the ablation was successful and that will only be clear in the next twenty-four to forty-eight hours."

She hugged me more tightly. "I'm so glad you were able to come after all."

"Of course I'd come. Ethan is like my own father."

When Elaine went back in with Ethan, Kate sat down on her chair once more. Then I had an idea. Kate was exhausted but wouldn't want to leave so I decided to reserve the extra on-call room for us.

"Wait here for a moment," I said and went to the nursing station. I spoke with the duty nurse and used the house phone to check on the schedule for the extra on-call room. Luckily, it was free and I asked if I could book it for use. I explained why and the clerk was happy to oblige.

I returned to Kate and sat down beside her, my arm around her shoulder. "You must be tired. I've been able to finagle one of the extra on-call rooms for you if you want to rest for a few hours. There's nothing much else to do here."

"What about you?" she said, rubbing my shoulder. "You must be just as tired."

"I'll lie down a little later," I said, shaking my head. "I want to go meet with Ethan's nurses and read his chart first."

"OK," Kate said and went into Ethan's room to let Elaine know.

When she returned, I took her hand and led her through the halls to the small room with a set of bunk beds and a night table and lamp. The room was where residents went to take a sleep break on their long shifts. We had it for the entire night.

Kate lay on the bed and I pulled the blanket up over her shoulder. I kissed her cheek and tucked the blanket in, hoping she'd be able to sleep so she could make it through the next day.

"I'll be in later to check on you or let you know if there's any news."

Kate nodded and closed her eyes, exhausted from the stress and long trip.

I knew our ordeal was just beginning for Ethan had a long road ahead.

KATE SLEPT the entire night through.

I spent the night checking on Ethan and making sure Elaine was okay. I caught a few moments of rest when I could, my feet up on the coffee table in the staff lounge where I spent so many hours when I worked at NYP. I felt at home there, and the staff pretty much ignored me, despite the fact I was on leave and didn't need to be there. I felt better that Ethan was at NYP for I felt more in control there, having access to Ethan's nurses and files, as well as his team of surgeons and neurologists.

I was speaking with Clark, Ethan's physician, when Kate arrived, looking quite a lot brighter than the previous day.

Ethan had a good night, but there was still a risk of another bleed.

"There's likely some permanent damage and Judge McDermott will have to undergo extensive rehabilitation. We think there'll be no cognitive impairment but we won't know for sure until later."

I thanked Aaron and we shook hands. He rested his hand on my shoulder.

"He's strong and generally fit so if there's no complications in the next day or two, he should do fine."

I waved Kate over, wanting to introduce them. She came to my side.

"Kate, this is your father's neurosurgeon, Dr. Aaron Clark," I said, gesturing to Aaron. "He's probably the very best in the entire country in dealing with your father's kind of stroke. Aaron, this is Kate McDermott, Ethan's daughter and my fiancée."

Aaron extended a hand and smiled warmly at Kate. "Your father is a strong man. I hear he's a former Marine. They're tough as nails so I expect him to pull through. Despite the second bleed, everything looks pretty good, so as long as the next few days are without any major complications, he should be fine."

"Thank you so much," Kate said and shook Aaron's hand. "We're so lucky to have you."

"Glad to be of help."

"You look very tired," Kate said. "Were you up all night?"

Aaron smiled. "Had an emergency surgery in the night. I'm on call this weekend and sometimes I don't make it out until Monday morning. Depends on what comes through the door." He turned to me once more and extended his hand.

"Well, I have to go check in on a patient. I'll let you know if anything changes."

We shook once more than then Aaron left, stopping in at the nursing station to speak with the nurses. I felt Kate's eyes on me and turned to her. Her eyes were brimming.

"I love you," she said, her voice catching.

I leaned down to kiss her, softly.

"Not that I'm complaining, but to what do I owe this declaration of your love, Ms. Bennet?"

She shook her head. Finally, she responded, her voice breaking once more.

"I'm so glad you're here. I don't know what I'd do without you. I'd be frantic."

"Of *course* I'm here," I said and frowned in surprise that she could imagine I'd stay in Nairobi when Ethan was so sick. "Do you really think I would have stayed in Nairobi?"

"But you have skills that are so rare and in demand. You have students who expect you to be in class to teach them. And you have patients like my father, and families who rely on you to save their lives."

I smiled at her. "I *am* pretty fabulous, if I say so myself."

"You *are*," she said, and punched my shoulder playfully. "You're amazing, Drake Morgan."

I touched her cheek. "How could I send you off by yourself, all the way from Nairobi to New York in the state you were in, alone? How could I *not* come with you, find out for myself how your father was so I could help you deal with whatever happened? I couldn't stand to be back there not knowing anything. Not able to see for myself. Not able to be with you." I shook my head. "*Nothing* could have kept me from coming with you."

I kissed her warmly, pulling her into my arms and against me.

201

"I love you," I said, holding her eyes. We stood with our foreheads pressed together, our arms around each other.

"Hey, you two lovebirds," Elaine said from the waiting room entry. "He's waking up."

Kate released me and followed Elaine.

"That's good, isn't it?" she said to me as I followed her. I reached out and took her hand.

"Yes," I said. "It's a good sign, but don't be upset if he has trouble speaking at first. There will probably be lingering effects from the stroke. It may take a while for his speech and other functions to come back fully."

Kate stopped at the window to Ethan's room. Inside, the nurse was talking to Ethan, whose eyes were half-open. She was checking a monitor, recording his stats.

"What's she doing?" she asked.

"Recording his vitals."

The nurse came out and stood with us. "One of you can go in with him. Don't try to make him speak too much. He can only whisper." She walked away with a smile.

Elaine and Kate looked at each other. "You go," they both said at the same time.

"I think we can break the rules this *once*," I said and shoved them both in. I stood in the doorway and watched as Elaine took one side of the bed and Kate took the other.

"Hi, Daddy," Kate said and leaned down to kiss his cheek. "I'm so glad you're waking up."

Ethan responded, but was unable to open his eyes completely.

"Chatty *Kathy*," was all he said, but there was a slight upward movement of the corner of his mouth on his unaffected side. He was smiling, or trying to and that was a good sign.

"You *heard* what I said?" Kate said in surprise.

"Every word," Ethan replied in his characteristic raspy

voice. Kate glanced over at me. I grinned at her, pleased that Ethan was so responsive.

Kate leaned down and pressed her forehead against her father's cheek, smiling back.

"Sorry I talked so much," she said, her voice soft and filled with emotion, "but I wanted you to know how much I need you."

"Wasn't going anywhere," Ethan said, talking out of one side of his mouth. Kate glanced up at Elaine, her eyes teary.

Then, the nurse returned and leaned in, giving me a mock-serious frown.

"Dr. *Morgan...*" Then she turned to Kate and Elaine. "OK, you two. Only one at a time."

Kate kissed Ethan's cheek. "I have to go now, Daddy, but I'll be back later. I love you."

"Love you," Ethan managed. Kate squeezed his good hand and then left Elaine alone with him. I put my arm around Kate and led her over to the waiting room. I pulled her into my arms and she finally broke down, crying against my shoulder, her tears of relief falling unrestrained.

"It's okay," I said and rocked her in my arms. "He's going to be okay."

She hugged me even more tightly and together we waited for Elaine to return.

"Feel like a coffee?" I asked. Kate nodded without speaking, still too overwhelmed after seeing her father. I led her down to the cafeteria and we got coffee for ourselves and Elaine as well as a few Danish pastries.

"Oh, thank you," Elaine said when she returned from seeing Ethan. "I'm exhausted." She ate her Danish in silence for a while. "Oh," she said after a moment. "The nurse said they'll be moving your father to the neurology ward later today. He's getting a private room with one of those recliners, so I can sleep in the room with him. It'll be so much

203

better than trying to sleep on the cushions from these couches."

"We should go and stay at 8th Avenue," I said, running my hand over Kate's hair affectionately. "It's pretty close and we can run back really quickly if needed."

Kate smiled, too tired to respond with more than a nod.

"I'll speak with the residents and see if the extra room is vacant tonight and you can sleep there if you want," I said to Elaine.

Elaine shook her head. "I'll be happy to sleep on the recliner in the room with Ethan. We haven't slept apart since we started to live together and I'm not going to start now."

"You haven't been apart a single night?" I said in surprise. "That's amazing."

"We haven't. I've gone to every convention and meeting he's had and he's attended all my family reunions. We've been so lucky that my work has never gotten in the way."

Kate took my hand in hers. "Drake will have to go back to Nairobi soon, so *unfortunately*," she said and looked at me. "We'll have to be separated for a while."

"What do you mean?" I said and frowned. "I'll stay until you're ready to come back. Ethan should be out of danger in a couple of days."

Kate was adamant. "I won't be going back for a while," she said, softly. "But you have to go back. You have students and patients waiting for you." She took my hand and squeezed, forcing a smile.

"I don't want us to be apart," I said, my voice low.

"We won't be apart for very long."

"How long?" I said, frowning at the thought of being separated from her.

"Not long," she said, her voice light. "When Daddy's back at home and everything's set up for his rehabilitation."

I shook my head, not willing to be apart that long. "That

could take weeks."

"Katie, you don't have to stay," Elaine said, calmly. "I can take care of your father. We'll hire private duty nurses, and will have the very best care. You should go back with Drake."

"No," Kate said. "I can't go back until I feel sure Daddy's OK. I'd fret and worry if I went back to Nairobi now. I'm alone all day when Drake's at work, and he works late every night. He's also busy on weekends grading and is on call once every three weeks so..." She shrugged. "I'm not going back until I feel completely satisfied that he's doing well. Drake will be fine. He's so busy, Elaine. Busier than he would be if he was here working. You don't know what it's like."

I said nothing, frustrated but not knowing what else I could say.

"Well," Elaine said and looked from Kate to me. "You two will have to sort that out between you, but really, Kate. There's no need to stay."

"It will only be for a couple of weeks." Kate turned to me. "You understand."

"Kate, I don't want us to be separated," I said quietly, trying hard to stay in control. I glanced at Elaine and she stood up.

"I'll leave the two of you alone."

We watched her leave, and then I turned to Kate.

"I don't want you to stay here without me," I said, emotion filling me. "I can take this week off if we're back by Sunday night. Michael's taking my classes, and Barnes is doing my slate for the week. I want you in Nairobi with me. We should know by Saturday at the latest how your father's doing."

Kate smiled at me, but I could see the resolve in her eyes. "What if he had a relapse? I can't be going back and forth."

"If you have to fly back, it's no big deal," I said. "We can afford it."

"It's not that," Kate said, shrugging one shoulder. "You

have to go back. You're needed there. I'm extra. I'm not needed there. My father needs me."

"*I* need you," I said but I knew when I said it that it was petty of me. Yes, I needed her, but I had to admit her father's illness trumped my needs.

She smiled and ran her fingers through my hair. "I'd be sick with worry if I went back too soon. I'd have nothing to do but sit around and think of all the bad things that could happen."

I said nothing, upset at the thought she'd be staying and I'd be taking the flight alone.

"Drake, you'll be really busy when you take on a full surgical load. Michael said he wants the two of you to go to the outlying provinces to do surgeries in the smaller centers during the breaks in the semester and you agreed. That would mean you'd be away for a week at a time and I'd be all alone..."

She was right of course but I still wanted to argue, see if she could be convinced.

"I can't help that I'm so busy. The patients," I said, my voice low. "They've been waiting so long for this surgery. And I want you to come with me when we travel."

"I understand that," she said and took my hand. "I can't leave here until I feel really certain that everything's OK. I read the articles on this kind of stroke. The risk of a re-bleed is still very high in the first few weeks after surgery. I'm not going to fly all the way to Nairobi and then worry every day and night that he's going to have another bleed and I'll have to fly back."

"That's too long," I said, a sinking feeling in my gut that she'd stay so long. "The semester will almost be over by then."

"Don't you understand? I'll feel useless there. All I have is my art and even that's in question after the safari," she said, her voice frustrated.

I exhaled loudly, my blood hot at the thought the bastard deVilliers had undermined Kate's already-weak sense of worth about her art. "What did that bastard Sefton say to you?" I leaned closer, staring in her eyes. "He must have said something to make you feel this way. It's like you're using your father's stroke as an excuse to stay here and not come back with me."

Kate closed her eyes, a look of pain on her face. I felt incredibly small but the words kept spilling out of my mouth, apparently beyond my control.

"Drake, my father and I only became close recently and then he almost died. I can't leave until I know he's no longer in danger."

"I can't stand the thought of going back without you." I couldn't. I hated the prospect of getting on the plane alone. I loved having Kate with me in Nairobi. Despite how busy I had been, each night when I was on my way back to the house, I felt incredibly lucky and happy to have her there and to see her, eat something with her, and if possible, make love to her.

Kate smiled softly. "I know. But you have to go back. And I have to stay. We'll only be apart for a few weeks."

Desperation filled me. "Elaine and Ethan were never separated."

"Yes, but her father didn't almost die while she was half way around the world!' she said, her frustration with me noticeable in her voice, her temper close to the edge. "What if your father had survived the crash and you had to leave Manhattan and go to Africa to see him. Would you have left him there and returned after only a week?"

I shook my head slowly. "OK," I said, my voice low. "All right. I understand." I glanced away from her face, trying to rein myself in, but failing badly. I felt like a jealous teenager but I was desperate to convince her. "You're not ready yet to commit completely to me. You're still torn between your father and me. But there will come a time when you have to choose, Kate. Me or him."

"I'm not *doing* that!" she said, sounding completely exasperated. "I'm not choosing him over you. And don't you *ask* me to do that. I *will* be with you – in a few weeks." She sighed heavily. "I'm afraid he'll die when I'm away and I won't get back in time to say goodbye." Her eyes filled with tears, and she bit her lip like she was trying not to sob out loud.

"That won't happen," I said, wanting to allay her fears.

"You can't promise it won't."

She was right. I couldn't promise it wouldn't but I felt pretty certain Ethan was over the worst of his illness. It would be a long slow process, but he would recover.

I took her hand. "You're not happy in Nairobi," I said and stroked her skin with my thumb. How could she be? I was away so much... She was alone so much... I'd felt it each time I left her alone—this lingering sense that I was making a huge mistake being away so long each day.

She sighed and with that sigh, I knew it was true.

"You're away so much," she said, admitting it.

I felt like a knife twisted in my gut.

"I'm alone so much," she added. "I have no one to talk to. Besides my few canvases, you're everything. At least in Manhattan, I have family and friends."

"Dawn is hardly a friend," I said quietly, a deep sense of defeat filling me.

"Well, acquaintances," Kate admitted. "At least I'll have someone to speak to. I go days sometimes with no one but you to talk to. You talk to people all day. You're probably never alone. Then you come home and I'm craving a conversation with you, but you're so late and you're so tired, we barely speak. Drake," she said, her voice lowering. "You probably see *her* more in a day than me."

That sent a jolt of ice through my veins. "Kate..."

She was right. There were days when I did see Sam more than I saw Kate.

"It's true," she said defensively. "Tell me it isn't true."

I shook my head and glanced away, unable to meet her eyes.

"Your work is so important," she said softly. "You have to go back. I have to stay."

"You're important to me." I glanced up at her. "Do you understand that?"

"Yes," she said, looking away. "Of course, I'm important to you. I'm right there, just below your career, your patients and teaching."

"There's no below, Kate," I said, feeling as if I had failed her. Failed to make sure she knew how I felt. "You're on the same level."

She looked in my eyes, but there was an expression of doubt in them, her brow knit like she was searching my face for truth.

"Do you believe me?" I said, taking her hand once more, rubbing her palm, needing the physical contact to counteract the sense of despair building inside of me. "Do you believe that you're as important to me as my career and my patients and my teaching?"

"If you say so," she said doubtfully, but I knew she didn't feel it.

"That's not a resounding yes." I exhaled slowly. "This isn't getting us anywhere. If you don't feel that I value you that highly, I'm doing something wrong. Kate, you're everything to me. I couldn't imagine not being with you, not loving you, not having your love."

Frustration filled me and for a moment I felt hopeless, as if I couldn't explain.

"I agreed to go to Nairobi when I thought you no longer

wanted to be with me," I added, hoping to make her understand. "I made a commitment to Michael and he planned the year based on my coming, arranged the class schedule so that I'd teach the surgical courses, and contacted patients who needed my skills to come to the hospital. I want to be with you more, but I can't let Michael down."

"Of course you can't!" Kate said, her emotions spilling over, her voice wavering. "I don't want you to. I don't expect you to leave Nairobi. My God, Drake. I know how important this is to you and to Michael, and to all your patients. But you have to understand that my father is sick and could die. I can't leave until I feel certain that he's going to be fine. I can't go back and sit all alone in Nairobi while you're away working, doing what you have to, doing what you love. I'd be so unhappy…"

"I understand." I stroked her hair. "You're upset now, because of what happened. You can't think rationally. Promise me this," I said and leaned closer. "Promise me that if your father is doing really well on Saturday, and if Aaron says you don't have to worry, that you'll return with me to Nairobi. If anything happens, you'll be on the next flight back, I promise."

She looked in my eyes like she was weighing her decision carefully. I knew she hated that I was trying to make her promise. I knew she might not be able to keep it, but it would make me feel better to hear her make it.

Finally she spoke, her voice soft. "I promise that if Aaron is happy with my father's progress, and if I feel that I can leave on Saturday, I will," she said finally.

"Thank you," I said, emotion filling me.

"But," she said and pulled her hand back. "If I don't feel that I can leave, you have to let me stay without any complaints."

I nodded, despite the fact I didn't want her to have that option but I had to fight my selfish desires. "Agreed."

Elaine walked up while we were still looking deeply into each other's eyes in hopes of seeing understanding.

"Either of you kids want to have coffee with Ethan? He wants some and needs help drinking it."

"I do." Kate smiled and stood up, but before she could leave me, I grabbed her hand. I remained in my seat and I stared up at her, her hand in mine.

"I'm sorry you're not happy in Nairobi. Don't give up on us, Kate."

She stopped and frowned. "Why would you think that I might give up on us? I'm staying because of my father, not because of you or how things are in Nairobi. If this never happened, I would never even think of coming back here until you were done with your term at the college."

I kissed her knuckles, and nodded, wanting to believe her, but a part of me felt that she was almost happy to have the excuse to stay.

She knelt between my knees and slipped her arms around my waist. "Drake, it isn't that I'm not happy in Nairobi. It's just that I couldn't imagine being there while my father's life is at risk. I'm happy there, but if I thought my father was dying..."

"I know," I said and smiled, although I felt a deep sense of dread at her staying. "I'm being selfish. I want you there all the time. That's all."

I bent down and kissed her, needing to feel some kind of physical connection to her to reestablish our intimacy. Finally, I pulled away and helped her up.

"You better go help your father with his caffeine fix."

She kissed me once more and then left me in the waiting room.

CHAPTER 17

THE REST of the week passed quickly as we spent time at the hospital, watching Ethan progress a little more each day. The nurses were great, making sure that Ethan pushed himself to keep moving forward. It would be so easy for someone with a stroke to lie still in bed, but that was dangerous. Besides loss of function, there was always the risk of blood clots due to inactivity. Finally, Ethan was well enough to sit on the edge of the hospital bed and dangle his legs over the side.

He still had a number of issues that would take time to address. He couldn't yet walk because of the paralysis on his left side, and he couldn't do much else besides kick his legs and move his arms for cardiovascular fitness. He had problems with solid food and had to have a liquid diet for the most part. His paralysis made half his face droop and his eye and mouth watered, but he was doing much better.

He spent a lot of time on the side of his bed, with a tissue in hand, wiping at his mouth and eye.

Dr. Clark was very good at explaining Ethan's illness. One day when Aaron was visiting to check on Ethan's status, Kate asked how long her father's paralysis would last.

213

"Difficult to say," Aaron said, stroking his chin thoughtfully. "The swelling is decreasing a bit each day and as long as no further bleeding occurs, your father should regain almost full use of his arms and legs. The swelling will fully resolve within a month or so, and then we'll know how much use he'll regain."

"What are the chances of another bleed?" she asked.

Aaron took a moment to consider. "Each year, he has a five to twelve percent chance of another bleed compared to someone who has never had a stroke like this. We think we got all of the malformation, but there could be an area that is still susceptible to bleeding. Only time will tell if we were completely successful."

THAT NIGHT, I wanted Kate to come with me to the apartment on 8th Avenue, but she refused my suggestion and slept in the extra resident's room instead. I tried to convince her to come with me, but she was a rock in her determination to stay at the hospital. She was afraid of being woken up at night and being called back to the hospital because Ethan was in crisis.

I insisted we speak with Aaron Clark once more to help allay Kate's fears.

"Kate's afraid that her father may have another bleed and so she's staying here at the hospital, but she's not sleeping well," I said, my arm around her. "Is there anything you can say to alleviate her fear?"

Aaron frowned and shook his head. "I really don't expect anything more at this point," he said. "Your father's made steady progress and the likelihood of another bleed at this point is very slim. Not zero, but I don't expect it. You should feel comfortable going home tonight. His vitals are all fine and the swelling is going down a bit each day."

Aaron turned and walked away, leaving us alone in the waiting room.

Kate turned to me and forced a smile, her arms crossed. "I'm fine here."

"You have to get used to being away from all this," I said, knowing that the hospital environment could make Kate more anxious than was warranted. "Ramp down the anxiety a bit. Being here surrounded by nurses and medical personnel all day makes your father seem more frail than he really is. Aaron doesn't expect anything more to happen. Come with me to 8th Avenue. We can have a nice warm bath and I'll give you a massage. You'll sleep like a baby."

Kate turned away from me and I knew she was fighting with herself, trying to come up with a good reason to stay.

Finally, she gave in. "I'll come home with you tonight but if anything happens, I'm staying at the hospital."

"Good," I said, relieved that she had finally agreed to come home with me.

Later that night, after Ethan went to sleep and after we sat and had a cup of tea with Elaine to discussed how the day went, we left to go back to the 8th Avenue apartment.

We drove through the darkened Manhattan streets to the apartment in silence. I knew Kate was still uncertain about leaving the hospital but I knew that she would eventually calm down and relax, especially after I gave her a nice massage and she had a warm bath. On the way, Kate took my hand and squeezed.

"So many good memories here."

I smiled and kissed her knuckles, glad that she was able to push thoughts of her father's well being aside for a few moments and remember. "The best," I said, warmth for her filling me. "I feel like when you walked up those stairs the first time, my life started again after being on hold for five years."

She said nothing, but I could see the emotion in her eyes. I leaned over in the car and kissed her tenderly.

I parked and the two of us got out and walked to the 8th Avenue apartment. I put my arm around Kate's shoulders and pulled her closer to keep her warm while we walked down the street. I fumbled to find the right key to open the front door and then led her up the flight of stairs to the third floor, remembering with so much happiness all the times I'd arrived there, trying to be late, but failing due to my eagerness to see her. It was supposed to be the other way around, of course. Kate should have been eagerly awaiting her Master, almost naked, on her knees by the bed the way I specified in our contract, but that wasn't to be.

Instead, I waited for her, a surge of lust in my gut when I heard her footsteps on the stairs. I admitted to myself that I was a very bad Dom, but I couldn't keep in my role. I wanted her too much.

Now, I opened the door to the apartment and turned to her, my arm under her knees and around her back so I could pick her up and carry her across the threshold. It was silly, of course, for I had done it many times, but it felt like a tradition. One day, I'd be carrying her across the threshold as my bride.

Kate buried her face in the crook of my neck, smiling. I closed the door behind us with my foot and then carried her to the bedroom, laying her gently on the bed.

I went around the apartment, turning on a few lights, while Kate removed her coat and boots, dropping them on the floor beside the bed. Before I'd even taken off my own coat and boots, I started the bath, wanting everything to be ready so I could treat Kate to a mini-spa experience. She'd been under so much stress and fear since we learned about Ethan's stroke, I wanted to pamper her.

I peeked into the room and shook my head when I saw she was about to get off the bed.

"You stay there and let me take care of you," I said with a mock frown. "You've been neglecting your health for the past week."

She obeyed happily, lying back and closing her eyes with a sigh.

I went to the living room as the bath was running and put on some music. Kate loved classical and so I picked a mix on my playlist I'd made especially for her. It included Debussy, of course. Kate's favorite.

I finally turned off the bath and went to the bedroom, remembering to take off my own coat and boots. Kate got up and tried to help me undress, but I stopped her.

"Let me do this, Ms. Bennet. You've been such a devoted daughter, you've hardly done anything for yourself. Let me pamper you."

She gave up and let me undress her. I took my sweet time, removing one piece of clothing at a time, pausing to kiss her naked skin when I did. I wanted to arouse her so that after the bath, she'd be eager to make love for it had been too long and I was aching to fuck her, hear her little moans of pleasure.

Once she was down to her bra and panties, I leaned over her, my hands on either side of her head and kissed her warmly.

"I've missed you," I said, my voice filled with lust I couldn't hide. "I often thought of sneaking into the resident's room and waking you for a quickie but I didn't have the heart to interrupt your sleep. You looked so tired and stressed out."

She sighed when I picked her up and carried her into the bathroom.

"Frankly, sex is the last thing on my mind and has been since I got Elaine's message," she said softly.

"I know," I said with a tinge of regret. "I won't push you. Let me take care of you."

She slipped out of my arms to stand in front of me, and let me remove the rest of her clothing. Then I helped her into the bath and rolled up my sleeves so I could wash her.

"You're not going to join me?" she asked, quirking one eyebrow.

I shook my head. "This is all about you, not me. If I was to get in with you, I wouldn't be able to hold back."

She smiled and watched as I took a bar of soap and started to lather up my hands. I took my time washing her body, starting with her shoulders and neck, then her arms. I didn't rush any part of the job, hoping to arouse her with my soapy hands so she would beg me to have sex. I felt her eyes on me as I bathed her, and tried hard to avoid looking at hers, so I could concentrate.

"Kneel," I said and helped her into a kneeling position. Then I washed her breasts, stroking them, my own lust rising, my dick hard as rock. Finally, I washed her back and buttocks, sliding my hands between her thighs to wash her folds, my eyes on hers now, unable to avoid gazing at her any longer. Her cheeks were pink from the warmth of the bath, her skin damp, her eyes languid. I poured fresh water over her to rinse her off and then helped her out of the tub. Her eyes slipped over my body to check out my groin and I smiled to myself. She was hoping to see if I was hard.

I was.

I toweled her dry, wiping her body gently before leading her back to the bed. I pulled back the covers and spread out a towel so the massage oil wouldn't stain the sheets. Then, I helped her lie down on her stomach.

"Massage time," I said. She sighed heavily and laid her

head on her folded arms. I took off my jeans but kept on my boxer briefs and shirt, my sleeves rolled up. Then, I straddled her hips, pouring massage oil onto her back before I began massaging her, keeping my hands firm but gentle. I started at her neck and worked my way slowly down over her shoulders and down her spine. I'd had many massages and knew the general principles, so I was able to almost replicate a professional job. Kate sighed in contentment and said nothing while I worked away at her muscles. When I was finished with her back, I started to roll her over only to find that she dozed off. Perfect. She was so relaxed, she couldn't stay awake.

"Falling asleep on me, are you?" I said with a grin.

"You give good massage," she said, smiling back at me, her eyes closed.

"Could you fall asleep right now?"

She yawned and nodded, snuggling down into the covers. "I'm so tired…"

I couldn't hold back a sigh of disappointment, but she had been under so much stress, I couldn't get too upset. I would have loved to lie on top of her and kiss her, for I knew I could arouse her enough that she'd eventually want to fuck me, but I didn't want to push as I usually would have. Not tonight. Instead, I pulled the covers up over her and left the bed. I went back to the bathroom and finished undressing, slipping into the bath for a quick wash. Once finished, I dimmed the lights and turned off the music. Finally, I crept into the bed, naked. Kate had turned on her side, her back to me so I spooned my body against her, my arm around her body, one hand under her breast. My erection pressed against her back, but she did nothing in response and so neither did I.

"Good night, my love," I said, and kissed the back of her neck.

219

"Good night," she murmured and together, warm from the bath, we nestled into the covers until sleep took us both.

The next morning, after a quick shower and breakfast, we returned to the hospital. Kate was eager to see her father and speak with the nurses to see how his night went. They informed us that Ethan had a very good night. His vitals were all normal and steady, and he slept reasonably well, considering he was in a busy wing of the hospital.

The nurses were even able to get Ethan up for a few moments, and he stood with the aid of a walker, his muscles straining, but his balance pretty good, considering.

Satisfied that Ethan was truly on the mend, Kate was far more eager for me that night when we returned to the apartment on 8th Avenue. A good sleep and a good report on her father, seeing how well he was doing, made Kate relax and so she was almost back to her old self. When I took her in my arms and kissed her deeply, she responded, her hands sliding up my back and then down to squeeze my buttocks, pulling my hips against her so she could feel my erection. Our mutual lust grew and soon, we were practically ripping each other's clothes off.

I walked her backwards to the bed while she unbuckled my belt and unbuttoned my jeans.

"God," I said, breathless with lust. "I feel like a teenage boy with his first girl."

"You don't *feel* like a teenage boy," she said, gripping my shaft with her hand and squeezing. "You feel like a very excited man."

"I am very excited, Ms. Bennet. So excited, I think I have to tie you up to keep you from interrupting me with your social commentary."

Of course, Fate had to intervene just when I thought I would get into my beloved's panties, when my hands were eagerly squeezing her beautiful breasts. I was busy devouring her mouth when the phone rang. Kate immediately jerked away from me and tried to get up, but I held her in place. The answering machine clicked on at the third ring.

Elaine.

"Drake, Kate, please call me right away. Ethan had another seizure and they've taken him down to get a CT."

Kate scrambled out of the bed to get to the phone but she missed Elaine's call.

"*Damn*," I said and got out of bed, pulling on my shirt and getting ready to leave. Kate was also getting dressed, her hands shaking as she tried to put on her bra.

"Oh, *God*," she said, her eyes wide, her skin pale. "He's had a seizure? Why? What would cause that? Another bleed?"

"Hard to say. After a hemorrhagic stroke, a patient is at a greater risk of developing seizures," I said, reaching for my jeans on the floor. "The area of the brain affected by the stroke sometimes misfires, leading to a seizure."

She stopped me as I bent to pull on my clothes, her arm on mine, her eyes on mine. "Will he die?"

I pulled up my jeans and shook my head. "If this is only a seizure and not the result of another bleed, he most likely will survive. But I can't say for sure unless I know the cause of the seizure. He's got the best surgeon in the country looking after him. If anyone can deal with this, it's Aaron."

We finished dressing, and went to the closet for our coats. I held Kate's coat out for her, helping her with it, squeezing her shoulders to show her some affection, but it was lost on her. Her mind was at the hospital with her father. I took her hand after I locked the door and together, we went down the stairs and down the street to the parking garage.

We held hands on the way to NYP, not speaking. I let Kate take the lead, and she preferred to remain silent, staring out the window at the passing scenery. The sky was dark, the streetlights casting long shadows over the sidewalks as we went to the entrance of the hospital and through the hall-ways to the ICU where Ethan would return after his test.

Elaine went to the radiology department to wait while Ethan had his CT. I sat Kate down in the family waiting room in the ICU and went to the nursing station to speak to Ethan's nurse.

"They got his seizure under control pretty quickly and he's sedated."

I checked Ethan's chart and read the nurse's notes, satisfied that he was being given excellent care by his team.

I went back to sit beside Kate, explaining to her about the CT to check for a new bleed or swelling on the brain that might have caused the seizure.

"I shouldn't have left the hospital," she said, her voice breaking. "I should have stayed here."

"Nonsense," I said softly and put my arm around her shoulder, pulling her closer to me. I lifted her chin with a finger and looked in her eyes. "This had nothing to do with you or me. It was a complication, not punishment from God. It was a setback. A certain percentage of people who have one event will have another. Usually, most don't. Ethan did. The surgeons will go in and fix it. End of story."

She nodded, but didn't look like she believed me. Her eyes were so wide and filled with fear.

We sat like that in silence, my arms around her, her head on my shoulder. About half an hour later, Elaine returned and sat across from us on a sofa, leaning back and sighing heavily.

"How is he?" I asked.

Elaine rubbed her eyes. "He's OK. There wasn't another bleed, so that's good. There was some swelling in the brain around the malformation, so they've got him on a medication to stop the seizures and reduce the swelling. They're going to keep him really sedated for a while, so he can recover."

"He's going to be OK?" Kate asked, her voice fearful.

Elaine nodded. "Dr. Clark said this does happen and they have medications to deal with it. He said Ethan should recover from this in a few days and then we can start over."

Kate nodded and I felt her body relax in my arms. She laid her head back on my shoulder and the three of us sat in silence in the tiny room, our minds on Ethan and the ordeal he was facing.

CHAPTER 18

THEY BROUGHT Ethan back to his room on the ward in about an hour and so we took turns visiting with him. I stood outside and watched as Kate sat on the chair beside him, her hand in his, rubbing his skin with her thumb. She was speaking to him in a low voice and I wished I could listen and see what she was saying to her beloved father.

When she was done, Elaine went in and sat with him a while. I went to get us all a cup of coffee and Kate and I sat and talked about old times when Kate was growing up and how her father would take the entire family to the coast for holiday weekends of beach bonfires and lobster feasts. As usual, I was envious of Kate's family life and childhood. It seemed idyllic compared to my own, which felt vacant and loveless compared to hers.

I made a commitment to myself that if – when – Kate and I had a family, that I would emulate Ethan, being there, being present for my wife and any children we might have so that they had such good memories.

My own childhood was stark by comparison after my mother left. I spent holidays alone with my caregivers. I was taken places, for sure. To the park, to the museum, to playgrounds, to the movies, but I was never with my father.

It was late Friday night when Kate finally said goodnight to Ethan and came out to the waiting room.

"We might as well go back to the apartment," I said, but I had this feeling that Kate wouldn't want to leave.

"I'll sleep in the extra resident's bunk, if it's available," she said without looking me in the eyes.

I sighed. "I'll go check."

I left Kate and Elaine and went to the nursing station and used the phone to check whether the resident's on-call room was free. It was, so I reserved it for the eight hour shift. I slipped down and got the key and then returned, handing it to Kate.

"At least let me sleep in there with you," I said. "I don't want to go back to the apartment alone, especially on our last night here."

"You mean *your* last night here," Kate said, her voice soft. "I'm not going back, Drake. I thought you'd already understand that. I can't go back to Nairobi now. Not after this setback."

I inhaled deeply and looked in her eyes for some sign that she might change her mind but there was none.

"No," I said, chopping my hand down, more upset than I realized at the prospect that Kate would not be coming back to Nairobi with me. "I don't want us to be separated. I told you that when I gave you that collar, and I meant it. Your father's better. Aaron said so."

"Drake," Kate said, her voice exasperated. "I have to stay."

"I have to go back. I've already taken a week off..."

"That's your choice."

I couldn't look at Kate, not wanting her to see me so close to losing control. I felt so certain she'd be coming back to Nairobi with me since Ethan had been doing so well...

"My flight leaves tomorrow morning at 7:00, which means I have to be there at 5:30. I have to go to sleep now, if I'm going to make it," I said with a heavy sigh. "I want to sleep with you."

Kate didn't resist and so together, we walked to the resident's on-call room. I brushed my teeth in the staff washroom, using a toothbrush from the dispensary, while Kate undressed, slipping into bed wearing her t-shirt and underwear. I turned off the room light, and crept under the covers, sliding over closer to her.

I wrapped my arm around her from behind, and kissed the bite mark on her shoulder.

"I hate this," I said, my voice soft. "I hate leaving you. I hate going back to our home without you."

"I can't leave now," she said defensively.

"You could if you wanted," I said, unable to keep the hurt from my voice.

"You could stay."

I tossed and turned beside Kate, upset and unable to relax.

Sleep was a long time coming as I imagined returning to Nairobi alone, to our house alone, to our bed alone.

MY CELL ALARM WENT OFF, waking me up with a start. I sat up and stretched, orienting myself to the location, remembering that I would be leaving very soon. My heart sunk at the prospect and I dragged myself out of bed with reluctance, and went to the bathroom to freshen up.

Kate took her turn in the bathroom while I went to get us both a cup of coffee. I needed the caffeine to wake me up after the horrible night I'd had, most of it restless, and getting very little sleep. I returned with two cups of coffee, and together we went up to the ICU to check on Ethan before I took a taxi to the airport. The duty nurse said that Ethan had a good night, with no further seizures and we would be able to see him after morning rounds.

"Can I pop in before I go?" I asked, leaning over the counter. "I have to leave now to catch a plane and won't be able to speak with Aaron."

She hesitated for a moment, but then she nodded. "Sure, Dr. Morgan. If you were still working here, he might even be one of your patients, so go ahead."

I slipped into the darkened room and stood by the bed beside Ethan. Elaine was slouched on a chair beside the bed, asleep. I leaned over Ethan and took his hand in mine, my fingers around his wrist so I could check his pulse. I glanced at my watch and counted.

Nice and steady.

"Well, Ethan," I said, my throat choking up a bit at having to say goodbye to him so soon after his seizure. "I'm off to Nairobi in a few minutes, but I wanted to stop by and see you first."

I glanced over his bulldog face, the salt and pepper brush cut, the jowls, the bristly eyebrows. There was still a bit of paralysis in the one side of his face, but it was improving steadily.

I leaned closer. "I just want to say thank you for everything you've done to help me with Kate. I can't stand that I have to leave her here and if I could, you know I'd stay and wait until you were better before going back to Nairobi, but I can't. Michael Owiti relies on me and there's no one else who can do all of my surgeries. That's why I'm there."

I saw Ethan's head nod just a touch as if he understood and approved. That made me feel somewhat better, but it wasn't enough.

"I also want you to know," I said, my voice lowering, tears biting the corners of my eyes, "that I love Kate more than anything. I'll do everything in my power to make her happy. You can count on that. I learned from my mistakes and won't make them again."

Then I leaned down and kissed Ethan on the forehead. The good side of Ethan's mouth turned up in a smile. He said something barely audible so I bent closer, my ear to his mouth.

"I'll hold you to that," he whispered. "If you ever hurt her, I'll kick your ass."

"Get better," I said softly. "You're like the father I wished I had."

"You're like a second son to me," he said. "I admired your father, loved him like a brother. I see a lot of Liam in you. I'm so glad that you and Kate fell in love."

"So am I," I said, surprised at the outflow of emotion in me.

"You should know this," he said, his voice starting to weaken. "Liam's one regret was that he failed to put your mother first in his life instead of his career. Don't make the same mistake."

I smiled and tears brimmed, blurring my vision.

"I won't."

I turned away quickly after squeezing his hand once more and left the room. I went to Kate but she wouldn't look me in the eye.

Finally, I sighed. "Are you even going to say goodbye?"

Kate glanced away, biting her lip to stop from crying but her lip quivered with emotion.

"Kate, come back with me *now*," I pleaded, filled with emotion—most of it regret and resignation. "I have two tickets."

She shook her head vigorously. "I can't," she said, her voice breaking. "I have to *stay*."

"I *have* to go," I said, but I felt that it was all so wrong. I *should* have been staying with her. We shouldn't be separated. I wanted to be like Ethan and Elaine – inseparable.

Kate still wouldn't look at me so I reached down and lifted her up, kissing her deeply, hungrily, my arms wrapping around her in a tight embrace. Finally, I pulled away and set her back down.

Then I grabbed my coat and left.

CHAPTER 19

I TEXTED Kate once I arrived at the airport and while I waited to be cleared through customs.

ALREADY MISSING YOU...

SHE RESPONDED IMMEDIATELY.

ME, too...

WHEREAS THE TRIP to Manhattan from Nairobi seemed to fly by, the flight back to Nairobi crawled along. I tried to sleep, but didn't have much luck. I tried to do some work, reading over lecture notes, but kept reading the same bullet point over and over again.

On the flight from Amsterdam to Nairobi, a woman with

231

blonde hair and pretty blue eyes sat beside me, iPod ear buds in her ears and apparently, an eagerness to chat me up.

I smiled politely, and unfortunately, she took that as an opening.

"You look busy," she said. "Are you working?"

I nodded. "Reading over my lecture notes." I pointed to my iPad, on which I had opened several files.

"You're a professor?" she said, her eyes widening. "You look too young."

"I'm a surgeon. I teach neurosurgery at the medical college in Nairobi."

Her eyes widened again, and I smiled to myself. Women and their mothers seemed to think physicians made the best husbands. I had to beg to differ on that point. Most of the physicians I knew struggled to keep their relationships healthy.

It was something I knew I would have to work on with Kate, but I was determined to make it not only work but flourish.

"You're a neurosurgeon? Wow," she said and eyed me more closely. "You do brain surgery?"

"I'm sorry," I said, a bit impatient and not wanting to talk further. "I've got cases to read over before we land."

She nodded, a bit of a sour look on her face and didn't bother me the rest of the trip.

I ARRIVED in Nairobi the next evening. For the taxi ride home, I was able to get Jomo. Despite his smiling face, I dreaded going to our house alone.

"Miss Katherine is staying in New York?" Jomo asked as he took my bag and put it in the trunk.

"Sadly, yes," I said, frowning. "Her father is recovering from a stroke and she wasn't ready to come home yet."

"Oh, that is so sad. Tell her that I am thinking of her."

I nodded and for the rest of the trip, I asked Jomo how his studies were going, happy to listen to him recount his test results and reading lists. I didn't feel like talking and luckily Jomo did. The trip passed quickly and then I was home.

I shook Jomo's hand and gave him a big tip, then waved goodbye as he drove off.

Alone again.

I entered the cool dark interior and stood in the foyer, inhaling deeply. I might have been imagining it, but I thought I could smell Kate's perfume and it made me feel even more morose.

I took out my cell and texted her, despite how late it was back in Manhattan.

WELL, I'm home. I miss you, Ms. Bennet. After this trip, I intend to never be apart from you again.

THERE WAS NO RESPONSE, of course. She'd be asleep.

I went to the bathroom and had a quick shower, and then checked my voice mail.

There was a message from Claire...

HI, Drake – just checking to see if you got my text about Sefton and Kate. Call me. We need to talk.

I TEXTED HER BACK.

I'VE SPOKEN with Kate and she cleared everything up. It was all a misunderstanding. But thanks anyway.

I SENT the text and put my cell away, wondering what she'd say in response. Then, I flopped into bed, sleeping almost immediately, exhausted from the trip and from all the difficult, mostly sleepless nights I'd spent in Manhattan.

THE NEXT DAY I went to the hospital early, reading over my lecture notes in preparation for a return to teaching. I had given a copy of my notes to my substitute, who taught in my absence, and so wanted to be prepared in case there were any questions on the material.

After class, and after my office hours, I went to the hospital cafeteria for a sandwich and was shocked to see Claire and Sam sitting at a table in the far corner of the dining hall. They were huddled together, talking, and didn't see me. I slipped out and went back to my office, frowning to myself that the two of them were spending time together. Of course, I knew they were acquaintances, because Claire usually had an end of term party at the house for all Michael's residents and students, but to meet and have a meal together meant they were closer than Michael's other students.

I wondered what the two were talking about and the idea that they were friends dogged me the rest of the day.

After my surgeries were over, I changed my clothes and spent a few moments at the nursing station, looking over patient files before I left for the night.

Serena, one of the nurses on the surgical ward, smiled at me when I handed back a file.

"Good to have you back, Dr. Morgan."

"Thanks," I said and smiled back. Before I was able to leave, she said something else.

"I'm so sorry to hear about your fiancée..." she said, letting her voice die off. She shrugged and had a sad expression on her face. "It's hard to make a new life in a completely different country."

"I'm sorry," I said and leaned over the counter to look in her eyes. "I don't understand. What did you hear about my fiancée?"

"It's really none of my business," she said, her cheeks red. "I heard that your fiancée didn't come back with you."

"No," I said, tilting my head to the side in surprise, for I hadn't spoken about Kate to anyone except Michael. Had he already told staff that Kate stayed behind? Why? "She had to stay because of her father. She'll be back soon."

"Oh..." Her eyes widened. "I'm confused. I thought you two had broken up."

I frowned at that. "Who told you that?"

"Dr. Cuttington. She said you two had broken up and your fiancée was staying in Manhattan."

I ground my teeth. *What the fuck...*

"You heard wrong. Kate stayed in Manhattan because her father is still recovering from a stroke. We didn't break up. She'll be returning to Nairobi in a week or two when her father recovers."

"Ah," she said and nodded. "It must have been a mistake."

I leaned my elbows on the counter. "Tell me, are Dr. Cuttington and Claire Owiti good friends?"

"I think so," she said and then I saw her hesitate, as if she shouldn't be talking about the personal lives of other staff. "I mean, they were friends before, when Sam, I mean Dr. Cuttington was here before. Back when you two were together..."

"We were never together," I said flatly.

235

Serena shrugged. "I probably shouldn't be saying anything, but Claire seemed to think you two would get together when you came back."

"Really?" I said, leaning on the counter.

"Yes," she said and glanced around. "She was surprised when you brought your fiancée along. She had a dinner at their house and talked with Brenda about it before you came. She was excited that you were coming back and let Sam know. She was really hoping you two would get back together. At least that's what I heard…" She made a guilty face. "Sorry," she said and cringed a bit.

I nodded. It all made sense now. Claire had contacted Sam to let her know I was coming back to teach. She told Sam I had a broken heart over Kate. They must have seen it as an opportunity for us to give it another try.

"Thanks for being honest," I said to Serena. "I'll make sure to keep this between the two of us. It was just a mix up."

"Sorry to be the bearer of bad news," Serena said.

"No," I said and backed away from the counter. "Really. I'm glad to know. Thank you."

I went down the hall to my office to collect my case and jacket. On my way out, I ran into Sam in the parking lot. The sun had set and the stars were starting to peek out from a darkening sky.

"Hey," Sam said as she caught up to me.

"Hello," I said and stopped at the door to my car. "Just the person I wanted to see."

"Me as well," she said, her voice all perky. "You know I scrubbed in on a lot of your cases while you were gone," she said and smiled. "You're welcome."

"Thank you," I said, and I meant it. The willingness of the staff and faculty to step in when I needed people to cover for me was a great show of collegiality. "I really appreciate it. It meant I could go back with Kate and be a support to her while her father was critical."

"Where *is* Kate?" Sam said, looking all innocent. "She didn't come back with you?"

I shook my head. "Ethan wasn't well enough yet. She'll be home soon." I opened the door and sat in the driver's seat. "Thanks for your help. Now, I have to go and try to catch up on my sleep." I smiled quickly and closed the door.

Sam knocked on the window and I inhaled deeply, trying to keep my cool. "Yes?" I said when I opened the window.

"Did Kate say how the safari went?"

"It went fine," I said and forced another smile. "She had a great time and got a lot of drawing in." I turned the car on and then glanced back at Sam. "Now I really have to go."

Sam put her hands on the car and leaned closer. "Did Kate tell you about Sefton deVilliers?"

I frowned. "Tell me what?" I said, playing dumb so I could see what Sam *thought* happened.

"You should come with me and have a drink," she said and made a face of sadness. "I have something to tell you that you might not like to hear."

I turned the car off and waited. "I'm all ears."

She shook her head. "You'll need a drink, Drake. Really."

"Tell me now," I said, my voice low.

Sam glanced around the deserted parking lot. "Can I get inside and sit down at least?"

I shook my head. "Whatever you have to say, you can say it from where you're standing. Now. I'm tired and want to go home so make it quick."

"Kate and Sefton deVilliers are having an affair. They had a tryst at the camp while on safari."

I said nothing for a moment, gripping the steering wheel in anger at the thought that Claire was passing around bull- shit gossip and lies about Kate. The woman was trying to

237

push Sam and me together and was intentionally trying to break up my relationship with Kate.

"I'm sorry to be the one to tell you," she said and tried to lay her hand on my shoulder.

I turned the car back on, not looking at her. I was angry at her, but I was angrier at Claire for telling Sam a lie and trying to make her think there was a chance for us.

"Are you going?" Sam said in surprise. "Don't you want to know more?"

I shook my head without looking at her. "I already know what happened. Claire is wrong. Sefton followed Kate into her tent and attacked her. Kate was just getting ready to scream when Claire walked in and misunderstood what she saw."

Sam said nothing for a moment. "And you believe that?"

Then I did look at her. In fact, I glared at her. "Of course, I believe her. She called and texted me right away to let me know what happened. Sefton has been trying to make the moves on Kate since he met her. He finally pushed things too far and Kate could have him charged with assault. That's it. End of story."

I shifted the car into drive.

"Believe what you want," Sam said, her voice petulant.

"I know the truth," I said and drove off, leaving her alone in the darkened parking lot. My blood was boiling in anger at the whole business. *Damn Claire!* I thought she was a friend, but I was wrong. She was a manipulative bitch who thought she could meddle in my life.

She was wrong.

I drove through the city to our neighborhood, having to taken deep cleansing breaths to calm down. It took a few shots of vodka back home and a lot of soul searching before I could go to sleep.

I knew then what I had to do. I had to give Michael my notice and go back to Manhattan to be with Kate.

She was my priority and I wasn't going to let my career get in the way of my relationship with her. My father had done that to my mother, and it cost him his marriage. It cost me a mother. I'd done the same with Maureen, putting career ahead of my relationship.

Ethan had done the same with Kate's mother and he regretted it more than anything.

I would *not* let that happen with the woman I loved more than anything in my entire life.

I SAT across from Michael the next morning and delivered the news. I'd already spoken to Bob MacMillan, a fellow surgeon, and asked that he take call for me and continue teaching my class until Michael found a locum tenens to replace me. He agreed and so there would really be only a very short gap in OR coverage.

Michael took it as well as could be expected, shaking his head, his fingers clasped in front of his face.

"I can't say this makes me happy, Drake. Things will be tight if you leave."

"Bob can take over some of my cases. He's experienced and has already accepted. I spoke with him before I came to you."

"Bob's great, but not as experienced as you. I'll have to find someone else. I'll take over your class."

I sighed. "I'm sorry. I'm not going to let my career ruin my relationship and right now, I need to be back in Manhattan."

Michael exhaled loudly. "I can reschedule a few surgeries until I get someone to replace you. Bob can't carry two loads forever. There are a few people I can call in South Africa who have expressed an interest in helping out. You were my first choice, Drake, but I would be happy to have them, if they're still available."

"Christiansen?" I said, thinking of other neurosurgeons in Pretoria who had my level of experience in robotics.

"Yes. Or Wangai," Michael said. "He's committed to coming next fall. Maybe I can get him here earlier."

I sat in silence for a moment, feeling guilty that I'd be throwing everything into chaos. "I'm sorry, Michael."

"We'll manage," he said and waved his hand in dismissal. "Claire will be sad to see you go. She was so happy about you returning, you can *not* imagine. I'm sorry if I worked you harder than you had planned. This is all my fault for not taking your personal circumstances into consideration when I arranged OR time for you."

"No, *no*," I said and shook my head. "It was just circumstances beyond our control. If this hadn't happened to Ethan, I'd have stayed. It may be that Ethan recovers fully in a few weeks, but I can't leave Kate there all alone and so you might as well replace me permanently."

"I'm sad to see you go."

I stood up and we shook hands. He took my hand in both of his and held it for a long moment.

"Really, Drake," Michael said, his voice emphatic. "I'm sad to see you go. I've enjoyed working with you. It's been good."

"It has and thank you. Working with you has made me realize I want to specialize in pediatric neurosurgery."

Michael nodded. "You'll be an asset to the profession, if so."

With that, I left Michael's office, a constriction in my throat, but a feeling of lightness now that I could see my way to leaving as soon as possible.

I slept well for the first time since Ethan's stroke, relieved that I'd soon be back in Manhattan at Kate's side. I'd miss

Michael, and I felt bad for my students and for the patients whose surgeries would be postponed, but this was my life and I had to do what was right. I knew this was the right decision by how I felt when I made it.

Relief.

IN THE MORNING, I rose early and had a shower, then dressed, planning on getting things squared with Jan regarding the house. I fixed myself a cup of coffee and called him to inform him of my plans to leave as soon as I could pack up the house. Our lease would not be up for another couple of months, so the house would still be ours until then, but I was happy to swallow the cost if it meant I could leave when I wanted.

Jan expressed his regret that we were leaving, but said he understood. I'd pack up as much as I could with plans to leave the rest for when Kate was able to return and we could finish the job. I wanted to leave in a few days, returning to Manhattan once I was satisfied with the packing of our most important possessions. Some of it would be shipped back to the states immediately. The rest would wait.

Once Kate was satisfied that Ethan had recovered enough, we'd come back for a week, finish packing what was left and then go on safari. It was something I wanted to do with Kate so that we had a memory of Kenya that was more than her being alone in the house while I was at the hospital.

In truth, I was jealous that Kate's memory of Africa would be of safari without me – and with Sefton. I wanted to over-write Kate's memories of the last safari, with Sefton, with happy memories of being with me. I wanted to see her doing something she enjoyed and share the experience with her.

The rest of the morning I spent going over my lectures, organizing them for Bob so he could take over permanently.

I had one class left before my flight to Manhattan, and would say my goodbyes to my students and wish them well.

With that out of the way, I went to the hospital to scrub in on a couple of surgeries with Bob. Once finished, we sat in the staff room and had a coffee, still in our scrubs, talking about the cases he would take over.

Sam came into the room a while later and leaned against the counter.

"I heard you're leaving," she said and shook her head. "What a waste…"

I frowned, not willing to put up with her disapproval but I didn't want to make a scene. Instead, I said nothing and sipped my coffee, studiously avoiding looking at her.

I caught her head shake out of the corner of my eye, and then watched as she fixed herself a cup of coffee. She turned around and leaned against the counter while she drank her coffee, eyeing me over the rim of her cup.

The door opened and a couple of the other residents entered. Naomi, one of the residents from South Africa, came right over. "I hear you're going," she said, her hands on her hips. "We'll miss you."

"Thanks," I said, smiling. "Sorry to leave so suddenly, but you're in good hands with Bob."

I turned to Bob. "Do you have any suggestions for a moving company? I have to do some packing before my flight."

"You should get the residents to help pack," Bob said and pointed to Naomi. "Order pizza and they'll pretty much do anything for free food and beer."

Naomi laughed. Older than the rest of the residents, she was in Nairobi with her husband and children.

"You know us too well," she said. "You say the word, Doctor D and I'll round up some able bodies and we'll help you pack."

"Sounds like a plan."

"When do you want people to come over?" Naomi asked.

"I have class tomorrow morning," I said, glad of the help, "but will be packing all day tomorrow afternoon."

"You leave it to me," she said and flopped down on the sofa beside Bob. "With free pizza and beer, you can expect quite a few residents will be willing to help."

"I'll order the pizza and have cold beer for anyone who comes."

"I'd like to help," Bob said with a mischievous grin. "But I'm taking over your entire surgical slate so…"

I smiled. "And I'm eternally grateful to you for that."

He shrugged. "I can use the OR time."

Across the room, Sam said nothing but she had this look on her face that screamed disapproval.

Maybe another surgeon would make a different choice, but I was lucky that money was not an issue. I could take as much time off as I wanted to deal with Ethan and be there for Kate. I could never work again, if I wanted.

Of course, I wanted to work, but I didn't face the same restrictions of needing to provide an income through my surgical case load that other surgeons might.

I sighed with relief and leaned back, imagining the look on Kate's face when I walked into the hospital to surprise her…

CHAPTER 20

THE NEXT DAY, after I spent time at the hospital wrapping up loose ends on my cases, filling out HR forms and packing up files, I met with a group of residents who had the afternoon and evening off. They were organized and were ready to work for pizza and beer.

I gave them directions, and we left the hospital for the house, ready to start packing. At the very last minute, as several residents were loading into my car, Sam walked up and tried to get in as well.

I stopped at the driver's seat door and frowned at her. "I didn't know you were coming."

"Drake…" she said, her arms folded across her chest. "I'm not going to accost you or anything," she said under her breath.

I exhaled loudly. I didn't want to create a scene in front of the other residents, so I gave in.

"Maybe you could catch a ride with Serena," I said, raising my eyebrows, hoping to send her a clear message. "My car is full."

"Fine," she said and turned away. I got in the car and

245

slammed the door a bit too hard. Then I took in a deep breath and tried to get control over myself. Fighting with Sam would do no one any good. She could help out if she wanted. Soon, I'd be on a flight to Manhattan and Sam would be far behind.

Once we arrived at the house, the mood was jovial. I had Mbecki's Cartage waiting so they could load up the van with furniture. I directed the residents to pack up the kitchen and bathroom, while I packed my office. Our most important possessions would go on the van to be shipped out as soon as possible. I would furnish the 8th Avenue apartment with the new pieces Kate and I bought together.

There were seven of us in total so the packing proceeded quickly. One of the male residents named Ben was in charge of the sound system. He plugged in his iPod and we listened to his playlists, which was mostly R&B and a bit of rap. It wasn't my choice of music but the workers ruled.

An hour in, I saw Sam standing in the open front door. I wasn't sure who she was talking to and thought perhaps it was a neighbor, curious about the moving van parked outside and nosing around for information.

I went over once she turned back to the living room, a smug expression on her face.

"Who was it?"

She shrugged. "Kate."

"What?" A surge of adrenaline washed over me and I pushed past Sam to the door.

What was Kate doing back? Had she returned without even letting me know?

I cursed to myself as I walked down the lawn to the small retaining wall that surrounded the property. There, Kate sat, her suitcase on the sidewalk beside her.

"Kate!" I said as I rushed down the driveway.

She didn't turn or acknowledge me. I sat down on the

wall beside her, leaning over, my elbows resting on my knees.

"*Kate...*" I said, my voice soft. "I didn't want things to happen like this."

"Like what?" She glanced at me, but quickly looked away.

Kate arrived home only to find Sam in the house... What must she think?

"I didn't think you were coming back so soon," I said, trying to handle things properly.

"Obviously," she said a bit tartly, but I could hear emotion in her voice and knew I had to explain, and right away. I reached out and took her hand in mine, stroking her palm with my thumb.

"You should have called me."

"I guess I *should* have," she replied.

"As soon as I got back, I gave Michael my notice and some of the residents are here to help me pack up the house."

Kate finally looked at my face, into my eyes. Her own eyes widened. "What?"

"I'm coming back to Manhattan."

I pulled her onto my lap, so that she straddled my hips, her arms around my neck.

"You should have called *me*," she said, shaking her head. "I would have told you that I was coming back to *you*."

"I thought you wouldn't come back for weeks because of your father."

"I realized that you're my life now," she said, her gaze moving over my face. "I couldn't stand to be apart from you even one more night."

I closed my eyes and then pulled her hand up to my mouth, pressing my lips against her knuckles. Tears bit the corners of my eyes.

"I gave Michael notice because I realized you're *my* life," I

247

said, choking back emotion, "and I couldn't stand to be apart from you even one more night."

Then, Kate wrapped her arms around my neck more tightly and kissed me and that kiss said everything. Hungry, needful. We remained locked in each other's arms, and I squeezing her so tightly, not wanting to ever let go.

I pulled back and brushed hair off her cheek, smiling when I realized what she must have thought finding Sam in the house.

"Why did you leave just now? What were you thinking?" I said, my eyes on hers. "You had to know there was nothing going on between Sam and me."

She nodded. "I tried *not* to think," she said, smiling a little guiltily. "I tried to hold back judgment. But I didn't know what to do so I thought I'd come sit here for a while."

"Of course, you would have to see Sam first before me."

"I would," she replied, and ran her fingers through my hair, which was hanging in my eyes. "You can imagine my surprise. When I saw her, I had this insane urge to run at her and claw out her eyes."

I laughed out loud at that. "Catfight?" I said, relieved. "I should be flattered, but really, Kate. I'm sorry you had to see her first. I didn't ask for any help, but the residents volunteered to come and help pack up, and she invited herself along with them."

She nodded.

"I hope you never ever worry about me," I said, keeping my voice soft. "I'm yours, *entirely*, Ms. Bennet." I smiled at that, my eyes narrowing. "Every single inch."

She couldn't help but smile back. "Call Michael and ask for your job back," she said and squeezed my hand. "We haven't even gone on safari together yet. We haven't slept out under the stars like I wanted us to."

"He may hate me," I said, grinning. "He called in a locum

248

tenens to help take on my caseload, and he was going to teach my classes himself."

"Then, I'm sure he'll be glad to hear you're staying."

I squeezed her, so happy that she wanted to stay. I nestled my face in the crook of her neck and just breathed in her scent.

"What will I tell him?"

She laughed. "Tell him you were temporarily insane but that you recovered your senses."

I sighed. "I guess I'll have to go in and stop the wrecking crew. Luckily, they haven't even started dismantling the kitchen."

"They'll all hate me," she said, her expression a bit reluctant.

"Nonsense," I said, smiling. "They'll be happy I'm staying. Besides, what the hell do we care what anyone thinks? It's what we think that matters."

"Will Michael give you your job back?" Kate said doubtfully.

I kissed her cheek. "The locum will want to keep a caseload so he'll get his salary, but I'm sure Michael will be glad that I'll take the classes back. I'll help Michael out where he needs me. It'll be fine. We'll stay and with the locum in place, I won't be nearly as busy."

We sat with our arms around each other and enjoyed the connection. After a few moments, I took out my cell and called Michael. I put the phone on speaker.

"Hey, boss," I said, keeping a playful tone in my voice. "Is there any chance you can rip up my letter of resignation?"

"*What?*" Michael said, his voice sounding shocked. "What happened? Why?"

"Kate came back and surprised me and she wants us to stay. So," I said, smiling at her, touching her bottom lip. "Can I have my job back?"

"Are you kidding me? Of course you can!" Michael said, relief evident in his voice. "I was dreading having to take over your classes. The students would be so disappointed to have an old geezer like me for their instructor instead of you. I already called Wangai and he'll want to keep the locum. You won't have any OR time unless you want to help me out. I'm sure we can find lots for you to do."

We spoke for a while about logistics and then I went into the house to let everyone know we were staying. Kate didn't want to come in with me at first, so she stayed outside and waited. When I told them, the residents let out a whoop, followed by applause. Finally, I went out and took Kate's hand, leading her inside.

Sam stood off to the side of the room, her arms crossed, barely even able to manage a half-smile.

"I'll order pizza," I said to them. "Do they even make pizza in Nairobi?"

The rest of the afternoon was spent unpacking and eating pizza. The movers took the furniture out of the truck and put it back inside the house, then had a beer with us.

Finally, everyone left and as I said goodbye, I thanked them for their help. Sam was the last to go, but our goodbye was quick and perfunctory.

Good. I hoped she got the message loud and clear.

I was Kate's. She was mine. There would be no one else taking her place.

I closed the door and turned to Kate, raising my eyebrows.

"I can relax," I said when I went to Kate, my hands on her shoulders. "Now that there's no fear you two will get into a catfight, although I must confess there's a little part of me that would have enjoyed it."

Kate laughed and slipped her arms around my waist and together, we enjoyed each other's warmth.

ONCE WE WERE ALONE, we sat on the couch, nestled in each other's arms. I pulled out a bottle of Anisovaya and we toasted each other before shooting back the vodka.

"I had an interesting experience when I got back to the city," I said, conspiratorially. "I happened upon Claire and Sam having lunch together. Claire was Den Mother to the residents at the hospital, but I didn't realize she and Sam were especially close."

Kate nodded and so I continued.

"One of the OR nurses and I got to talking about office politics. Seems Claire and Sam became pretty good friends when Sam was here two years ago. Apparently, she wanted Sam and me to get together and wasn't happy when we broke up. In fact, Claire said something to Sam even before she got back from the safari. Sam seemed to think you and I would break up."

"I *knew* it," Kate said, her eyes wide. "I mean, I didn't *know* it, but I felt something was off with Claire."

I nodded. "She called me and left a message on the voicemail wondering if I had received her text about you and Sefton. I texted her back saying that I had, that I had spoken with you and cleared everything up. It was all a misunderstanding. She never responded."

"Do you suppose Sam told Claire about you being in the lifestyle?"

"If they know, neither Michael nor Claire said anything." I shrugged and said nothing for a while, still not sure if Michael was aware of Claire's machinations or whether he was simply completely self-absorbed in his world.

"She wanted you to be with Sam instead of me," Kate said softly.

I exhaled. "Too bad for her then," I said and turned to face her. "I'm *glad* you're not in medicine. It would drive me crazy to come home to more of the same. Neurosurgery is intense and I need to escape. I escape into *you*."

I kissed her, cradling her face in my hands. Then I pulled her more tightly into my arms.

"I haven't found my passion yet," Kate said, her voice doubtful.

"Not painting?" I asked, sad that she felt uncertain about her art.

She shrugged. "I have to rethink what I'm doing."

I caught her eye and frowned. "Don't let Sefton undermine your confidence. Both your teachers asked you to be in the Master Class. That's a huge compliment. Obviously, you have talent."

"Talent isn't enough," she said plainly. "You have to have a voice."

"Kate, forget all that mumbo jumbo Sefton said. All that really matters is that you love what you do," I said and stroked her cheek, remembering how she looked when she was wrapped up in her art. "You looked so happy that day I saw you in the studio, and after a long day painting. I think you *have* found your passion. You have to let yourself enjoy it and don't let what others think affect you. You can't really ever know what other people are thinking. You can only know yourself and how you feel. That's what matters."

"How will Claire knowing about us affect your relationship with her and Michael?"

I took in a deep breath. "I'll wait and see if she does or says anything else. But maybe from now on, turn down her requests to go out and do things."

"What about going on safari? She said she and Michael would arrange something for the four of us. Will we refuse to go with them?"

I shook my head. "I don't want my friendship with

Michael to be strained, so I'd be willing to go on safari with them, but don't get too friendly with her, in case she really is that manipulative."

Kate nodded. "She was trying to break us up. She always said these things that made me feel insecure about our relationship. I took it as friendly advice from someone with experience, but now that I think of it, I think she was laying a foundation of doubt in me."

"I still can't believe it," I said, angry that Claire could be so manipulative, but I was finding out a lot about her that I didn't know before. "I hope Michael wasn't part of this," I said with a sigh. "I don't believe he'd go along with it, but still... to be so unaware of what your spouse is doing."

"You said he's very busy."

I shrugged. "I'm glad you're here," I said and pulled her onto my lap. "We were each thinking the same thing, not wanting to be separated any longer."

"We were," she said and smiled. Then she pulled back. "What were you and my father talking about before you left?" she asked, looking into my eyes. "I asked him but he wouldn't tell me. He told me to ask you."

I smiled. "I told him," I said, and paused, remembering. "I told him to make sure and get better because he was like the father I wished I'd had and I didn't want to lose him, too."

"What did he say?"

"He said that I was like a second son to him. He admired my father, loved him like a brother. He saw a lot of Liam in me and was so glad that you and I fell in love but that Liam's one regret was that he failed to put my mother first in his life instead of his career. He said I shouldn't make the same mistake. He was right. That's why I decided to come back to Manhattan. I didn't want to make the same mistake my father did."

Kate squeezed me more tightly. "I can't believe you

would have really left Nairobi," she said softly. "I'm glad I came back when I did. I'd feel terrible if you quit because of me."

"I'd *only* leave because of you, Kate. I realized that I can't stand to be apart from you. I don't have to be, and I don't want to be. I want to be like Elaine and your father. Not one night apart by choice. Do you understand?"

"I understand," she repeated and we kissed, our hands reaching out, needing to touch each other.

Then I pushed her down on the couch, my hands beside her head, my fingers lacing with hers. "I love you," I said, holding her gaze. "Never leave me again."

Kate's eyes filled with tears. Soon, we were lost in each other as the African night fell around us.

Over the next couple of weeks, our lives fell back into a familiar routine, but I made it my goal to spend more time with Kate. Kate kept busy at her art classes, working in her studio, and shopping. I worked much less because of the locum tenens and so we were able to enjoy each other the way we hadn't before.

I still taught classes and was away several nights a week, but was home more often.

One night after I arrived home, we sat down to eat. Kate was quiet for a moment and then finally, she turned to me.

"Sefton and I spoke today," she said. Immediately, my pulse increased but I tried to keep my breathing under control.

Kate proceeded to tell me how Claire had encouraged Sefton to pursue her.

"She said we were having problems and it wasn't certain that we'd marry. She said I was unhappy because you worked so much and I felt neglected. She said that the relationship was shaky and that he should be there for me in case we broke up."

"What?" I said and put my fork down. "I can't believe she'd do that."

"She did, or else Sefton is lying," Kate said. "But considering what you heard from the nurse at the hospital, I believe him. He's probably embellishing, but I think she hoped that Sefton would get in between you and me."

I took a long drink from my glass of wine. "I wonder if I shouldn't have a little talk with her the next time I see her."

She reached out and took my hand. "No, don't," she said, her voice soft. "I don't want any hard feelings between you and Michael. It's best you let this die a natural death. We still have to go on safari with them."

"How can we even socialize with Claire after this?" I asked, shaking my head.

She squeezed my hand. "We don't have to invite them over, and I'm sure Claire won't be inviting us over anytime soon. Let's just let this go."

I nodded, but I would have preferred to confront Claire. Still, Kate was right. Claire wasn't likely to invite us over any time soon.

Still, it made me so angry that someone could be so manipulative. Claire encouraged Sam to return, and then she encouraged Sefton to purse Kate.

She lied to them both about us.

I sighed and pushed the thought out of my head and tried to enjoy my meal with Kate.

It was the least that I owed her, now that I had time to spend with her.

Claire was not going to ruin things.

IN THE END, I didn't have to confront Claire because Kate did it for me. One evening when we were lying on the couch watching television, Kate related a conversation with Claire, word for word. I listened and my heart rate sped up, but I took in several deep breaths.

"How did she seem?" I said, stroking Kate's hair. "I wonder if she'll say anything to Michael."

"She seemed insulted that I would suggest she might get in between you and Michael. Let's hope that shuts her up."

I sighed and kissed her forehead. "I've had my fill of interfering friends. When we go back to Manhattan, I want us to marry right away so we can end any speculation about our relationship – with anyone."

"Will we invite Michael and Claire?"

"Of course. I want to invite Michael. Claire can come if she wants, but I have a feeling she'll be unable to."

"I'm sorry," Kate said, her voice sad. "I wish things could have been different between the four of us."

I hugged her more tightly. "We have each other," I said and ran my hand down her back. "We love each other. Madly. Deeply. In the end, that's all that matters to me."

"Madly," she said, echoing my words, tears springing to her eyes. "Deeply."

I pulled her against my body, needing her touch, her kiss. Soon, my anger at meddling friends and colleagues faded into nothingness. I was happier than I had ever been in my life, as I basked in the warmth of Kate's love.

EPILOGUE

Seven Months Later

THERE WAS no difficulty in choosing a wedding date.

Exactly one year since we bumped into each other in the pub before Ethan's fundraiser, three-hundred and sixty-five days after I tried to peek under her skirt to see her garters while attending to her wounded knees and ankles, twelve months since I looked on in shock to learn that *she* was Katherine. This luscious, curvy, chestnut haired and green-eyed beauty that I wanted to possess was Ethan's beloved daughter.

Ms. Bennet, Katie, the love of my life.

I'd fallen in love with her a little before I even met her as I listened to Ethan describe her. He told me tales of her as a child, tomboyishly trying to keep up with her older brother, striving to impress him with everything she did, working hard at her studies, volunteering in Mangaize, crying during performances of her favorite music.

Once I met her, felt her in my arms outside the restroom

257

at the pub when she stumbled into me, carried her to the bedroom to patch up her bloody knees, and then inhaled the scent of her perfume when I helped her on with her coat, it was game over.

There was no hope for me.

I had to possess her.

So it was a year to the day we met that we would marry in a small ceremony for family and friends at Ethan's apartment on Park Avenue.

Kate didn't want to stay with me the night before the ceremony, but I was having none of that.

"I said I didn't want us to be separated again, and I want it to stay that way," I said sternly when she suggested she spend the night at her father's apartment. "To hell with your silly superstition. I'm a scientist, and there's simply no convincing evidence that allowing the bride and groom to see each other before the ceremony leads to a failed marriage."

"But it's a tradition!" she protested, pouting.

"It's a tradition based on a time when the bride and groom had never even seen each other and was intended to prevent one or the other from running off in horror when they did. We've both already seen every single naked inch of each other so there's no fear of that," I said, looking down at her from under a frown, my hands on her shoulders. "Besides, look what happened to my *first* marriage. We followed all the rules."

Kate relented and stayed with me the night before the ceremony, but she refused to look at me the entire evening. When we made love, I blindfolded her, and then I had to lead her around afterwards, helping her into the bath, washing her off tenderly, before helping her back into our bed.

Usually, when we made love, I would untie the blindfold just before she came so she would be forced to look into my eyes. I loved the intimacy as she fought to keep them open and stare into mine, but that night I had to give that up. One night wouldn't hurt.

I even tickled her in the hopes that she'd lose control while in a fit of giggles and look at me, but she was determined not to look me in the eyes and kept hers squeezed tightly shut.

She woke early on the day of our wedding, and slipped out of the 8th Avenue apartment before I even woke up. So it was that I didn't see her at all the day of our wedding until just before the ceremony.

I spent the day with Dave Mills. We had lunch and then went to an old-fashioned barber and did the whole hot towels, shave and haircut routine, before going to his house to put on our tuxedos.

About fifteen minutes before the ceremony, we took a limo to Ethan's apartment and went upstairs, where we were greeted by one of the staff. We were escorted into a spare bedroom, where we were to stay until it was time to take our places in the living room.

I had a bit too much coffee at lunch and needed to take one last bathroom break before the ceremony. It was then I saw Kate in all her glory.

And she was glorious.

Dressed in a floor-length white wedding dress with a corset-style bodice, she looked spectacular. The back of the dress had a long line of tiny satin covered buttons and the dress even had a long train that spread out behind her a full five feet. Ethan helped Kate pick it when we returned from Africa and I was sure he was so incredibly happy and proud to see her wearing such a dress.

She was a vision.

A vision hopping down the hall in the other direction, holding up the dress and then falling against the wall with her dress bunched up around her.

"Oh, *Damn*..." she muttered as she tried to remove her foot from the poufy material under the skirt.

She groaned and squeezed her eyes shut when she saw me.

"*Dammit!*" she said, covering her eyes with a hand. "I didn't want to see you yet!"

"Well, nice to see you, *too*, Ms. Bennet," I said, grinning at her predicament. "Falling over in the hallway, are you? I don't see any high heels on you this time. Or any bloody knees and hands but I do hope you're wearing some nice garters and stockings..."

She smiled but kept her eyes covered. "Only my usual deft footing to blame, I'm afraid. *Please* go away so I can go to the washroom without seeing you."

"You already saw me," I said and bent down, helping free her foot from the skirt. When she still tried to avoid my eyes, I took her hands in mine, prying them away from her face. She kept her eyes shut. "If you're right, you might as well accept that our marriage is over, and we might as well break up right now."

She opened her eyes immediately.

"I *knew* that would work," I said and held her out at arm's length. Then, I turned her around in a circle, and watched as the train of the dress twisted around her ankles. She bent down to free it and when she did, her delicious décolletage was on display.

I groaned a tiny bit at the sight of her, a twitch in my groin in response.

"Is that better?" she asked, adjusting her breasts under the corset.

"You look..." I said and shook my head slowly. "You look like you're covered in icing sugar and ready to be licked all over. How will I make it through the night?"

She smiled. "Do you like it? My father picked it out."

I clicked my tongue. "The man has wonderful taste." Then I pulled her against my body. "Speaking of taste, I want one…"

I kissed her, pressing my lips against hers, a swell of emotion filling me to have her in my arms before the ceremony, just the two of us alone.

I couldn't stop from touching her, my hands slipping over her bust, trailing along the tops of her breasts.

"It's a beautiful dress, but to tell you the truth, I can't wait to strip this off you."

Then I reached into a pocket and pulled out the gift I bought for her. I had intended to give it to her earlier, I even insisted that she wear nothing around her neck precisely so that she could wear my gift, but she'd run off without giving me a chance.

"Here," I said. "Your neck is bare."

"As you commanded," she said.

"Since you slipped out this morning before I was able to give this to you, I had to sneak past the guards to get this to you before the ceremony."

I handed her the velvet box and she eagerly untied the ribbon, her fingers trembling. Inside was a necklace encrusted with tiny diamonds, a large red teardrop diamond dangling from the center. It would be her new collar.

"Oh, my *God*, Drake." She held up the box and admired it.

"Come here," I said and pulled her into the bathroom. I stood her in front of the mirror and removed the necklace from the box, placing it around her neck so that the large diamond hung in the hollow at the base of her throat.

"It's *beautiful*," she whispered.

"Look at yourself," I said, my face next to hers. "*You're* beautiful, future Mrs. Katherine Marie McDermott Morgan."

She smiled at me in the mirror.

"Hopefully, every man you meet will think this necklace is

just an indulgent extravagance on my part," I said somberly, "but this is your new collar." I adjusted it on her neck. "Now you'll truly be mine."

"I already was yours, Drake," she said, tears brimming in her eyes.

I stood behind her, my eyes moving hungrily over her reflection, as I slid my hands over her shoulders and down to her hands, threading my fingers through hers, our eyes meeting in the mirror.

Then, I released her hands and slowly turned her around, pulling her into my arms.

I kissed her deeply and passionately.

Finally, a year to the day after we met, she was truly mine.

THE END

ALSO BY S. E. LUND

THE UNRESTRAINED SERIES:
   THE AGREEMENT: BOOK 1
   THE COMMITMENT: BOOK 2
   UNRESTRAINED: BOOK 3
   UNBREAKABLE: BOOK 4
   FOREVER AFTER: BOOK 5
   EVERLASTING: BOOK 6

≈

STANDALONE ROMANCE:
   MR. BIG SHOT
   MATCHED

≈

THE DRAKE SERIES: (FROM DRAKE'S POINT OF VIEW)
   DRAKE RESTRAINED: Book 1
   DRAKE UNWOUND: Book 2
   DRAKE UNBOUND: Book 3

THE BAD BOY SERIES:
    BAD BOY SAINT: Book 1
    BAD BOY SINNER: Book 2
    BAD BOY SOLDIER: Book 3
    BAD BOY SAVIOR: Book 4

THE BRIMSTONE SERIES
    IF YOU FALL: A Brimstone Series Novel (standalone)
    IF YOU STAY: A Brimstone Series Novel (standalone)
Coming 2018

PARANORMAL ROMANCE:
    THE DOMINION SERIES
    DOMINION: Book One
    ASCENSION: Book Two
    RETRIBUTION: Book Three
    RESURRECTION: Book Four
    REDEMPTION: Book Five

ABOUT THE AUTHOR

S. E. Lund is a writer who lives with her family of humans and pets in a century-old house on a quiet tree-lined street in a small city in Western Canada. She writes erotic, contemporary and paranormal romance and dreams of living in warm climate beside the ocean where snow is just a word in a dictionary.

Sign up for the S. E. Lund Newsletter and get free eBooks, updates on new releases, upcoming sales and giveaways as well as sneak previews before everyone else.

I hate spam so I will never share your information!

Sign up below:

http://eepurl.com/1Wcz5

For More Information:
www.selund.com
selund2012@gmail.com